SIDNEY CHAMBERS AND THE PROBLEM OF EVIL

SIDNEY CHAMBERS AND THE PROBLEM OF EVIL

THE GRANTCHESTER MYSTERIES

JAMES RUNCIE

ISIS
LARGE PRINT
Oxford

First published in Great Britain 2014
by
Bloomsbury

Published in Large Print 2014 by ISIS Publishing Ltd.,
7 Centremead, Osney Mead, Oxford OX2 0ES
by arrangement with
Bloomsbury,
a trademark of Bloomsbury Publishing Plc

CIP data is available for this title from the British Library

ISBN 978–0–7531–9250–4 (hb)
ISBN 978–0–7531–9251–1 (pb)

Printed and bound in Great Britain by
T. J. International Ltd., Padstow, Cornwall

For Marilyn

"It is said that we are a great literary nation but we don't really care about literature . . . we like a good murder."

Walter Sickert

Contents

The Problem of Evil

Canon Sidney Chambers was thinking about the nature of forgiveness. He was on his way to the consecration of Coventry Cathedral where he had worked shortly after the war. Now, seventeen years later, a new building had arisen from the bombed remains; a symbol of defiance against the horrors of history. How much, he wondered, could people recover from the evil of so terrible a time; and were some crimes so great that they could never be forgiven? How could a God of love have allowed such suffering and what steps could be taken to ensure that those agonies could be prevented in future?

It was a bright afternoon in late May. Sidney had opted not to robe and process with the other priests for the service, having been specifically asked to sit beside his German wife in the nave. As a couple, he and Hildegard had been identified as a living embodiment of post-war reconciliation, proof that humanity could heal itself, recover and find love; and that a new generation could rise from the destruction.

Although Sidney acknowledged the need for hope, he believed that it would not do to be too confident about any prolonged peace. The current tension with the Soviet Union was proof of that and he understood enough about human character and international diplomacy to recognise that "never again" might prove overly optimistic. Evil could seed itself in the quietest places and grow unchecked for years, spreading its malevolent influence until it was too late to stop. Even here, in a rebuilt city centre and within a positive sign of faith at its heart, it would pay not to be complacent about the lasting power of goodness.

Sidney was pleased and touched at the good turnout by the clergy from his own diocese. There was his former tutor Simon Opie, now principal of the theological college Westcott House. He was a small, bald man with a crumpled face like a baby who spent as much time with his budgerigars as he did on religion. Following him in the procession came Philip Agnew, a former missionary who lived a life of such simple asceticism that he carried no money and so hardly ate anything at all. Then there was Isaiah Shaw from St Bene't's, a great biblical scholar who was prone to depression and sought consolation in the bottle; and in the pew opposite sat Patrick Harland, a fastidiously effete lay-reader who loved suede shoes and was rather too evangelical for Sidney's taste. This little Cambridgeshire group, Sidney mused as he watched them, were a microcosm of the Church of England as a whole, doing their best to promote the faith in different ways, sometimes serious, at other times charmingly amateur and other-worldly, ignoring the uphill nature of their struggle to bring grace to an increasingly secular world.

Sidney explained to Hildegard that the idea behind the resurrection of the Cathedral was that the building would open out like a flower as the visitor entered, revealing beauty with gentleness. Men who had been responsible for designing camouflage in the war had contributed to the overall design, a modern variation on turning swords into ploughshares. Sidney and Hildegard had approached through the old lace-like walls towards a charred cross, then through the Queen's Arch into the glass west front of saints and angels before spotting the great Graham Sutherland tapestry of the risen Christ above the High Altar; a figure of victory, serenity and compassion.

"He has a particularly English face," Hildegard whispered, and she laid her head for a moment on Sidney's shoulder, making him smile.

The congregation of the great and the good stood to sing the hymn "All People that on Earth do Dwell", and the Dean gave his welcome. The Archbishop of Canterbury preached a sermon in which he argued that the building echoed the words of the prophet: "This house of God was glorious; now it will be more glorious still." The choir sang the Magnificat and the Mayor of Coventry collapsed, overcome with the emotion of the day. For Sidney the ceremony was both an affirmation of faith and a statement of national identity; and as he shared these thoughts with his wife when they made their way out of the cathedral, Hildegard reminded him that a special service was also taking place in the Kaiser Wilhelm Memorial Church in Berlin. Prayers were being offered up to the same God, at the same time, in countries that recently had been violent enemies, in the hope of a lasting peace.

There was the usual bun-fight at the deanery afterwards. The Coronation Chicken was washed down with a Riesling that some of the guests considered to be taking Anglo-German relations a little too far, and Sidney was able to see a few old friends, show off his new wife (they had not yet reached their first anniversary) and quell any speculation that he was considering leaving the Church for a career in criminal detection. Those rumours, he insisted, when his fellow clerics teased him and clinked their wine glasses in salutation, were unfounded. All he wanted was a simple life in a small parish and soon, perhaps, he said, glancing at Hildegard, a family of his own.

His wife smiled quietly. She had already reminded her husband that she was in her mid to late thirties and the odds of having more than one child were long; almost as unlikely as Sidney refusing to involve himself in any more of Inspector Keating's inquiries. She had tolerated the continuation of the two men's weekly backgammon sessions at the Eagle, but had asked that any subsequent investigation would need to be approved by her in advance. She was prepared to accept that she might, at times, have to come second after God in Sidney's life but she was not sure that she was going to take third place after petty criminals and felons.

In the secular world, at least, she was always to be considered first. There were to be no secrets between them. Sidney could preach about forgiveness for as long as he liked in the pulpit but he would not find it at home if he ever deviated from the straight path of his marriage.

"Is there to be no let up?" he had asked in a tone that was mock forlorn.

"I need to know everything you are thinking, *meine Liebe*. And if your conscience is clear then you have nothing to worry about."

"I think I'll always worry about something."

"But not ever, I hope, about my love."

"Sometimes I can't believe my luck in finding you."

"Then imagine what it is like for me, Sidney."

Hildegard's first husband, Stephen Staunton, had been murdered by his first lover after dallying with a second, and she had never expected to marry again. Now she had done so she was determined to enjoy the happiness of their union; even if others had warned her that no marriage was ever plain sailing.

Mrs Maguire, for example, Sidney's former housekeeper, had already given Hildegard a crash course on the inadequacies of her new husband. He was, allegedly, prone to dreaming, hopeless at cooking, vague, untidy, and he spoilt his dog. He was easily bored, too often distracted and never appreciated the food she provided although he did like a pork pie, preferably with a gherkin, as well as sausage and mash, fish on a Friday and lamb on a Sunday and that was helpful because it would always do for the shepherd's pie the following day and she would show Hildegard how the mincer worked. Mr Chambers had to be made to sit down for meals because otherwise he forgot or lost his appetite and then he went and bought a bun at Fitzbillies cake shop (because he had too much of a sweet tooth) which filled him up so much he then either left his dinner or burnt it. He liked his tea milky, hated cabbage and Brussels sprouts although he would manage carrots and peas, and he never ate much fruit because his friend Amanda Kendall couldn't tolerate bananas not that they would be seeing so much of *her* these days. His curate, Leonard Graham, was apparently no better and even though, Mrs Maguire was at pains to point out, no one would call him a ladies' man, he was pale from being indoors and not taking any exercise, he smoked a pipe that was bad for his asthma and he kept referring to books in Russian about which no person in their right mind could make neither head nor tail. Both men needed *watching*, she had opined. *They could not be trusted.*

Hildegard had thanked Mrs Maguire for the information and quietly decided how different things would be without fully explaining what her plans were. Although she was prepared to support her husband, she intended both to continue her career as a piano teacher and retain a little bit of mystery to keep him interested.

Simon Opie gave the couple a lift home from Coventry, driving erratically in an excess of clerical absent-mindedness, dawdling at thirty miles an hour through Warwickshire and into Northamptonshire, passing Kettering and then on to Huntingdon with an alarmingly sudden turn of speed as the afternoon drew to a close. Hildegard had announced her intention of having a little sleep in the back seat while the two men talked shop about the order of service and their expectations of the forthcoming Vatican Council.

"I have always wondered," Simon Opie mused, "how the Pope can have both a piscatorial ring, representing St Peter's trade as a fisherman, and the good shepherd's pallium, woven of white lamb's wool from sheep raised by Trappist monks. How can the supreme pontiff be both shepherd and fisherman?"

"Ah ... you are worried about the mixing of metaphors?" Sidney asked.

"Exactly. Surely they need to make their minds up? You can no more catch fish with a crook than you might herd sheep with a fishing rod."

"Perhaps you are able to do so if you are the Pope; although that might be taking infallibility a little far."

"At least he's not an aviculturist as well. I'd find that very irritating." (Simon Opie kept his own private aviary in the grounds of Westcott House.)

"No," Sidney concurred. "That's best left to St Francis; and, of course his contemporary successors, Simon."

"I wouldn't put myself in the same bracket as the humble St Francis, Sidney."

"Of course not," his colleague smiled. "But we can all aim low."

After two hours they reached the outskirts of Cambridge. Sidney was looking forward to a consoling whisky after a long day. Hildegard woke and told them that she had dreamed of planes flying low over Berlin and dropping children in parachutes rather than bombs. What could it mean? Sidney wondered silently if it was a sign that she wanted a child of her own more keenly than she had previously admitted.

Simon Opie pulled up outside the vicarage, applied the handbrake, and stepped round to the back to let Hildegard out as Sidney collected their things from the boot. After bidding them a fond farewell, and vowing to see them again before too long, he started the car once more and prepared to drive off. The sound of the engine almost obscured the little cry, halfway between a gasp and a scream, that Hildegard made.

On the doorstep of the vicarage lay two dead doves.

Sidney put his arm round his wife, looked down, and then turned to see Simon Opie's Humber recede into the distance. He told Hildegard to go into the house. He did not want her to be distressed. He tried to think of the most natural and least upsetting explanation for the dead birds at his front door. Perhaps his beloved Labrador Dickens had found them, or they had been left as a present from Jerome Benson, the local taxidermist? Did people eat doves? he thought wildly. Perhaps they were like quail or duck? Could he separate the idea of a dove as a symbol of peace from its culinary potential? He inspected the birds for signs of shot but there were none; nor were their necks broken. In fact it was no clearer how they had died than why they were on his doorstep. The only certainty was that this was not an accident: two doves, slain and laid out for discovery. There was no note.

He fetched a spade from the shed and buried the birds in the garden, praying not only for their souls but also, as he remembered the solemn ceremony of dedication that afternoon, for peace; in his own life and in the wider world.

Hildegard tried to banish the vision of the doves, so still and dead, by making some ham sandwiches and a pot of tea. A cheerful Leonard Graham had popped in to see how the day had gone. He asked if Sidney had "passed on the news".

"What news?" Hildegard asked, having been unable to concentrate on anything Sidney's curate had said.

"I'm going to be a vicar."

"Where?" Hildegard asked.

"It's a parish in North London. Holloway. A bit different from here."

"I had no idea."

"Didn't Sidney tell you?"

His colleague looked abashed. "I was waiting for the right moment."

"You forgot."

"Of course I didn't forget."

"Cup of tea, Leonard?" Hildegard asked. She stood by the window, unable to settle.

Sidney looked at the book his curate was carrying. "You'll have to pack up your Dostoevsky in your old kit bag."

"But I don't think I'll be smiling."

"No, perhaps not." Sidney could not forget the dead birds. "Leonard, there's something I need to ask you. Is this the first time you've been to the vicarage today?"

"I was here earlier. Why?"

"It's just that Hildegard found a couple of doves on the doorstep."

"A gift?"

Hildegard handed him his tea. "Not a very welcome one."

"I think you can cook doves, you know. The Russians have a dove-like dish with white cabbage. *Golubtsy*, I think it's called . . ."

"Yes, I can believe that," Sidney cut in. "But this looked very different."

"What do you mean?"

"I'm not sure."

"An omen? Surely not?"

"Possibly, but I can't imagine why. I don't think I've done anything wrong; at least not recently."

"Are you going to tell Inspector Keating?"

"I thought I might."

"Sidney . . ." Hildegard interjected.

"Just to be on the safe side. Even if we have to solve the mystery ourselves."

Hildegard put her arms round her husband's neck. "Perhaps we should ignore them. I don't want you getting into any trouble, *meine Liebe*. I know what you're like."

Sidney kissed his wife on the cheek, and held a lock of her hair in his hand. "Please don't worry, my darling."

Leonard was always touched by these small demonstrations of love between Sidney and his new wife. He saw that it was time to go. "I am sure there's a perfectly plausible explanation. But I should leave you love-birds to it," Leonard observed before realising, as he walked down the vicarage path, that it was not the most helpful remark he could have made in the circumstances.

It was almost eleven o'clock. Sidney turned on the wireless and listened to the news on the Home Service. As well as telling listeners that it was Marshal Tito of Yugoslavia's birthday, that Soviet ships were monitoring nuclear testing by the United States at Christmas Island, and that Sussex had beaten Pakistan by seven wickets, there was also a report of the Queen's attendance, accompanied by Princess Margaret and Lord Snowden, at the service they had attended that very morning.

Sidney sat at his desk in his study, looked over his correspondence, and then knelt at his prie-dieu to say his prayers. He asked for mercy, forgiveness and understanding, and prayed that the birds that had been left on his doorstep were not a sign of more ominous things to come.

"O God, from whom all holy desires, all good counsels, and all just works do proceed; give unto Thy servants that peace which the world cannot give . . ."

Hildegard always liked to be first into bed and Sidney listened to her humming as she climbed the stairs; at first he thought it was a German folk song until he recognised "The man I love". It was extraordinary that he was that man. No matter how badly a day went, or how worried he was, he knew that she loved him absolutely and that he loved her. It was the most precious thing in his life and he would do nothing to harm it.

Hildegard was almost asleep when he finally came upstairs, giving her husband a drowsy kiss before turning away from him, on to her side. Sidney listened to his wife's breathing as she fell asleep. It was erratic and rose in volume the deeper she slept (had she begun to snore?) and Sidney worried then that one day he might be in her presence when her breathing stopped altogether. They had only been married for six months but he could no longer bear any time they spent apart. He had never felt that his existence on this earth could be so complete. He was even afraid of his own happiness. He worried that it might not endure; he almost expected it not to last, perhaps believing that he didn't deserve it, and it was all an elaborate joke to make the pain of any eventual loss far worse. Strange, he thought, that a man could not trust contentment or appreciate it for what it was.

Sidney tried to let his own breathing fall in with hers, imagining his wife's rhythm could help him sleep and they would be synchronised through the night. But Hildegard's breathing was fitful, filled with long silences that were then broken by a loud shudder as if she was dreaming so deeply she had forgotten how to inhale and only remembered just in time. Sometimes she gave a little cry, or adjusted her position, lying first on her back before turning towards him, oblivious, lost in dreams or the past, unaware of any waking present, safe from danger, warm in the half-light.

It was love, he thought, to lie like this, listening to his wife so near.

Contentment was a gift that Sidney knew was hard won, but he was grateful for it, and he fell asleep musing on other small areas of life where he felt simply, and easily, at peace with the world; not least the regular Thursday evening backgammon session in the RAF bar of the Eagle with Inspector Keating.

They arrived at the pub together and in the rain. Even though it was almost June, Geordie was fed up he still had to wear a battered raincoat and worried that he was beginning to appear middle-aged. After they had got in the first of their regulation two pints and sat down by the window he complained that his grey hairs were edging remorselessly upwards, his belt had loosened not one but two notches in the last few years, and that his need for reading glasses made him look like a civil servant. "And not a very well-dressed one, either." He sighed.

"That's true," Sidney said absent-mindedly as he laid out the backgammon board.

"Are you agreeing I'm scruffy, Sidney?"

"Your clothes are well-lived in."

"That's because the only people who get new clothes on my salary are the children. Not that I see that much of them."

"The demands of the job."

"It never stops, you know."

Sidney told his friend about the two doves that they had discovered on his doorstep and was alarmed when

Keating began to take a particular interest. He assumed that he would have been accused of being overly suspicious but in fact the reverse was the case. The Inspector was all ears.

"This worries me, Sidney. I think you need to be very careful here."

"I am always careful."

"No, this is serious. I don't quite know . . ."

"You hesitate, Geordie."

"I am afraid I do. I have been wondering whether to tell you this or not."

"I thought we had no secrets from each other?"

"That is the idea, and I know the news will get out anyway so you had better hear it from me first. The fact is that there has been a murder: a dead body has been discovered in the Round Church."

"That's terrible."

"It is."

"And are you sure that there were no natural causes?"

"No, Sidney, I am afraid not. The victim had been suffocated. We don't know how long it took or how conscious he was when it happened but he also seems to have been tortured; a pattern was scored on his chest with a knife."

"What kind of pattern?"

"Like an animal's claw. It's definitely some kind of insignia. The pathologist says he has never seen anything like it."

"The mark of the beast?"

"Perhaps. I'm not sure what that looks like."

"This is so upsetting. And I wonder, do you believe this may have any connection with the doves I have just been telling you about?"

"Yes, well, I'm afraid that's the thing . . ."

"You are being unusually evasive, Geordie."

"The victim of the crime was a vicar."

"No."

"He's called Philip Agnew. I am sure you must know him."

"Good heavens," Sidney replied. "I saw him only last Friday at the service in Coventry."

"What was he like?"

"Sidney paused, still moved and saddened by the news of Agnew's death. "He was a very good man. A holy man; almost too good for the world."

The victim had been a bachelor in late middle age, a man who welcomed the homeless into his church, and who gave most of his money to the poor. He had believed that the Church should be a "work of art" and an "offering of love" rather than an institution or a "cause". His was a frugal life, and he denied himself both meat and alcohol in an attempt to stay alert, believing that the wiles of Satan must be fought with a clear head and a light stomach. Sidney had once heard him preach a sermon based on five words in the gospel before Christ's arrest in the garden of Gethsemane: "And then there was night." Philip Agnew had argued that the sentence was not a simple description of the time of day and the rise of darkness at the moment of the arrest but an announcement of impending and absolute evil.

Sidney took a sip of his beer. It was less consoling than it had been when he had started it. "This is terrible. Do you have any suspects?"

"There had been reports of a vagrant in the area. It's possible the vicar had looked after him for a while. We are carrying out investigations on his whereabouts, of course . . ."

"And in the meantime you suspect there may be a killer on the loose?"

"There's definitely a murderer in this area, and he may or may not have it in for vicars. I'll need your help."

"I wouldn't want Hildegard to be troubled by this."

"She already knows about the doves . . ."

"Yes, but hearing about Mr Agnew will alarm her."

"I think it's the talk of Cambridge already. It will alarm everyone, Sidney. That's why we have to find this vagrant."

"It seems improbable, though, that he would . . ."

"Who else can it be?"

"I mean it is unlikely that a vagrant would go as far as carving something on a man's breast, don't you think? Stabbing is one thing, for money or in a kind of wild revenge against his life. But the carving of a symbol . . . This seems different. The mark of the beast . . ."

"Steady, Sidney . . ."

"The Book of Revelation; the coming of the end of the world. It could be the work of a man with delusions . . ."

"Which doesn't rule out a tramp."

16

"No, but the motivation may be more complicated than it first appears."

"It's always more complicated than it first appears. That is the nature of crime, Sidney. It's not in the perpetrator's interest to make it easy for us."

"And there is no obvious motive? No money missing or anything untoward?"

"Nothing that stands out. Perhaps it's simple wickedness." The Inspector rose to order a second pint. "It makes you think, though; why a loving God allows the killing of one of his own? It's evil. Why doesn't he intervene to stop it? I thought that was what prayer was all about."

"You have to remember, Geordie, that we cannot always judge God's acts by human morality."

"But what other standards do we have?"

"In terms of faith there are truths other than the factual. Mysticism. Metaphor. Imagination. Unknowing. Some people believe that evil is not a problem to be solved but a mystery to be encountered and lived through."

"Well I'm certainly mystified by this; let alone the appearance of those bloody doves. I presume you'll work on the case with me?"

"I don't appear to have any choice," Sidney answered ruefully.

He tried not to let the conversation with the Inspector haunt him but he was still unsettled when he took his Labrador out for his morning constitutional the following day. News of the murder had begun to spread and Sidney thought that he could detect people looking oddly at him, as if they believed that vicars might even be harbingers of murder. He tried to concentrate on his day-to-day duties — the next PCC meeting and the sick members of the parish who needed him to visit — but his mind kept returning to the death of Philip Agnew, one of the kindest of men, who should have ended his life in the serenity of aged holiness rather than being suddenly attacked, suffocated, cruelly mutilated and stabbed to death. Who could have wanted to do such a thing and what could his profession as a priest have done to provoke it?

Dickens was nosing his way gingerly, and with endearingly doggy circumspection, round a sheep which was lying down, very still, at the far end of the field. Sidney could only hope it was not dead, a "lamb that was slain" perhaps, and decided that, for once in his life, he would not investigate but leave things be.

He reconsidered the doves that had been left on his doorstep and was thinking that he should perhaps visit the local taxidermist, Jerome Benson, and seek his opinion, when he saw the man himself walking towards him with a bag slung over his shoulders. He was a little smaller and thinner than Sidney had remembered, with a more roseate face.

"Do I know you?" the man replied to the priest's greeting.

"I certainly hope so. You will recall we had those conversations a few years ago about Daniel Morden and the fire in the summerhouse?"

"I think you must mean my brother."

"I'm so sorry." Sidney realised that he had made an elementary error. "You are not *Jerome* Benson, the taxidermist?"

"No ..." The man did not appear to want to volunteer any more information and appeared irritated that he had been stopped. He looked to left and right, working out the quickest way to skirt round Sidney and continue his journey.

"You are not from these parts?"

"No."

"Visiting? Or perhaps working?"

"I'm a musician."

"My wife is a musician."

"Not the same kind, I imagine."

This was not going well. Sidney was aware that he should wrap up the conversation and move on but could not resist adding, "She's a pianist." He paused. "She teaches the piano," as if Benson's brother needed an explanation of what she actually did. He was sounding foolish, he knew, and the awkwardness was not improved by the return of Dickens with a ball in his mouth.

"I do jazz."

Sidney's eyes sparkled. If there was one thing he liked talking about it was jazz and the opportunity to do so was all too infrequent. He threw the ball for Dickens to chase and asked, "What kind?"

"I play the horn. When I can."

"I'm a great fan of Lester Young," Sidney began.

"I wish I could play like him."

"Are you performing round here?"

"Not at the moment. I've come to see an old friend. Staying with my brother. He helps me out when I'm running out of money."

Sidney checked. "Your brother being Mr Jerome Benson?"

"That's right."

"I imagine it's hard to make a living from jazz."

"You're right there."

Sidney was determined to keep cheerful and remain friendly. "Where are you going next?"

"Birmingham. A friend is in a quartet. They're probably going to ditch the sax player; although they might not when they see me."

"I wouldn't be so hard on yourself."

"It's a tough life. But then no one said it would be sweet."

Sidney wondered if the man was going to ask him for money. He didn't carry any with him when he was walking the dog. "Jazz has always been the music of hard times, I suppose."

"'*Brother, can you spare a dime. Money gettin' cheaper.*'"

"'*Sixteen Tons*' . . ."

"My brother's probably waiting. I should go."

"Then I must not detain you, Mr Benson."

"Jimmy," the man replied. "The name's Jimmy."

When Sidney returned to the vicarage he found that Hildegard had been wondering where he was. She had been into town and had just met Helena Randall, an ambitious young journalist on The *Cambridge Evening*

News, in the market square. The reporter had asked Hildegard whether her husband was investigating the murder of a local vicar and if he had any leads. Could she perhaps come to the vicarage that afternoon and talk about it?

"Why haven't you told me anything about this, Sidney?"

"I didn't want to alarm you."

"I don't see how you were going to keep it a secret."

"I wasn't expecting you to go into Cambridge."

"Is this connected with the doves? Should I be worried?"

"I knew you would be. That's why I wanted to keep it quiet."

"But if you don't tell me anything, or if I only hear a little, then I will always think there is more to know."

"It's difficult . . ."

"Tell me everything," she asked.

Although he dreaded doing so, Sidney knew that he still ought to visit Jerome Benson, if only to ask about the dead doves and to discount the possibility that his brother was the vagrant seen near Philip Agnew's vicarage.

It had been a few years since he had last been inside the ramshackle dwelling on the edge of Grantchester that served as both home and workshop. Dickens, however, remembered it well enough and was scared to enter. The walls of the front room were decorated with traditional examples of the taxidermist's art and concentrated entirely on fish: a pair of perch, three or four pikes, a thick-lipped mullet, a brown trout, a carp, a roach and a flounder. The inner room was more haunting, featuring picturesque narrative attempts (a fox with pheasant prey, two sword-fighting stoats) and what could only be described as the macabre: a two-headed lamb, a mummified cat, an armadillo holding a soap dish and a model of the human eye.

Benson stood throughout their encounter, restlessly tidying the glue pots, small chisels and pliers which littered his work bench, and was defensive when Sidney began talking about the doves on the doorstep and the sight earlier in the week of what he had imagined to be a dead lamb in the meadows.

"I am not sure what you are implying, Canon Chambers, but surely I cannot be responsible for every creature that has died? There may be a special providence in the fall of a sparrow, but that is your department rather than mine."

"Of course."

"As I have told you before, I only use animals that have died naturally. I don't go round killing them."

"I admit that I am unclear about the legal implications of taxidermy."

"I recall that you once accused me of shooting an owl."

"I did not accuse you . . ."

"Any illegality involving my art would put me out of business. Please could you get to the point? In the past our conversation has not been as congenial as it could have been and, at the moment, the chance of improvement seems unlikely."

"I'm afraid that this encounter may be no better. A vicar in my diocese, Philip Agnew, has been found murdered."

"I'm sorry to hear that, but death comes to us all eventually."

"Indeed; but the combination of all these events seems strange."

"Does it, Canon Chambers? To people who deal with mortality as we do, surely this is little more than nature running its course?"

Sidney changed tack. "I wondered. Is your brother still staying with you?"

"Why do you ask? Have you met him?"

"I thought he was you."

"We are often mistaken for each other. Although Jimmy is a wilder spirit than I am. The police have called him in more than once."

"I imagine he has had his troubles." Sidney knew that the underlying tenor of their exchange was almost certainly about drugs but neither man was prepared to say so.

"You probably don't need me to tell you about them. People suspect Jimmy of all manner of crimes just because he is an outsider."

"I do not suspect him of anything, Mr Benson. I gather he is a jazz musician."

"That does not give him immunity from prosecution."

"It gives him a good start as far as I am concerned."

"Not everyone is as open-minded in their assumptions as you, Canon Chambers. He has sometimes been in the wrong place at the wrong time."

"Do you know if he ever visited the Reverend Philip Agnew? The priest was a good friend to many troubled souls."

"I very much doubt Jimmy was among them. We were brought up as atheists. That may of course be why you appear to us as someone whom we mistrust, and from whom we also expect forgiveness."

"That is my primary task. But I must hate the sin even if I love the sinner."

"My brother may have sinned, in your terms, but I can tell you that he is not a murderer."

"But he will fall under suspicion. He was seen in the area, he is a man of no fixed abode, and he has had his run-ins with the police in the past."

"Then that is why he needs support."

"Provided that aid is within the confines of the law."

"Or, I would argue, natural justice." Benson walked towards the door and held it open.

Dickens began to bark at one of the displays. It was a panorama involving a selection of seabirds: a puffin, razorbill, guillemot and red-throated diver. The dog was clearly as unsettled by his immediate environment as Sidney had been by the conversation. There was little more he could get out of the situation and his interlocutor had made it clear that it was time for him to leave. There would be no more information from him that night.

★ ★ ★

Sidney resumed his parish duties but let the crime worry away at his subconscious. He hoped he might have something helpful to say the next time he saw Inspector Keating and was looking forward to some time on their own. He was therefore more than irritated the following Thursday when he arrived at the Eagle to find that Inspector Keating was already *in situ* with an empty pint glass in front of him and Helena Randall at his side. "I was just leaving," she smiled.

Sidney was determined not to succumb to her wiles. "I wasn't expecting to see you here."

"I am not intruding, I hope. We've had our little chat, haven't we, Inspector?"

"And very pleasant it has been, Miss Randall."

Helena reached forward and brushed the shoulder of her companion's jacket. "You've got a bit of fluff. Is it a dog hair? Someone needs looking after."

"I know . . ." Keating acknowledged.

"I'm going to have to keep an eye on you," said Helena, as she blew the Inspector a kiss and wished both men a pleasant evening.

Sidney raised a metaphorical eyebrow.

"Whatever you're thinking, don't. She's a good girl."

"She works for the newspapers, Geordie. Any secrets can hardly be safe with her."

"We have to help each other, Sidney. These are difficult times."

Sidney was unsure of Helena Randall. She was a woman whose fragility and long, fair pre-Raphaelite hair disguised a steely ambition. She was unnaturally pale, extremely thin (what did she ever eat? he wondered) and her face was held in a state of almost permanent curiosity, with brows raised over unsuitable yellow eye shadow. She had long fingers that either played with her hair or held a poised biro that moved between her thin mouth and a reporter's notebook. Although she wore a duffel coat it was never seen to be toggled, and the skimpy blouse, thin cardigan and pleated trousers that she wore underneath were hardly sufficient to keep out the cold. As a result, she was frequently prone to sniffles, and even bronchitis, which Sidney had thought that previous winter, uncharacteristically uncharitably, could be construed as a deliberate appeal for sympathy.

Inspector Keating admired her "critical intelligence" (she could, apparently, grasp things before anyone else did) and he was happy to admit that her attractiveness to him resided both in her resemblance to the great Waterhouse painting *The Lady of Shalott* and in her ability to listen with what appeared to be rapt admiration to everything he said.

Sidney acknowledged that it was unchristian of him to harbour such dislike but there was something about her voice (simultaneously too high and too flat), her unconvincing laughter and her wheedling manner that got his goat. His distrust was compounded by the fact that he suspected that she didn't like *him*. Keating had confessed that she had already asked several times what on earth a priest was doing involving himself in criminal affairs and "getting in the way of professionals who knew better".

His friend said that he had defended Sidney. "Of course I put her right as soon as she started on that line of thinking."

"But did you hesitate at all? Did you give her cause to think you might agree, perhaps?"

"Not at all. Don't be so touchy. She's a bright girl."

Sidney did not think that he was the one being touchy. Now that he was more experienced as both a married man and a priest, he had learned to detect the danger signs at both the beginning and the end of relationships; a look that was held too long at the start and then not at all when a couple were hardly speaking; quiet intimacies such as a covert touch or glance; the public sharing of food, crossword puzzles and wine glasses; and the difference between a companionable and a hostile silence. The fact that Keating had not referred to Helena's quiet brushing away of the dog hair had made it obvious that they were on dangerously familiar terms and Sidney knew he was going to have to be ever vigilant if he was to protect his friend from the destructive foolishness of an affair.

He spoke to Geordie about his encounters with both of the Benson brothers and was surprised by the ferocity of the response.

"Why didn't you tell me straight away?"

"You were otherwise engaged."

"That is nonsense, Sidney."

"And I believe there is nothing to suggest that Jimmy Benson is the homeless stranger who was seen near the Agnew vicarage."

"He is a vagrant . . ."

"He is a jazz musician."

"That is almost the same thing."

"It certainly is not."

"So where do you think your wandering minstrel is now?"

"I think he is en route to Birmingham."

"You mean he's left the crime scene already?"

"I don't think he's committed any crime."

"That's for me to judge."

"Technically it's for a judge to judge."

"You might at least have let me get the cut of his jib."

"I will ask Jerome Benson when his brother is coming back."

"No, Sidney, we will ask that question. I'll send the boys round right now. It may not be too late. Honestly, you've been very slow about this man. Helena was on to it like a flash. She must have asked every member of the congregation of the Round Church if they'd seen anything suspicious. It's good to have her as an unofficial member of my team. She keeps everyone on their toes."

"So you will be involving Miss Randall in your investigation?"

"I'd like to keep her on my side. Besides, she is as entitled to follow the case as you are."

"I only hope she does not prove a distraction to your work on it, Geordie."

"You don't need to concern yourself about that."

"I think you should be very careful in your dealings with her."

"I am."

"It doesn't look like it."

"Perhaps not. It's only that, well, to be honest, there are times when I must confess that I do need a bit of cheering up."

"I thought that was my job."

"Of course it is. But female company does have its charms, Sidney, as you well know. I get so discouraged these days. It's just one thing after another and then, when I go home, it's more of the same. Noise, arguments, nagging; children wanting things all the time; there's no peace. Family life is more exhausting than work."

"Really?"

"You'll find out about all that soon enough. I just think I need a bit of a treat from time to time; a little holiday from everything that's going on in my life. And Helena's very easy on the eye, Sidney. I bet you've spotted that."

"I only have eyes for my wife."

"Give it a year or two and you may change your tune."

"I very much doubt it."

"Then I look forward to seeing whether you're proved right or not."

Sidney was not in the best of spirits when he returned home. He told Hildegard that Geordie had undermined his confidence and that he had felt like a gooseberry in Helena's presence.

His wife did not understand the term and so he tried to explain. "I think the phrase originated in the nineteenth century when a chaperone accompanied two lovers into the garden and was supposed to pick gooseberries while the couple did whatever they had to do; in France the best man had to 'tenir la chandelle', to light the way for newlyweds. I wonder if there is a German equivalent."

"Yes, there is something like that: 'drittes rad am wagen,'" Hildegard answered. "It's like being the extra wheel on a cart. It's not needed. You felt like that when you were with them? Is Inspector Keating keen on this woman? I can't understand what he sees in her."

"Youth. Attention."

"Is that what most men want?"

"I wouldn't know, Hildegard. My only contentment is with you."

"That is a good answer. We don't have any need for gooseberries in this house."

The telephone rang. It was Keating. They had gone to the taxidermist's but Jimmy Benson had fled. Someone had evidently tipped him off, Geordie was certain. "Could it have been you, Sidney?" he asked.

"Don't be ridiculous."

"I was just checking that the comfort you give to the afflicted does not involve helping them resist arrest."

"You were going to arrest him?"

"We were going to call him in for questioning. Now his behaviour is even more suspicious. He's a fugitive."

"Perhaps he is frightened."

"How do you think he knew we were coming?"

"His brother probably advised him to leave pretty quickly. He knows how easily loners and outsiders get blamed for things they have not done."

"Only if there's a good reason. Strong evidence."

"That is not always the case. Sometimes they're made scapegoats. We can't be at all sure Jimmy Benson has anything to do with the Agnew murder. You can't assume a man is guilty just because he likes jazz and lives the life of a drifter."

"What did he say to you? Did he ask you for money?"

"He knows he's unlikely to get much off a priest."

"You lot are a soft touch, though. And there's always a bit of silver in the church."

"It's mainly plate."

"He might not know that."

"I don't think he's our man."

"But you can't know that, can you, Sidney? Miss Randall is convinced we should follow it up."

"And does she have any expertise in criminal investigation?"

"No more than you."

"I'm not sure that's true."

"She wants to be a crime reporter. I've already said she can follow the case, as you know."

"I'm sure she'll be glad of your company."

"That is none of your business."

"It's never quite clear what's my business and what is not," Sidney replied.

"My friend, it may have escaped your notice but we have a murder victim — a man of God, like yourself —

and now we have a suspect on the run. There's enough to worry about without you casting any aspersions about Miss Randall's motives for helping me. Perhaps you're just jealous."

"For heaven's sake, it's not that at all . . ." Sidney began but the Inspector had put down the receiver.

Philip Agnew's funeral took place in the middle of June. It was a hot, dry and airless day, as if the life had been sucked out of it. There was no breeze, simply the remorseless heat and the threaded hum of a town that stopped only briefly to acknowledge the arrival of the coffin and the shock of a murder.

The congregation was filled with priests who had known, respected and loved the victim, and there was an uneasy solemnity to the occasion. Sidney took the service, assisted by both Leonard Graham and Patrick Harland, the lay-reader who had sat beside them in Coventry only a few weeks previously. Harland was a small thin man with quick-moving eyes, dressed in a cheap suit that had started to shine at the knees and elbows and whose pockets had slackened. He prepared for the service with meticulous attention to every detail of the liturgy. Sidney wondered why he had never become a priest.

"He gave up his training after a year," Leonard explained. "I think he found the academic side a bit too taxing after the excitement of divine revelation. But he's a good sort even if he is prone to certainty."

"We all know what an error that can be," Sidney replied.

He decided that his sermon would reflect on Philip Agnew's goodness in the face of evil. He would talk about how a God of Love could have allowed something so terrible to happen. One had to make a distinction between moral evil (that human beings originate) and natural evil such as disease, flood and earthquake. Sidney began to argue, as he had done before, that the problem of goodness was just as intractable as the problem of evil. In the words of the old Latin phrase: "*Si Deus est, unde malum? Si non est, unde bonum?*" He was even tempted to leave his Latin untranslated but he knew that Mrs Maguire and some of the regulars would be in the congregation, and it would not be fair to show off his donnish capabilities in her presence. "If there is a God, why is there evil? If there is not, why is there good?" The mystery of evil was complex upon the basis of a good God, but the mystery of goodness was, he suggested, impossible on the basis of no God.

"That was very thought-provoking," Patrick Harland told him after the service. Sidney thought there was a slightly patronising tone to his voice but told himself not to be over-sensitive.

"Of course it's such a terrible loss. Agnew was a good man. Sometimes naive, of course . . ."

"Goodness and naivety often go together, I find," Sidney replied. "The holiest men are often thought simple."

Leonard hung up his robe, glanced at both men and muttered something about Dostoevsky's novel *The Idiot* before leaving the vestry to meet some friends.

Sidney, who wondered how keenly Harland might really be feeling about the loss of Agnew's fellowship, took the opportunity to ask how often he helped out at the Round Church and whether he had seen the victim on the day he had died.

"A few hours before. He was talking to one of those waifs and strays who always want money. So many of them do. I think it's better to give them food. You know they're only going to drink any cash. You might as well throw it all into the lavatory."

"Have you told the police this?"

"I didn't think that it would make much difference to their line of enquiry."

"They haven't interviewed you?"

"I have been away for a few days."

"You could at least have provided a description."

"There were so many of them. Mr Agnew was always entertaining strangers."

"I'm not sure I would refer to it as 'entertaining'."

"They stayed long enough."

Sidney pressed. "About the visitor that you saw on the day of Philip's death . . ."

"He looked very much as they all do. He was very thin and he had a loping gait. You would think that he had become so adept at asking for money that his features had fixed into a permanently servile humility. It was not attractive."

"But this man might either be responsible for Philip's death or know something very important. We have to find him."

"I don't think that's our job."

"It is our duty to share any knowledge with the police. I must insist that you tell my friend Inspector Keating what you know."

"Very well. But I fear we may be barking up the wrong tree. Rather like your dog, I should imagine."

"Dickens doesn't bark very often. Only when he senses something is very wrong."

"Perhaps he is like his master in that respect, Canon Chambers. Now, if you'll excuse me, I must attend to the candles and check the hassocks are all in the right place. I like to leave things tidy. Good day to you."

"Mr Harland, you seem to be reluctant to confront some aspects of the way in which our poor friend Philip left this world. What is on your mind, I wonder?"

"Not at all. I merely ask myself if the crime was not perhaps sexually motivated in some way. You know that Mr Agnew was a confirmed bachelor. He never married."

"But that does not make him a homosexual."

"We all know that he was."

"I always think it's better not to ask," Sidney replied.

"Canon Chambers, for a man of such curiosity you seem very squeamish about things that might matter."

"I don't see how this could possibly be construed as a sexually motivated crime and this is hardly the place to be talking about it."

"Then I apologise, Canon Chambers. I was merely making a suggestion."

"However, I do not shy away from pursuing questions that may lead to some kind of truth. Did Philip Agnew have any particular friends?"

"No. I rather think that was the problem. Because there was not one person, there were many."

"I'm not sure how you can know that."

"Trust me, Canon Chambers. I do."

The next day, Helena Randall stopped Sidney in the street. She wanted his thoughts, both on the murder and on the missing vagrant. He told her firmly that he was not ready to share them because he was inwardly uncertain if this was a deliberate crime against a possibly homosexual priest, or a consciously misleading suggestion by Patrick Harland who might, or might not, have been a spurned lover himself.

"And so," Sidney replied, "I don't think I can have much to offer Inspector Keating. In any case, I think we are both peripheral figures in his life . . ."

"You may be, Canon Chambers, but I am not. It's my job to report. It's Inspector Keating's to investigate and solve the case. Perhaps you could remind me of your vocation?"

"I am helping a friend . . ."

"And so am I."

"I worry that in so doing you may, in fact, be distracting him."

"You're being very solicitous."

"I don't want to intrude . . ."

"You are intruding. But there's no need for you to worry about Geordie and me. There's nothing going on, you know. It's only a bit of fun."

Sidney remembered being with a London girl, Janet, during the war before he went off to fight. His friends had told him that he could not die without knowing a woman first. Then Janet had said the same thing. He shouldn't worry about making love to her. It was "only a bit of fun".

It was so long ago and he had never told anyone about it. He wondered what had happened to her: if she still lived in the East End, if she had survived the Blitz, if she was perhaps married with three children, or if she was alive at all.

Helena looked at him quizzically and he realised he had repeated the words "only a bit of fun" out loud. She shrugged and turned away. Sidney watched her go, and then pushed his bike forward into the road, towards home.

He missed Hildegard, though it wasn't even lunchtime. He remembered her coming naked to bed the previous night and saying, "Don't look at me. I'm shy."

"I can't help it," Sidney had replied. "It's the best bit of the day."

That afternoon, Jerome Benson was taken to St Andrew's Street police station and questioned about his brother's disappearance. Despite the heat he had persisted in wearing his hunting clothes. He would not sit down or accept a glass of water and it was clear that he did not intend to be persecuted on account of his profession or appearance. After a series of "No Comments" he finally snapped, "I don't know why you are asking me all these questions. I am not my brother's keeper."

Keating remained unusually patient. "We need to know where your brother might have gone . . ."

"He told the clergyman Birmingham . . ."

"Do you believe he has got anything against priests?"

"No more than most people."

"You think most people don't value priests?" Sidney asked.

"They are tolerated. I don't think many people take what you do seriously. Look at how much spare time you have to go meddling in other people's lives . . ."

"I don't see it as meddling."

"Well, I do. My brother and I have done nothing wrong. We're both pretty anti-social . . . a bit misanthropic, I suppose, as you may have noticed; and we are likely to become more so after all this."

Keating began to pace around the room, leaving Sidney to continue with the questioning. "Your brother is a jazz musician?"

"That is no insurance against misanthropy."

"But he gets out and about. He goes on tour. He plays nightclubs. People applaud . . ."

"And then he has to face himself again when all the clapping stops. We are both prone to depression, if you must know. Jimmy has more ups and downs than I do. But that is probably because he uses chemicals rather differently. I use them for my taxidermy whereas he . . ."

"Injects straight into his arm?" Keating cut in.

"I leave you to fill in the blanks. You don't need me to tell you about that kind of thing."

There was a pause that Sidney soon remedied. "A long time ago, you told me that birds are your favourite form of taxidermy. 'They die so beautifully,' you said. I wondered if you could help us consider the implications of one element of this case. Dead doves have been left on my doorstep. Do you think that this particular choice of birds is significant?"

"As a portent or warning, you mean? I would have thought a raven might have more significance. Or a bird of prey — a falcon, for example, or even a vulture."

"They may not be so easy to come by."

Inspector Keating stopped his pacing round the room. "Have any of your animals gone missing recently?"

"None at all."

"Is your brother homosexual?"

"What's that got to do with anything?"

"I just need to know."

"We don't talk about things like that. Even if he is, it's legal now. You can't do anything if it's between consenting adults."

"Are you?"

"That is none of your business."

"Neither of you are married." Keating continued.

"That does not make us homosexual . . ."

"I am aware of that."

"What am I being accused of?"

"Nothing."

"I would like a lawyer if you are going to question me in this way . . ."

"We are not accusing you of anything, Mr Benson . . ."

"But you are asking leading questions. I prefer to live on my own without men or women. It is easier that way: protection from the false hopes and disappointments of love."

"And you have been let down in the past?"

"My mother left my father. It broke his heart. Ever since then I swore that such a thing would never happen to me. Solitude makes life safer."

"You don't feel that you are missing out?"

"Never."

"And your brother is the same?"

"I cannot speak for him. I've told you."

Sidney was wondering where all this was leading but before they had finished what was intended to be a full interrogation Inspector Keating glanced at the clock and announced that he had to leave. He had an important meeting to attend. Sidney had assumed they would discuss matters informally in the pub and was therefore surprised by his friend's imminent departure. As soon as they had left the room he asked Keating the obvious question. "Who are you going to see?"

"Never you mind. In any case, it won't take long." Keating smiled unconvincingly. "I'll see you in the Eagle later on."

"But we haven't finished the Benson interview . . ."

"You get the pints in. I'll worry about the investigation."

Sidney walked out of the police station and made his way towards Corpus to call in on some friends, but found himself waylaid by a chance encounter with the

Inspector's wife outside the butcher's shop. Cathy Keating was a dark, handsome woman with a natural authority, taller than her husband, a fact only accentuated by her beehive hairdo, and cheekbones that were almost as high as her heels. Every time Sidney met her he was reminded both why his friend had so many children and, at the same time, why he spent so much time away from home. The woman was simultaneously attractive and terrifying.

"I'm surprised that you're so out and about after the recent murder, Canon Chambers. I would have thought you might want to stay indoors until the culprit is brought to justice."

"We cannot live in fear."

"And a low profile doesn't really suit you, does it?"

"What do you mean?"

"You like to be at the centre of things. Are you going my way?"

"I'm not sure. I thought I'd look in at Corpus."

"Then I'll walk with you to the end of Pembroke Street. Have you been seeing my husband again?"

"I hope you don't disapprove of our friendship?"

"Of course not. He enjoys your company. It keeps him out of the house. Although I didn't know you were now meeting him twice a week. Tuesdays as well as Thursdays."

Sidney was about to say, "I'm not", when he realised what was going on. Geordie was expecting him to cover his meetings with Miss Randall. "Is that what he said?"

"You mean you are not?"

"I don't think we had quite settled on making it a regular thing."

"Are you hiding something from me? What plans are you two cooking up?"

"Nothing more than the usual."

"That's often too much. I know about the journalist, if that's what you're worried about. I can tell she's trouble and I've warned Geordie that I'll change the locks and boot him out if there's any nonsense."

"I don't think it'll ever come to that."

"He wouldn't be so daft but I don't like people *talking*."

"I understand, Mrs Keating."

"He says she's helpful. I know he just likes being with a pretty girl. It's hard when you've got three children and you feel yourself getting older. Sometimes I think I can't keep up. Men assume they get more attractive as they get older. Perhaps it's just a question of confidence. Some people find certainty alluring, don't they?"

"I suppose they do."

"But you're not that confident, are you, Mr Chambers?"

"I try to be so about my faith."

"But you are reluctant to judge. You like to give people the benefit of the doubt."

"I hope I do."

"And do you think the best of that girl? Tell me truly."

"I'm afraid I don't."

"You don't like her either?"

"I'd rather not answer that question, if you don't mind."

"That means you don't. Will you tell him?"

"I think it would be better if he found out for himself."

"I don't want him making a fool of himself," Cathy continued.

"Perhaps if we allow events to take their course, common sense will prevail. You see, this is a tricky situation."

"I'm sure you've seen it all before."

"I mean the case. The murders. There is evil involved. I don't think either Miss Randall nor your husband know exactly what we are up against and there's certainly no time for distractions. We'll be too busy to go to the pub or worry about gossip. They're underestimating everything."

"But if the devil makes work for idle hands . . ."

"Then the way to combat him is to make those hands less idle and fight evil with all the strength that we can muster."

They had arrived at the turn into Trumpington Street where their paths diverged. "You're a good man," said Cathy Keating before leaning forward and giving her confidant an unexpected peck on the cheek.

Sidney collected his post from the Porters' Lodge, looked it through and then proceeded to the Eagle, where he intended to question his friend. Inspector Keating was, however, properly preoccupied. A decapitated blackbird had been left outside Helena Randall's front door.

"She's frightened, Sidney. She needs a bit of comfort."

"That is bad. But you'll have to work out how much comfort you are prepared to provide."

"For God's sake, man, she's a worried woman."

"We mustn't be distracted."

"I've already told you. Miss Randall is a help and not a hindrance. She is a vulnerable young girl and a material witness. How many people do you know who have had dead blackbirds left on their doorstep? And dead doves too, for that matter? Look what happened after you found them."

"We don't know the birds are connected with murder."

"I don't know how much more evidence we need to draw that conclusion."

"Nothing more has happened since the blackbird was found. And I still think it's a mistake to see too much of Miss Randall."

"What do you mean?"

"It's a matter of reputation. You don't want to be seen with her in off-duty situations that might be compromising. Your wife . . ."

"What's Cathy got to do with it?"

Sidney realised he had put his foot in it and that it was now too late to retract. Why had he brought Geordie's wife into the conversation?

"She's worried," he answered, rather too firmly, remembering how his father had once told him to be particularly emphatic when you already know that you are in the wrong.

"Have you been talking to my wife?"

"I bumped into her outside the butcher's."

"That's very convenient."

"It was a coincidence, I can assure you. We had a very good chat."

"My marriage is private, Sidney, as is yours," Keating snapped. "That's one thing I can teach you: stay out of any relationship that's not your own. You never know what goes on in other people's bedrooms and never will. What we have to do is solve this bloody case before it gets even more out of hand than it is already." He slapped a half-crown on the bar. "Now get me a pint, for God's sake, and have one yourself. You look like you need it and we have to sort this out."

Later that evening, as Sidney cycled slowly back to Grantchester, he considered the choice of birds in the case. Dead doves could simply be a warning of a shattered peace. Surely, he thought, a raven should have been next, the bird that never returned to Noah's ark, scavenger of carrion, and, in some cultures, the ghost of a murder victim. So, why a blackbird? And did it provide any clues as to who might be the next victim? A journalist perhaps, since his own warning placement of doves had preceded the death of Philip Agnew, a man in the same profession as Sidney. He decided to make a few enquiries about the editor of the *Cambridge Evening News* and, even though he knew such thoughts were despicable, he might also find out if the man was married. Although he did not like Patrick Harland's insinuations, he could not ignore them, especially if homophobia were to prove a motive for murder.

Hildegard was working her way through a particularly stormy bit of Beethoven when he arrived home and Sidney was just thinking that it would be safest to let her get on with it and tiptoe to his study when she stopped playing and called him into the drawing-room.

She did not move from the piano. Her hands lay on the silent keys and she stared at him over the music rest as he stood in the doorway. "Where have you been?" she asked.

"I was a little delayed coming home."

"So . . . have you walked Dickens?"

"No. Why? Have you?"

"I just want to know what you have been doing?"

"I've been out and about. The usual things. I can't really remember all the details but I'm home now. There's no need to worry."

"Don't be evasive. I just want to know where you have been this evening?"

"I was with Geordie. You know that."

"The whole time?"

"Yes, just about."

"You didn't see anyone else?"

"Not really."

"Sidney, I want you to think very hard about this."

"I've got so much else to worry about. There have been developments."

"You can say that again. What were you doing with Mrs Keating?"

"Oh, that? I just met her outside the butcher's. It was nothing."

"Nothing? I think you gave her a little kiss."

"She gave me one. I haven't done anything wrong, Hildegard."

"You are sure?"

Sidney hesitated. "I suppose someone has said something. Is this Mrs Maguire being helpful?"

"I'm grateful to her. She saw it all."

"It was a peck on the cheek, nothing more."

"People will talk."

"I could hardly cut her dead. Besides, it is my job to give pastoral care."

"When people are sick and distressed. There's nothing wrong with Cathy Keating."

"You are right. There isn't."

"Then why did she kiss you?"

"Because I promised to help her. It's difficult to explain, my darling."

"Have a try."

"I'm worried about Geordie, if you must know. He seems to have taken a shine to a local journalist."

"The one I met?"

"Yes. Helena Randall."

"His wife is more attractive."

"Yes, that's what I think."

Hildegard smiled at her husband. He had walked right into her trap. "What am I going to do with you?" she asked.

Dickens brought them his favourite shoe, then his old red sock and finally his squeaky rabbit, forcing the couple to think of other things and take him for a brief walk to the end of the road and back, before the ritual of evening cocoa.

All was calm once more, and Hildegard had gone up to bed when the fragile peace of the vicarage was broken by a knock on the door from a police officer. He had time for neither friendliness nor formality. Earlier that evening, the body of another clergyman, Isaiah Shaw, had been discovered on Jesus Green. At first it appeared that it was suicide. He had hung himself from a tree. Then the same hatched stab marks were found on his chest: the mark of the beast.

Sidney asked for a few moments alone before accompanying the police officer to the station. He went upstairs, kissed his sleeping wife, and left her a note in case she woke up.

Even though it was almost midnight, he wanted to pray before he did anything else. He knelt briefly at his prie-dieu and remembered the dead.

Isaiah Shaw had been a studious, hard-working clergyman with skeletal features, a slightly hooked nose, and dark recessed eyes that gave the appearance of never seeing daylight. He was a somewhat tortured man who was perhaps too sensitive to his own flaws, and who took to the bottle when he worried how far he fell short of living in God's image. He felt the cold easily, complained of poor circulation and was well known in clerical circles for greeting friends and neighbours with "the icy hand of doom". This was unfortunate because although he had neither small talk nor a sense of humour, preferring books to people, Sidney recognised that Isaiah's heart was in the right place and that his patient, prayerful worship of God and the saving of souls was far more important than easy popularity.

He had also had his troubles: a dead wife (cancer at thirty-two) and an estranged son who worked as a builder, with no interest in his father's vocation to the point where Isaiah had once confessed to Sidney that he was not sure if he had ever been "the right father for the boy".

Sidney was desperately sad as he made his way to the police station to talk to Inspector Keating. He was then asked if he wanted any protection. "There's a full-scale manhunt for Jimmy Benson on now and we have to remember that he's met you already and knows where you live. The doves were an omen. The blackbird was a warning. Miss Randall has been provided with an officer of her own. I could give you one of my constables."

"That would look like favouritism. You can't protect every priest."

"But you have been warned specifically, Sidney. There were dead doves outside your door. It would give Hildegard some reassurance."

"I think a police presence might alarm her even more."

"I will need to know where you are at all times."

"That shouldn't be too hard."

"And I'll certainly ask my men to keep a look-out. I don't want to lose you, Sidney."

"Or anybody else, for that matter. This is evil, Geordie, pure evil."

49

★ ★ ★

The following evening, Sidney confided his darkest anxieties to his curate. He did not want to appear frightened in front of his wife or his parishioners but he was fearful none the less. "Perhaps this is something we can't ever fully comprehend, Leonard; evil without any rational explanation."

"I am never quite sure, Sidney, if people are wicked from birth or if they become so. I'm interested in how the good can turn or become possessed."

"Or if evil can be disguised or hidden beneath an apparent normality; that humanity pivots between the two."

"'This supernatural soliciting cannot be ill, cannot be good.'"

"*Macbeth*. Exactly."

Hildegard called out that supper was nearly ready. If the men could come and lay the table that would be helpful.

Leonard continued. "I have always been interested in the theory that we are not made in God's image at all. Instead we are deliberately created incomplete."

"That is not the traditional Augustinian position, of course," Sidney pointed out. "As you recall, according to the great church father, we are creatures who have sinned, whether literally or metaphorically, thereby disrupting God's plans. We have fallen from grace."

"But if we are now born sinners, if we have already sinned, why then should each generation be punished for the wickedness of their fathers, yea, even unto the end of time?"

Sidney thought for a minute. "Because it underpins the idea of redemption."

"But why should we have to redeem ourselves? Are not human beings created innocent rather than sinners?"

"As you know, there is an alternative argument."

"I remember this from theological college; it's the idea that we are created neither innocent nor guilty but immature, and yet to be fully formed. One has to decide if human beings were once good (and have fallen) or if they have *yet to be* good? Perhaps this life is not meant to be lived as punishment for the evils of the past (and therefore is our chance to make amends) but is, instead, a vale of soul-making that offers us the chance to *evolve* into goodness? In this tradition, humankind is still in the process of creation. We look forwards to a future life instead of backwards to a life for which we must atone. Life becomes a classroom, or a laboratory, in which we acquire moral discipline as we live, testing both good and evil."

"Are you coming?" Hildegard called once more. "I am dishing up."

Leonard showed no sign of moving. "God is then fully aware of evil; it is not the work of the devil or any other agency."

"He is responsible for evil?"

"He has to be. He accepts it as the price of soul-making."

"Even if there are casualties?"

"It is, of course, a perilous adventure in intellectual freedom. But the key question to ask, and perhaps the foundation for Christian theodicy, is this: can there be a future good, 'set free from its bondage to decay', that is so eternal and so complete that it compensates for all previous suffering and wickedness?"

"A heaven that makes up for the hell of life on earth?"

"Not exactly heaven, but a state of perpetual grace."

"That is a long promise. I'm not sure how we can ever justify pain and suffering, cruelty and wickedness by an end-state; however good that might be."

"THE SUPPER WILL BE COLD WHEN IT IS SUPPOSED TO BE HOT."

"We are on our way," Sidney answered.

Leonard kept talking. "Dostoevsky asked this in *The Brothers Karamazov*; could an architect build a heaven based on the unavenged torture of a baby?"

"'No, I would not consent, said Alyosha softly.' I have read it, Leonard. But Christianity is predicated on the idea of waiting: as Christ waits in the garden of Gethsemane, embracing the agony of suffering, as a father waits for his prodigal son, as we wait for those who matter to us and those we love, and as God waits with man for the secret of the world's power of meaning; its wonder and terror, vastness and delicacy, good and evil."

"AND I WAIT WITH YOUR DINNER," Hildegard answered as they entered the kitchen. "You men. I think I am going to start pretending supper is ready when it is not. It is the only way to get you here on time."

"I am sure this will be delicious, my darling," Sidney replied before looking at the confection on the table. "Shepherd's pie! What a treat."

"It's your favourite and so I'd like to know what have you been talking about that's so important?"

"Ah," said Leonard. "Let me fetch the Worcester sauce."

Sidney confessed. "We have been discussing the problem of good and evil."

"I see." Hildegard met his look and made her challenge public. "I imagine that you have been referring to the murders?"

"I'm afraid so."

"I should have guessed."

"I'm sorry."

"You know that I was thinking as I was cooking," Hildegard mused. "Even though Isaiah Shaw was married, do you think the murderer could have been mistaken about him?"

"Do you mean people might have thought him queer?" Sidney asked.

"It being a potential motive for murder."

"That and, it seems, a hatred of priests."

Leonard poured out the water. "Why do people despise us so?" His companions were not sure that he was talking exclusively about the priesthood but let the remark pass. "We are only trying to do good."

"It's not 'people', Leonard. It's one particular person. We just have to find out who it is."

"And you don't think it could be Benson?" Hildegard asked.

"Which one? It could be either of them."

"Or both, perhaps? One could be killing the animals, while the other commits the murders?"

Sidney looked at the shepherd's pie on his fork and decided to speak instead of eating it. "Although they were brought up as atheists they don't seem particularly hostile to priests, do they? Eccentric loners perhaps, but not murderers."

"I presume Jimmy Benson is still on the run?" Leonard asked.

"He may not be consciously 'on the run' but I'd be surprised if we found him in hiding near here. I just need to think what links the birds to murder."

"They are omens, of course," said Hildegard. "I suppose Inspector Keating will find one next."

"A dead bird? Do you think so?"

"I do," said Hildegard. "The murderer is taunting you."

"It looks like it."

"And I think you can assume it's a man. But is there anything that links the two victims apart from the fact that they were both priests? Were they friends? Did they move in the same social circles? Did they know people in common?"

Leonard answered, "We are all friends, of course."

"But some more than others."

"That is true. The main thing that the two priests shared was that they were known to take in vagrants and they both had an air of holiness about them. They were, and I think Sidney will agree, far more spiritual than we might be; and that may put us out of danger. You, at least, Sidney . . ."

"What do you mean?"

"You are a man of the world and are married: unlike the victims."

"I don't see how that makes a difference."

"Well, I can. If I was naive and a little more devout, I'd be worried that I was next."

Hildegard gathered up the plates. There was treacle tart to follow. "You're not frightened, are you, Leonard?"

"I am a priest and a single man. Furthermore people do suspect . . ."

Sidney interrupted. "There's no need to go into that."

Leonard looked to Hildegard. "I wouldn't want you to think . . ."

"We are friends here," Sidney reassured him. "Your feelings are private, Leonard. At the moment I think the aim is to get at priests in general. Perhaps the murderer is someone who has been badly let down in the past."

"And these two in particular?"

"What would inspire a man to hate a priest?" Hildegard asked.

"And what would make him so desperate that he would choose evil over good?" said Leonard.

"Hate over love."

"And death over life," Sidney mused.

By the time they had finished the treacle tart they were no nearer an answer.

★ ★ ★

For the next few days, Sidney tried to concentrate on the quiet rhythms of life but everything he did could be construed as banal in comparison to his investigation. He used his regular walks with Dickens to think through the possibilities of the case. It was just after his return from one such ramble that the telephone rang in the vicarage. A muffled voice that was trying to disguise itself asked if he was Sidney Chambers and if they could meet.

"Who is this?"

"I can't say. But I know the man you're looking for."

"Who are you?"

"Never mind who I am. There isn't much time. I'm staying in a boarding house in the centre of town. There's a café round the corner. Meet me in Christ's Lane at four o'clock. Don't bring anyone else."

"Why me?" Sidney asked, but the caller had hung up.

He was not sure how to fill the time before the appointment, but when he made his first move Hildegard asked why he was going out again so soon after he had come in. How many walks did Dickens need and why was her husband being so evasive? She wanted to check that in this troubled time he wasn't putting himself into any more danger. Sidney assured her that he knew how to avoid getting into a scrape.

"It only takes one mistake."

"I am aware of that."

"I don't want you assuming that you are immune to bad luck. We're happy together. Do you sometimes think that we're too happy?"

"So happy that there's bound to be a massive amount of ill-fortune coming round the corner? I do think that sometimes, I must admit, but then I hope that in the past you've had enough for both of us."

"You take on my burden."

"I take on everything about you, my darling. We are one."

"Then don't leave me half a person by dying."

"I have no intention of doing that."

Sidney kissed his wife softly on the mouth. He wished he could stay. He even wished they could go upstairs in the middle of the afternoon. That was the kind of thing louche people did, and if he was a jazz musician like Jimmy Benson he could probably stay up all night and then spend all day in bed with a glamorous singer or, even more appealingly, his wife. He looked her in the eyes. "Until tonight then."

"I'll make a special supper."

Sidney was worried that he was going to be late and began a reckless bicycle route across the meadows, scattering a group of picnickers who were just leaving the path, ringing his bell, and apologising to parishioners who wanted him to stop for a chat. He was going to be five minutes overdue and he was trying not to think about what else he could be doing as he freewheeled into Christ's Lane and left his bike against the railings. He was just about to enter the café when he thought he noticed something in the adjoining alley.

He was aware before he knew.

The slumped figure was of a man whose tongue had been cut out. His shirt had been ripped open and the mark of the beast was upon his chest.

It was Jimmy Benson.

A woman screamed in the street.

Sidney asked the café proprietor if he could borrow his telephone and told Keating to come round immediately.

It was impossible to keep the crime scene secret and Helena Randall arrived shortly after the police. Sidney had just finished making his statement when she started on a few direct enquiries of her own. "You had the doves. I had the blackbird. Then, and he won't have told you this, someone left a dead bird at Geordie's house."

"That could still be a coincidence."

"No, Sidney. It can't be, and you know it."

"What type of bird was it?"

"A canary. And it was nailed to his front gate. We are being taunted, Sidney. All three of us."

"But it's curious, isn't it? We are not the victims."

"Jimmy Benson was killed because he was about to talk. That would make the canary significant. Had he been in touch with you?"

Sidney paused, uncertain whether he could lie. Helena read his hesitation. "My God," she said. "You were on your way to see him, weren't you?"

"I was."

"Then people might even think that you could be the killer yourself."

"I don't think that's likely."

"Two priests and a vagrant. You knew them all. You have to be careful."

"I think I can look after myself."

"That could be what the previous victims thought. We don't want anything happening to you."

"I'm grateful for your concern, Miss Randall."

"I care about you more than you think."

After being told of the death of his brother, Jerome Benson was questioned in his workshop for several hours. The small cramped room smelled like a post-mortem laboratory and its working light was illuminated despite the sunshine outside. Keating sought out the information he needed about Benson's movements that day while Sidney asked about the birds. Was any special knowledge of taxidermy required to prepare them in the way in which they had been left, and how easy would it be to capture and kill specific types? Was there a connection, he wondered, between the type of bird chosen and the manner of death of the victim? The doves before Philip Agnew's suffocation, the decapitated blackbird before the hanging of Isaiah Shaw, a canary nailed to a gatepost before the stabbing of a man who was about to talk?

"How much do you think your brother knew about the previous murders? Did he discuss them with you?"

Benson did not stop to offer Sidney a cup of tea, or even to concentrate on the questions he was being asked, but continued cleaning an otter skin. "He was a very clever man; far more than me — until he got into difficulties."

"When was that?"

"Five or six years ago now. I think love had something to do with it. That and the late nights. I didn't see him that much."

"But what did he tell you?"

"We're not close, Canon Chambers."

"But he came to you for help."

"He came to me for money."

"Who else did he go to?" Keating continued.

"You'd have to ask him that."

"I can hardly do so now."

"If you'd reached him sooner . . ."

Sidney knew that it would not do to respond to such a provocative remark. Grief could make people vindictive, and he didn't want Jerome Benson taking the law into his own hands. Keating, however, had no such qualms. "If your brother had come in for questioning then he might still be alive."

"You mean it's his own fault? He was scared."

"Did he tell you that he was?"

"He didn't need to tell me. He ran off."

"Do you know where he went?"

"No I don't. How much longer is this going to take?"

Sidney sat down on a low bench. "Quite a few priests like jazz. I am sure that if he'd spoken to one or two of them, and asked them for help, he would have been given charity; either food or a bed for the night."

"He didn't go round killing them, I'll tell you that much."

"But perhaps he knew who did?"

"You won't get that from me."

"Is that because you are the very man we are looking for?" Keating asked.

"Don't be daft. Why would I want to kill my own brother?"

"I don't think you did. But I think Jimmy knew his killer. He recognised the danger that he was in," Sidney continued. "There's something we're not being told."

"How can you be so sure?"

"Because if he did not have a secret then he would have had nothing to fear. Do you think he met both Philip Agnew and Isaiah Shaw?"

"It's unlikely he knew one priest; let alone two."

"You mentioned love." Sidney said quietly.

"There was a girl."

"Who was she?"

"She's called Bianca. Jimmy was always cagey about her. I don't know where she lives. Somewhere round here."

"So your brother is not a homosexual after all?" Keating pressed.

"No. Although I don't see how that can have anything to do with it."

"We think it can, Mr Benson. We think this could be a hate crime."

"My brother didn't hate anyone; not homosexuals nor vicars. He just didn't fit in. Neither of us did. But we don't do harm. The world is full of hypocrisy, don't you find, Canon Chambers? Sometimes those that look as if they've slept in a hedge do so because they really have slept in a hedge. They've got no money. They're down on their luck. What you see is what you get. But then that's not the case with so-called respectable people at all, is it? You can't ever tell what they think or what they're doing. They've got so much on the surface you can't even begin to know what's going on underneath."

"And what do you think is 'going on underneath', Mr Benson?"

"The power of all evil, Canon Chambers. That covers it, by my reckoning. The power of all evil."

The theological college of Westcott House was an unassuming nineteenth-century building in Jesus Lane, with an old Tudor brick courtyard and a refectory that contained a life-size image of the Crucifixion. Simon Opie, or *Princeps*, ran the college as erratically and eccentrically as he drove his car, never appearing to concentrate on the job in hand. He divided his time between his study, the chapel and the aviary he had built in the college gardens.

Opie had written one great classic work of theology in his youth, *An Enquiry into Suffering and Omnipotence*, and despite his inability to settle down to anything for any great length of time, he had a deep knowledge of human deviance and the nature of evil. If anyone would know how to deal wisely with the problems that they were facing and form some kind of psychological profile of the killer then it was surely Sidney's former tutor.

Many of his students regarded the man as a latter-day St Francis, who preached to the birds in the valley of Spoleto, praising God for making them the most noble of creatures, quietening them when they were noisy, invoking them as evidence for the glory of God's creation; and indeed Sidney could hardly stop his friend talking about his fine collection of cockatiels, kakarikies and rosellas.

"I named the first generation after the church fathers," Simon Opie explained, "but then I thought that it was all getting a little pretentious. You can't really have a parakeet called Polycarp of Smyrna or a budgie called Tertullian."

"I think I'd name them after cricketers."

"No, I'd never remember all that. I think I'm going to call the next batch after the great poets. I'm going to have to have a think because I've lost quite a few birds recently."

"Nothing serious, I hope? No disease?"

"Nothing like that, fortunately, and at first I did think it was just a question of fate. There really is a special providence in the fall of a sparrow, you know. But then, this morning there was something unusual."

"And what was that?"

"I found a dead robin inside the aviary. It could have got in of its own accord, of course, but I don't see how. I would have noticed, I am sure of it."

"You mean it did not seem a natural death."

"Indeed it did not."

For a moment neither priest spoke.

"Who killed Cock Robin?" Simon Opie asked after a while.

Sidney felt cold. "Not the sparrow with his bow and arrow, I imagine."

"It all seems so spiteful. I suppose I must be the rook, with my little book, and bury him."

"Then if it's not in the dark I'll be the clerk. There's a great deal I need to ask you, Simon. There's more to this, you know."

"I was afraid that you were going to say that."

"I am *extremely worried*. I cannot exaggerate."

"Then we should have a cup of tea and discuss the matter. Do you have time? I will ask Mrs Maguire to see to it."

"You have employed my former housekeeper?"

"The very same. She told us that after your marriage she missed the company of clergy . . ."

"That doesn't sound like her at all . . ."

Sidney remembered overhearing Mrs Maguire complaining to his wife. "There's another thing I should tell you. Both men leave the toilet seat up and their aim isn't as good as it should be so there's always a mess on the lino. They just don't *concentrate*, that's their problem."

"She works here part-time," Simon Opie continued. "She's a lively presence, as I am sure you will remember. I can always count on her for an opinion."

"I am sure you can, Simon, but it's not her opinion I'm after. It's yours."

"Then proceed."

Sidney filled his former tutor in on the facts of the case, concentrating particularly on the idea of animal sacrifice. What were these portents or warnings? The dove was the representation of peace and purity, the blackbird's dark feathers were a reminder of the darkness of sin, and the canary was self-explanatory, but Sidney was extremely worried by the robin.

"There are several mythologies about his red breast," Simon Opie answered. "One is that it was scorched after taking water to the condemned in hell; another is that it was pierced and bled when removing the thorns from our Lord's crown on the cross. You also know the legend of animals talking at the moment of the nativity, the robin being one of them . . ."

"I remember something from Martial. 'I magpie, a talker, greet thee, O Lord.'"

"Speaking of talking . . ." Mrs Maguire entered the room with a tea trolley. She nodded to Sidney, put out a plate of pink Peek Freans biscuits and proceeded to pour out two cups while muttering that there was a man outside waiting to see the Principal.

"Did he say who he was?"

"He speaks a bit too fancy, if you ask me."

"Never mind about that. What is his name?"

"I think he said his name was Harland."

"Ah yes. He will have come to discuss his offer of lay-reading."

"Did he study here?" Sidney asked.

"For a short while. I am afraid he did not find it congenial. I think he had a bit of a breakdown. Not all that are called are chosen."

"Would you mind if I spoke to him too?" Sidney asked.

"I have no objection. But why would you want to do that? I am sure that you have parish duties to attend."

"He assisted at Philip Agnew's funeral. He didn't strike me as a man who had suffered a nervous breakdown."

"Sometimes people emerge from their setbacks all the stronger. With God's help."

"They are changed, I know, but not always for the better."

"That's rather uncharitable of you, Sidney."

"I sometimes think there is a reason people don't find themselves . . ."

"You have always preferred a life in doubt and mystery. I know you of old."

"Plato, of course . . ."

Mrs Maguire hovered. "Shall I show him in or not?"

Simon Opie smiled and gave her a little nod. "So good to see you, Sidney. I am only sorry about the circumstances."

"These are very worrying times."

Patrick Harland was wearing a three-piece pin-striped suit that was too hot for summer, and there was a light sweat across his forehead. He was surprised to see Sidney. "I hope I am not interrupting."

Simon Opie decided to forgo the introductions. "I believe you two know each other?"

"Not well."

"I thought you lived in London?" Sidney asked Harland.

"I do. But I'm spending the weekend with my sister. She and her husband run a boarding house off Midsummer Common."

"I must take a look at it. People are always asking where they might stay. What's it called?"

"The Willows. I'm sure she'd be glad to be of service."

"I'll be in touch then. What did you say her name was?"

"I didn't, Canon Chambers."

"Then would you mind telling me?"

"She's Mrs Jay. Bianca Jay."

"A bird's name," said Sidney. "There's a coincidence."

"I don't see what makes it so."

"We have just come from the aviary and we were talking about Christian symbolism. Is that a subject which interests you, Mr Harland?"

Mrs Maguire trudged into the room without knocking, a cup and saucer in her hand. "Would you care for a cup of tea, Mr Harland? There are some quite nice biscuits there if you fancy them. Peek Freans wafers. Popular with all the vicars I've worked for. They can't get enough of them."

When he returned to the vicarage Sidney was relieved to find that Hildegard had gone out. She had left a note on the table saying that she was seeing an old friend. Sidney wondered who that friend might be and felt an unexpected pang of jealousy before being thankful that this would buy him time to talk to Leonard. It was such a pity he was leaving. He would miss the company of his curate and only hoped that he could find a suitable replacement, especially one with whom he could discuss his criminal cases.

He wanted to explore all the issues surrounding Patrick Harland, Bianca Jay and Jimmy Benson. It was clear that they knew each other and that there could have been something going on between Jimmy and Bianca. He made a pot of tea in the kitchen and tried to sum up his thoughts.

"The intriguing factor in all of this is that Bianca Jay is married," said Leonard. "Are there any biscuits? I was hoping for a flapjack."

"I had a Peek Freans with *Princeps*. A married woman can still have a boyfriend, of course."

"Or a former lover. That would be more likely. Ah, I see we have some Garibaldis."

"Hildegard doesn't approve of shop-bought biscuits. I wonder where they could have come from?"

"I think that's a mystery we can leave aside at the moment. We have to assume, I think, that Jimmy Benson's love was either unrequited or at an end."

"And he, being spurned, turns up on the doorstep . . ."

"With a bit of blackmail, perhaps? If he suspected Bianca's husband was the murderer . . ." Sidney continued.

"Although he may not have been the blackmailing type. Do you think Hildegard could make some Garibaldis? They are quite ordinary run-of-the-mill biscuits but with lots of raisins."

"I prefer shortbread. Mrs Maguire, of course, made the most marvellous shortbread. Do you know they've employed her at Westcott House?"

"Perhaps we could ask her to keep an eye on developments there."

"I'm sure she's already doing that. But I think we should try and speak to Bianca Jay about Jimmy and then find out more about her husband. We have no idea of who he is or what he is like but perhaps he has something against priests?"

"It's a bit of a long shot and it's hard to see how we can justify a visit. He's not in our parish. Surely he will smell a rat?"

"That is true. But he could very well be our man. If only we had more information."

"Do you not think we are out of our depth, Sidney?"

"The police need all the help they can get."

"But neither you nor I, nor Miss Randall for that matter, are trained detectives."

"But we are trained priests, and priests have been the victims. Miss Randall is an investigative journalist."

"I see your position towards her is softening."

"She's very bright."

"That's what Keating says. I wouldn't admit as much to Hildegard."

"What do you mean? She approves of intelligence in a woman."

"When a man praises a woman's intelligence, Sidney, he is normally acknowledging how attractive he finds her."

"The intelligence being part of the attraction."

"Yes, but only a part. Be careful."

"I don't think you need worry about my having the wrong kind of feelings. But it's kind of you to be concerned. I know you're not so interested in women yourself, Leonard."

"They do interest me. It's simply that I don't understand them. I think I must be scared of them."

"They can be distracting, of course."

"You mean Miss Randall has been distracting?"

"Don't start on that all over again. I'd rather talk to you about biscuits."

"I think we have had a tinful of that, Sidney. But what do you think about the religious aspect to all this? Do you think it could be a case of demonic possession of some kind; or that it is being made to look like that? I am remembering the animal sacrifices as well as the murders."

"Perhaps it could be someone who is theologically aware?"

"You don't mean a fellow priest?"

"No, Leonard, but someone who might once have been a priest; or someone who thinks he has been treated badly; rejected, perhaps, personally, sexually, or even from the priesthood itself."

"A former ordinand who turned against us?"

"Having been rejected. And that expulsion from our midst then fuelled his resentment and his fury?"

"I don't know, Sidney, I am thinking aloud. I need more time to consider."

"I am not sure Inspector Keating is up for waiting. Can you tell me a little more about Patrick Harland?"

"Why are you asking about him? He is an over-enthusiast for God rather than the devil."

"I'm not so sure about that," Sidney replied.

"You don't think he can have anything to do with this, do you? He trained as a priest."

"But he didn't become one. Simon Opie told me he had a nervous breakdown."

"Something like that. An occupational hazard for evangelicals who run out of certainty."

"He was a late convert?"

"God has spoken to him, yes. He had a road-to-Damascus moment on the A1, I believe."

"A near-death experience?" Sidney asked.

"A blinding light. And a voice telling him to turn back. He was on his way to join his father's firm in the Potteries but he gave it all up to work with the poor. He wanted to do something more profitable than make plates."

"You don't mean 'profitable'; you mean socially useful."

"Yes. He wanted to change the world."

"How do you know all this, Leonard?"

"Some of his behaviour was cited in our tutorials as an example of how not to be a clergyman."

"The idea being that just because you think you have been given the gift of revelation, it doesn't give you carte blanche to become a cleric?"

"Or that it was even revelation in the first place," Leonard continued. "It could have been a fantasy; or even a migraine. Harland was never named but I knew that it was him. One of the tutors let it slip when we were talking about the difference between revelation, inspiration, creativity and madness. How can we know which is which? It's a theme that obsessed Dostoevsky, of course . . ."

"Yes, I am sure it did. Who were his tutors; can you remember?"

"Well, of course Philip Agnew was there at the time, and, oh my, of course, Isaiah Shaw came in and gave a series of meditations on suffering in the Easter of 1957. He was on the examining body too. Oh, Sidney, you don't think . . .? Patrick Harland may have been a bit zealous but he's not behind all this, is he? Benson's our man, surely; and if not him, then Mr Jay. I can't imagine a Christian committing all these crimes."

"I know. But we may have to. I think I will go and see him."

"Then I should come with you. After supper, perhaps?"

Sidney wondered about the nature of inspiration and revenge. Could God be blamed for putting an idea into someone's head; whether it was the desire to become a priest or its perverse opposite? Could Harland have changed his passion and impetuosity from good to evil? Had there been voices in his head and, if there had, what had they been saying?

Would a man such as Patrick Harland argue that he was fulfilling some supernatural instruction? Was evil, such as murder, a choice or could it be excused by possession, madness? How responsible are we for our actions? How far can we use reason to understand the irrational? Is to understand all to forgive all?

By no means, thought Sidney. We cannot excuse our actions, however evil or possessed, if we have free will; and even if God knows what choices might be made from that free will, his knowledge does not impinge upon our actions.

Leonard left to visit old Mrs Royston who, at the age of ninety-eight, was considering a last minute conversion to Catholicism, and Sidney was just going to telephone Keating and make his suspicions clear when the vicarage doorbell rang. It was Helena Randall. She wanted him to join her immediately. When Sidney asked her why, she pulled a map from her bag and pointed out that the location of each crime scene conformed to a pattern that must have been deliberately designed by the killer.

"There is a straight line down from where Isaiah Shaw was found on Jesus Green to the place where Jimmy Benson was discovered in Christ's Lane. If you then take another line from the Round Church where Philip Agnew was killed and bisect the previous vertical, as if you were drawing a cross, you will notice that the fourth point of the crucifix is Westcott House. Your friend Simon Opie will be next: unless we can stop it."

"Have you told Geordie?"

"He's still at the Benson crime scene. He's in a panic and won't listen to anything I say. We have to get to Westcott House immediately. I've got my car."

"But why do you need me?"

"Because you're the only man who understands what's going on and, if we're not too late, you can talk the killer down."

"You may have too much faith in my abilities."

"You're the one with the faith," Helena snapped, before leaning over and opening the car door. "Get in."

Even though they drove with the windows open, the air in Helena's Morris Minor was uncomfortably oppressive. Sidney didn't know whether it was the heat of the Cambridge summer or his own fear in the face of evil. Were they about to intercept a murder and, if so, who was the killer: Harland, Jay, Jerome Benson, or somebody they hadn't yet contemplated? Sidney's thoughts had become so confused that he had started to suspect everyone.

Helena's driving was aggressive and she used her horn at every corner, overtaking a tractor on a bend and narrowly missing a cyclist outside Queens'. "We've been several steps behind all along. I don't know what Geordie's been up to."

"We pursued Jimmy Benson for too long."

"You know who's behind this, don't you?" Helena asked.

"I have an idea but it's so perverse I can't be sure."

Helena hooted her horn, cut in front of a delivery van, and turned into Market Square, swerving to avoid a pedestrian before accelerating down Sidney Street and into Jesus Lane. Sidney was now too terrified to speak.

At last they pulled up outside Westcott House, and Helena slammed the car door behind her. "Where now?" she asked.

Sidney pointed in the direction of the refectory.

Inside, the crucifix had been taken down from the wall and lay on the floor. The figure of Christ had been removed and replaced by the unconscious body of Simon Opie, who had been tied to it by his arms and legs. A liquid circle surrounded him. Patrick Harland was straddling his chest with a knife in his hand and had made the first incision of the mark of the beast. He stopped when he saw Helena and Sidney.

"You are not just in time but just too late. I couldn't wait. I wonder what took you so long. I gave you enough clues."

"You left a robin . . ."

"With a breast as red as this man's chest is about to be. I hope you appreciate the symbolism."

"In the past, the omens have not been left in the homes of the victims."

"That would be too obvious, wouldn't it? Besides, I wanted to test you as a little trio. I know that you two both fancy yourselves as detectives."

"We did not set out to investigate these things," Sidney replied. "But when a good priest is killed . . ."

"As opposed to a bad priest. Are you sure he was good?"

"These are dedicated holy men."

"We are all flawed, Canon Chambers."

Helena interrupted. "Why did you kill Jimmy Benson?"

"Because he blabbed to my sister. He said he was worried about me. He thought I was going to do something stupid. Well, there's a surprise."

"Bianca," said Sidney.

"You were very slow, Canon Chambers. I told you her name and even where she lived. Yet you didn't find the time to see her. I imagine many of your parishioners must feel the same way: neglected."

"Jimmy Benson was in love with your sister."

"All his life. But he wasn't suitable. Not good enough, you understand. We like a bit of propriety. That's why, when we don't get it, it upsets us. Then we have to force people to give us the respect we deserve: like Mr Opie here."

"Don't touch him," Helena shouted.

"Oh but I already have. Do you think I should stop?" Harland began carving again. Simon Opie's body twitched. "Don't worry. He's still alive."

"What have these priests ever done to you?" Helena asked.

"What have they not done? That is the question you should be asking."

"There's no need for this."

"But there is, Canon Chambers. Mr Opie, here, would not let me become a priest. None of them would. I am the most despised and rejected of men."

"But that is no cause to kill. You can still do God's work. As a lay-reader and as a Christian."

"It was not enough. And these men themselves are not good enough to serve."

"That is for God to judge."

"I cannot wait that long. I have to take the law into my own hands. And what fine strong hands they are, don't you think? Such clean lines. My father was a butcher. Don't you think he'd be proud if he could see me now? Perhaps he can gaze in wonder through the flames of hell. That's how Mr Opie is going to see me. This liquid, as you can see, is petrol. I have a match. The devil has taken possession of a body where Christ should be. Serpents writhe inside me. I must burn them out, kill the devils that you will be purged. You may believe in prayer and fasting and medicine, but you do not know evil as I do. You have failed to heed it and I have shown you what it is like. Now I will show you more; your Church, your life with mine, must burn."

"Let us pray first," said Sidney.

"It's too late for that. There is no God. His only defence is that he does not exist. And without God, everything is permissible."

"Without God there is only the terror of absence; a chasm without love."

"And I am in that chasm."

"Then let me help you out of it."

"There is nothing you can do, Canon Chambers."

"You won't even let me pray for you?"

Patrick Harland stopped. "You would still do that? After all that I have done?"

"I pray for everyone." Sidney knelt down. "Come. Kneel. You too, Miss Randall."

"What?" Helena asked.

"Please. Kneel down."

Helena did so.

"Mr Harland, put your knife aside. Please. Kneel. Close your eyes."

It was not a request but an order.

"Let us pray."

Sidney began the Lord's Prayer, buying time, hoping for an act of God, anything to stop the evil that lay before them. The important thing, he had been taught, was to lead. This was no time for public doubt. He spoke clearly and loudly, already planning which of the familiar prayers he would say next, asking for mercy, hoping for understanding.

A sparrow flew through the open windows of the hall. Harland looked up, surprised by the interruption, as Sidney kept praying. "When the wicked man turneth away from his wickedness that he hath committed, and doeth that which is lawful and right, he shall save his soul alive."

Then Simon Opie, revived by the words and rescued from death, began to pray from the cross. "Rend your heart, and not your garments, and turn unto the Lord your God: for he is gracious and merciful, slow to anger, and of great kindness, and repenteth him of the evil."

Harland opened his eyes and looked back at the dying man, praying confidently in the hope of mercy, and began to weep.

Sidney let the tears fall into the silence. Then he walked over to Harland, knelt down beside him, and held him in his arms. "It's all right," he said. "It's over now."

A few days later, two couples spent a sunny Saturday together, lunching in the gardens of a local restaurant.

Geordie was reflecting on Patrick Harland's eventual arrest, Simon Opie's miraculous recovery, and Helena Randall's quick thinking. She was quite a girl, he continued, and Sidney had to agree, as Cathy and Hildegard smiled indulgently.

On tackling his second pint, the Inspector then began to muse on the trouble caused by religion and asked how a loving God could allow such evil.

"That is complicated," Sidney answered. "However, instead of trying to justify the ways of God to man we should perhaps think more of justifying man's ways to God."

"That would take for ever."

"An eternity, I suppose."

"And so evil people like Harland will still be forgiven in the end?" Keating asked.

"Possibly," Sidney continued. "I've been reading a text from the early Middle Ages, the *Vision of Saint Paul*, which is an account of the apostle's journey into the underworld. There he meets a man engulfed in the fires of purgatory. But the man is not in pain. Instead he is smiling. Why? Because he knows that three thousand years later one of his descendants will become a priest and, at his first Mass, that same priest will pray for him and release him from his suffering. St Paul realises that three thousand years in purgatory is nothing in comparison with eternity. The sinner has taught him the meaning of patience."

"I'm not sure I'd be prepared to spend three thousand years in pain. It would be simpler not to sin in the first place."

"That is rather the idea," Sidney assured his friend.

Keating fetched them all more beer and wondered whether, as he put it, God could ever be happy. "He must be a miserable old bugger, really, when you think of the wickedness human beings get up to; all that sin."

"That may be true," Sidney replied. "If God is aware of the human condition then how can he be content? But perhaps we have to think about the divine presence in a different way; not as what he is, but what he is not. In other words, not human, and not liable to emotion. The concept of happiness perhaps has no subject. It exists outside ourselves, unrelated to any specific human being."

"Then why do we all want to have it?"

"Because we are human."

"And therefore we suffer."

"Yes, Geordie."

"So what you are saying is that God does not know happiness; even though he is supposed to be omniscient? I don't understand how that works."

"John Stuart Mill argued that happiness is not something that can be achieved by striving for it. You have to pursue some other goal and 'if otherwise fortunately circumstanced you will inhale happiness with the air you breathe.'"

"So happiness is an accident?"

"Possibly. Schopenhauer defined it as the temporary absence of pain."

"And that is the best we can hope for?"

"Perhaps, but not necessarily."

"Oh, Sidney, this is all too deep for me."

"And me. Life still has many pleasures; not least the company of our delightful wives. Let us enjoy that while we may."

Hildegard leant forward and whispered to Cathy Keating. "How do you put up with it all?" she asked.

"To tell you the truth, Mrs Chambers, most of the time it's best to ignore what they get up to. It gives you time to yourself. They're out of the house and don't get in the way. That's the consolation. You've no need to be jealous of any of it. They'd be lost without us. They always know what's best for them in the end."

As Cathy Keating finished speaking, Helena Randall walked past. She was wearing a diaphanous green summer dress, her arms were bare and she had just washed her hair. It hung, still damp, in soft waves almost to her waist, small stray tendrils framing her face. She had not noticed the party at the table and the four friends did not ask her to join them. Cathy Keating remarked that even though it was a warm day Helena would catch her death of cold dressed like that and that her uncombed hair would lose its shape if she didn't watch out. It was a pity, she observed. Miss Randall could be quite a pretty girl if she just made more of an effort.

The two men looked at each other and knew that it was safest to say nothing.

A gathering of swallows flew above them, away and then into the distance, twittering in the skies. The sun had begun its decline. Sufficient unto the day, Sidney thought to himself, was the evil thereof.

Female, Nude

It was midday in October and Sidney was waiting for his good friend, the art historian Amanda Kendall, in the upper galleries of the Fitzwilliam Museum in Cambridge. They had arranged to view the new acquisition of a painting by Matisse, *The Studio Under the Eaves*, before enjoying a leisurely lunch at Le Bleu Blanc Rouge. That afternoon, Amanda had an appointment to see the director of the museum in order to confirm that the collection's portrait of William Fitzwilliam, Earl of Southampton was painted "after" Hans Holbein the Younger and was therefore of considerably less valuable than the museum had hoped. Such a possibility might diminish the reputation of the collection but at least it would save on the insurance.

It was a long time since Sidney had spent any time in the galleries and he had forgotten that the Fitzwilliam contained works of art that were far more impressive than many people imagined. There were paintings by Italian Renaissance artists, particularly Venetian, a superb collection of landscapes of all schools, a distinguished group of portrait miniatures by British artists and a remarkable range of French Impressionist paintings which were like old friends: a lilac-washed Monet scene of springtime, a simple plate of Cézanne's apples, and a Matisse portrait of a woman, *La Blouse Bulgare*, that always made him think of Amanda. He was reminded of the fact that the greatest paintings could always sustain repeated viewings. Like a classic book or a Shakespearean play, they were open to multiple interpretations. What mattered in art was not impact but resonance.

That autumn, there was a special exhibition on the female nude with works by Rodin, Whistler, Burne-Jones and Augustus John. Sidney passed the time waiting for his friend by imagining what it might be like to take a life drawing class. It would have much to teach him about patience, the art of looking, and the nature of human anatomy. He wondered how closely the eye of the artist should mirror that of the clergyman or the detective. Perhaps he could try to be, in Henry James's famous phrase, "one on whom nothing is lost".

He had just stopped to look more closely at two studies of a female nude by Eric Gill when he heard someone singing. It was a female voice; both high and delicate.

"Mon amant me délaisse
O gai! Vive la rose!
Je ne sais pas pourquoi
Vive la rose et le lilas!"

He turned round. As he did so, a young blonde girl undid her fur coat to reveal that she was naked underneath.

83

She draped the coat over her right shoulder and walked slowly round the room, still singing.

> "Il va-t-en voir une autre,
> O gai! Vive la rose!
> Qu'est plus riche que moi
> Vive la rose et le lilas!"

A guard called out. "Stop that. Put your clothes back on, Madam."

The girl continued:

> "On dit qu'elle est plus belle,
> O gai vive la rose!
> Je n'en disconviens pas . . .
> On dit qu'elle est malade
> O gai! Vive la rose!"

The guard shouted for help. "Omari! Come quick!"

Bemused visitors from the surrounding galleries were summoned by the girl's voice.

> "Peut-être elle en mourra . . .
> Mais si elle meurt dimanche
> O gai! Vive la rose!
> Lundi on l'enterrera . . .

She circled the room twice.

> "Mardi il r'viendra m'voir
> O gai! Vive la rose!

> Mais je n'en voudrai pas
> Vive la rose et le lilas!"

Then she walked out, her fur coat still over her shoulder, and disappeared.

Sidney was just beginning to compose himself when Amanda arrived. "What is it?" she asked. "You look as if you've seen a ghost."

"She was more beautiful than any ghost; a spirit from another world . . ."

"Who?"

"Was it a vision or a waking dream, I wonder?"

"What are you talking about?"

"Fled is that music — do I wake or sleep?"

Amanda was exasperated by her friend's distraction. "Pull yourself together, Sidney."

He was unable to do so. "I'm sorry. I've just seen the most extraordinary thing. A beautiful woman gliding, yes *gliding* . . . "

"Stop it. It's quite insulting to get all soppy about one woman whilst in the presence of another. Besides, you're a married man. Are you going to take me out to lunch or not?"

It was only after the waitress in Le Bleu Blanc Rouge had taken their order of pork cutlets with mushrooms that Sidney recovered sufficiently to explain why he had been so unsettled. Amanda listened with as much interest as she could muster but admitted that she could not concentrate because she was bursting to tell him that she had recently had dinner with Gerald

85

Gardiner QC, the defender of *Lady Chatterley's Lover* at the notorious trial.

"Such a clever man," she began. "I wish I'd discovered him earlier."

"Isn't he in his sixties?"

"I think I prefer the more mature generation. They're more stable, more charming, and generally I can be sure that they're not after my money."

Sidney tried to get back on to the subject of the girl in the art gallery. Could it be some kind of contemporary "happening", he wondered, or was it something more sinister?

"Honestly, Sidney, I don't know why you are preoccupied. Some girls are just show-offs."

"I think she must have been French."

"There you are then."

"Not all Frenchwomen are exhibitionists."

"Have you been to Saint-Tropez?" Amanda asked.

"No, of course I haven't."

"Well, there are plenty of them there, I can tell you. Had she shaved her armpits?"

"I don't know," Sidney answered forlornly. "I didn't look."

"Nonsense."

"It was embarrassing, Amanda. But also strangely brave. I wonder what makes a woman want to do such a thing?"

"I'm sure she'd tell you if you ever had the chance to ask her. Was she dark or blonde?"

"Blonde."

"Naturally?"

"Yes, Amanda, ash blonde."

"That's probably why you didn't notice the armpits. Aren't you going to eat those mushrooms?"

Sidney was trying to find something on which to concentrate other than the girl. "The choice of setting was clearly deliberate. An exhibition of nude paintings."

"Perhaps she was making some kind of political protest, or she was drawing attention to the conflict between art and life, the real and the imagined, the naked and the nude? Kenneth Clark was always going on about it when I was a student."

"I imagine that the male students must have enjoyed such a concentrated form of study?"

"Yes, the ones that weren't pansies, of course; sum total, three, by the way. I went to one of the lectures when Clark explained that 'nakedness' is the unadorned body viewed with embarrassment, whereas 'the nude' is the body re-formed as art; a refined vision, balanced, prosperous and confident. Do you think your new friend was naked or nude?"

"Somewhere between the two, I should imagine. But she's hardly my friend."

They finished their cutlets and were waiting for the chocolate mousse when Inspector Keating arrived. "At last," he said. "I've been all over the place looking for you. I had to telephone Hildegard."

Amanda was amused. "Normally it's we who seek you out, Inspector."

"Well in this case you might be relieved that I am coming to you, Miss Kendall. I believe you have an appointment with the Director of the Fitzwilliam?"

"At three o'clock," Amanda answered.

"He may be delayed."

"On what grounds?"

"On the grounds that a painting has been stolen from the museum."

"What?"

The Inspector turned to his friend. "Sidney, I believe you were there at the time?"

"I can't think . . ."

"It was when some French girl was making an exhibition of herself. She was a decoy while, two rooms away, a thief was snatching a Sickert."

"An odd choice," said Amanda. "You'd get more for a Matisse."

"That's as maybe. But it can't be a coincidence. The girl and the thief must have been in cahoots. And you, Sidney, were a witness."

"Not to the theft."

"I want you to tell me exactly what happened. And I'd like you, Miss Kendall, to ask the Director a few questions on the side. Is he all he's cracked up to be? Does he know more than he is letting on? I can brief you on the way over."

"Have you spoken to the security guards?" Amanda asked. "These things are often inside jobs, you know."

"Only too well. We're talking to them now; but none of them have done a runner and the painting's vanished. It can't have been the girl because she had nothing on; but we'll have to find her. Sidney, I presume you can give me a description?"

"Well . . ."

"In considerable detail, I would have thought," said Amanda.

The stolen picture was called *The Trapeze*, a circus scene at Dieppe which the painter had visited from 1919–22. It had been bequeathed to the gallery in 1939, and was considered to be one of Sickert's finer and freer works. The subject was a young woman, seen from far below, preparing to swing across the highest part of the tent. It was a portrait of drama, risk and bravura, filled with the painter's love of the theatre, but it was unclear why anyone would want to steal this work rather than a nearby Monet. Amanda thought perhaps that it would be easier to fence, but Sidney had begun to consider the painting's theme. Perhaps an exhibitionist, like the girl in the gallery, would be attracted to a painting that displayed similar daring?

He recognised that, against his will, he was getting carried away by the prospect of a mystery to solve, and he told Inspector Keating firmly that he was already late for home. "I should get back to my parish duties now."

"Nonsense. You like this kind of thing."

"I may enjoy the intrigue and the thrill of the chase, but I am not sure that my life should be such a slave to excitement."

"Don't be absurd."

"And Hildegard will not take kindly to the idea of my running round the country looking out for women who take their clothes off so readily."

"But I haven't asked you to do that, Sidney. Don't get your hopes up. I simply requested that you come back to the museum."

"Very well."

The Director of the Fitzwilliam was a well-groomed man called Graham Anderson, with hair the colour of beach sand after rain. He had a naturally tanned face, good teeth, and a rather stylish moustache that he clearly waxed. This was a man who had perhaps been told once too many times that he looked like a matinée idol and had started to believe it; a minor vanity that had become more pronounced after he had twice been mistaken for David Niven.

He also had one of those extraordinary hard handshakes which Sidney disliked, the kind his namesake, the Victorian clergyman Sidney Smith, had once referred to as the *shakus rusticus*, "in which the recipient's hand is seized in an iron grasp, betokening rude health, warm heart and producing a strong sense of relief when the victim finds his hand has been released and his fingers blessedly unbroken".

Graham Anderson talked through the daring nature of the crime. He told Amanda and Sidney that he was puzzled by the theatricality of the theft. It would surely have been simpler to break in after hours or to organise some kind of inside job with one of the guards. Instead there had been an elaborate ploy of distraction, during which the painting had been cut from its frame. Amanda asked if she could take a look at what remained while the Director continued talking to the police.

Sidney accompanied her to the crime scene. "How long do you think it would take to cut it out?" he asked.

Amanda inspected the empty frame. "You could do it in under a minute with a Stanley knife."

"Does it require a special technique?"

"Yes, if you want to preserve the painting. You are obviously reducing its size by missing out the edges under the frame, but a thief might not worry about that."

"Can you tell the level of expertise of the thief from the manner in which the painting was removed?"

"You can distinguish between care and clumsiness."

"I presume it's too cumbersome just to lift the painting off the wall?"

"It is if you want to hide it easily. The Sickert isn't that big, around two foot by three foot. You could roll it up inside a copy of *The Times* if you wanted. All it requires is daring. And probably a change of clothes for the girl."

"With a second accomplice waiting in a car?"

"Possibly not. It doesn't take too many people to do these art thefts. It's a question of confidence. No gallery can protect every painting."

Graham Anderson returned with Inspector Keating and nodded as he heard Amanda's words. "We just don't have the staff," he explained.

"But who was on duty at the time?" Keating asked.

"It was one of our newer guards: a fellow called Omari Baptiste. He's only been with us a short while so it's been a bit of a shock, I'm afraid."

"And did he see anything?"

"He says not. He was called in to see the uproar the girl was creating. Deserted his post to do that. Then he came to fetch me. I don't think he can have had anything to do with the theft. He's a very Christian man. Came over from Antigua on the *Windrush*."

"I'd like to talk to him," said Sidney.

"Are you sure it's necessary?"

"If you don't mind . . ."

Graham Anderson looked surprised that a clergyman should be involving himself so closely in the inquiry. "He is a Jehovah's Witness, you know?"

"That makes no difference to me, Mr Anderson."

"When he started here I told him that he could say what he liked outside the museum but I didn't want his religion interfering with his working day."

"Yes," said Sidney. "It's interesting how religion is often considered to be something of an inconvenience."

Keating gave his friend one of his "don't start" looks, before the Director made an immediate peace offering. "I can give you his address if that would be of help."

"He's not here?" Keating asked.

"He requested the afternoon off. He was a bit upset."

"Can the whole experience have been that disquieting? It was only a girl removing her clothes."

"I think the Director is referring to the theft of the painting rather than the naked woman, Inspector," said Amanda.

"Actually, I'm not so sure you're right about that. The man clearly has a strict moral code and is easily shocked; so I said we could do without him for the afternoon," Graham Anderson continued. "We've had to close the museum in any case." He turned to Keating. "I think your men are interviewing everyone who was here at the time."

"And you say there were no witnesses to the actual theft?" the Inspector asked. "There must have been seventy or eighty people in the gallery. Someone must have seen something."

"It appears not. They were too busy looking at the girl."

"We'll put out an appeal," Geordie continued. His face brightened as a thought occurred to him. "I'll talk to the local paper. Miss Randall can help."

Amanda cut in. "I wonder if Sidney is right and that the choice of painting is significant?" she asked the Director. "It was painted in Dieppe and the woman was singing in French. And it's a Sickert. Not something more precious. There are others here of far more worth."

"Although this is valuable enough," said the Director. "It's insured for over a thousand guineas."

Amanda was thoughtful. "You know, Inspector, that there's a man doing the rounds in London who claims that Walter Sickert was Jack the Ripper?"

"I hadn't heard that."

"He claims he's the illegitimate grandson. He points to the fact that one painting is called *Jack the Ripper's Bedroom*."

"I don't see what that can have to do with the theft of this painting, Miss Kendall."

"I just thought it might be a clue. Perhaps the thief is a known murder suspect, Inspector. Then you'd have him in your records."

Inspector Keating tried to remain calm. "Miss Kendall, it's probably best if I have the theories on this crime. That kind of thinking is the last thing we need at the moment. The history of art and the nature of police procedure are very different matters. It would be extremely foolish to confuse them."

Hildegard was unimpressed when Sidney returned from his lunch at six o'clock in the evening. She was not jealous of Amanda, she said, as she pointed a colander at him in what could only be described as a threatening manner; and it wasn't, she assured him as she rinsed the vegetables, that she minded them spending so much time together, but her husband had completely forgotten that they had arranged to have tea with one of the most boring couples in the village.

She took the vegetable knife from the drawer and explained that she had been stranded with the said couple for almost an hour and a half before she could make her escape and also, she reminded Sidney, waving her knife at him, he had still done nothing about finding a new curate to replace Leonard Graham who would have been able to go in their stead in the first place.

Sidney apologised. He took the vegetable knife from her, kissed her, and then solemnly put the colander on his head.

"How do I look?"

His wife relented a little. "Ridiculous."

"Good."

"It's all very well, Sidney. I'm not going to make a fuss and I don't want to turn into one of those wives who sigh every time they talk about their husband . . ."

"I should hope not."

"But I do expect you to pay the same level of attention to me as you do to your investigations . . ."

"I am sorry, my darling," Sidney began. "You know how I get carried away."

"Only because you want to."

"But you must know that I can only be myself when I am with you . . ."

"But you still think nothing of leaving me with what I think I heard you once telling Leonard were 'the lame ducks of the village'. You cannot delegate the parts of your job that are unrewarding, Sidney. You have to see them through."

"I'm sorry, Hildegard . . ."

"It's all right. Now tell me what has happened."

"Very well."

"And take that colander off, *Dumm-kopf*."

Sidney obeyed and talked through the events of the day, explaining that it wasn't anything very dramatic at all and he didn't have to involve himself in the case, but he was aware of his responsibilities as a citizen, his friendship with Inspector Keating and the fact that he was a material witness.

"And tell me," his wife asked. "Do you think you would be taking such an interest if the figure walking naked through the art gallery had been a man?"

★ ★ ★

The following day Sidney tried to concentrate on his parish duties. He needed to catch up on his correspondence, see to the church rota, delegate tasks and, of course, pray. There were times when he worried that he had neglected to do this and he knew that he had been sidetracked yet again by the excitement of a criminal investigation. He only hoped the Archdeacon was away, because if any inkling of his activities with a naked French girl reached the ears of his superior, not of course that there were any actual *activities*, then it would land him in the steamiest of hot waters.

Getting through his daily routine and keeping his spirits up was, however, a hard slog, particularly when his parishioners were more interested in gardening than God, but at least it was a Thursday, and he had his regulation two pints and a game of backgammon to look forward to. When he reached the Eagle, he was pleased to find that the Inspector had already set out the board and got the pints in.

"It's all about seizing the opportunity, Sidney," said Keating as he began the game. "Knowing when to make your move. That's what the thief did. You can't have any doubt. You just have to pounce, like a poacher potting a pheasant, or a rugby player making a tackle . . ."

"Or even, I imagine, a trapeze artist such as the one in the painting: knowing when to jump . . ."

"I can't see you as a trapeze artist, Sidney."

"I said: '*I imagine.*'"

"It's what the thief must have done. There's no doubt in my mind that he knows the naked girl."

"Do you think so?"

"She's his accomplice, of course. I wish I'd seen her too."

"Talking of girls," someone said from the doorway of the bar. "I was wondering if you could help me."

It was Helena Randall.

Geordie Keating was discombobulated immediately. "Oh, Helena, it's you . . ."

"I've just called in on Mr Anderson, although I have to say I'm clearly no Mae West. He wasn't remotely pleased to see me."

"I can't imagine how he managed to control himself," said Sidney. He noticed that Helena was still wearing the tatty duffel coat that she must have had for at least six years. Her hair was unbrushed, she had put on a bit of weight, and was decidedly spotty. Perhaps his perception of her charms had been spoilt by his glimpse of the French girl the previous morning.

"The missing painting is a Sickert, isn't it?" Helena continued. "Do you know that some people think he was Jack the Ripper?"

"Have you been speaking to Amanda?" Sidney asked.

"We met at the station. Such a nice woman. She was incredibly helpful."

Keating cut in. "It's not helpful at all."

"I'm sorry you feel that way when we've both been so good to you in the past. I suppose that, as a result, you won't be interested in the fact that my friend Basil Bonney is a well-regarded art critic."

"And how is that relevant?"

"He lives in London and is a specialist in French painting."

"Sickert was English," said Sidney. "Although Amanda tells me he was born in Munich."

"I can't see what any of this has to do with the price of fish," Keating complained.

Helena looked at him with amused and patient scorn. "The subject of the painting was French, the girl was French, and Basil knows everyone in the art world. If that girl is part of the London scene then he will be able to point you in the right direction. Would you like me to help or not?"

Omari Baptiste, the security guard, lived with his sister Francelle in a two-bedroom flat in a converted terrace house at the end of Bateman Street. The living-room was a riot of pattern and colour; from the red floral carpet to the yellow lampshade on the standard lamp, the crimson blanket and white lace cover on the settee, the pink flock wallpaper and the vases of artificial flowers that had been set out on each surface. Framed photographs of ancestors and family relations hung on the walls together with sunset scenes of the islands back home, as if one room had condensed all their noise and sunshine. A large pile of the *Watchtower* magazine lay on a side table and the smell of rice and peas from the kitchen combined with the aroma of the paraffin lamp in the fireplace. There was no television or wireless.

Once Sidney had explained that he had come only to ask if there was anything he could do to help Omari get over the shock and outrage he must be feeling, he was offered a glass of lemonade and allowed to sit down.

"I gather you came over on the *Windrush*," he began. "Have you been in Cambridge long?"

"We started in London," Omari answered. "Then the Lord sent us here. There's plenty of His work for us to do. At times it's a struggle but we manage."

"I suppose your job gives you less time to witness?"

"A man's gotta eat, Canon Chambers, but we still put in the hours telling people about the *Kingdom*. Ain't no good doing nothing."

Francelle moved a vivid-blue blown-glass fish to one side and placed the tray of lemonade on the sugar-starched crochet cover of the coffee table. After Sidney had made a careful point of gently asking Omari's sister if it was all right to talk of the naked girl in the gallery in her presence, he sipped his lemonade and began.

"I wonder if you can tell me something. I know this must be difficult and that you probably didn't look at all, but I wonder if you had seen the girl in the museum before?"

"I'm not sure I want to talk about it."

"You mean you can't be sure?"

"It's not that."

"You mean you *had* seen her before?"

"I wouldn't like to say."

Sidney produced one of his kindly confessor looks. "As a man of God, I hope you can trust me."

"Well then I think so, sir. Yes, I have."

"And when would that have been, if you don't mind my asking?"

Francelle interrupted. "Be careful what you say this day, Omari. We don't want no trouble."

Her brother was less concerned. "Trouble comes and trouble goes. It's only this world. We're not here for long."

"But what we do while we are here matters," Sidney cut in. "Our actions have implications."

Omari relented. "It was last Saturday I saw her first, sir. The girl was looking at the painting that's gone. *The Trapeze*, they call it."

"You're sure it was her? The same girl?"

"Pretty sure."

"Could you swear in a court of law?" Sidney asked.

"I wouldn't like to go to no court of law, sir. I could swear on the Bible."

"That is good enough for me. And was she on her own, this girl?"

Omari paused. "I cannot tell a lie. But I don't like to speak the truth about this."

"Then let me speak it for you. I imagine she was not."

"You could be right assuming that."

"And who was her companion?" Sidney pressed.

"That's hard for me to tell you out loud."

"I don't think it is."

"I don't want to get in no trouble. I can't lose my job."

"It was a man?"

"I can't answer, sir."

"I think you are telling me that it was a man. Did you know him?"

"Again, I wouldn't like to say."

"That means, Omari, I think, that you did know him. Could you hear what they were saying to one another?"

"I could hear but I couldn't always understand."

"And why was that?" Sidney asked.

"They were speaking in French."

"You are sure?"

"As I say, I don't want to get into no trouble."

"You won't. I can assure you."

Francelle was not convinced. "I don't know how you can assure us. The police have been here talkin' all kinds of things already, treating us like criminals when we're no such thing."

Sidney thought to himself that there were only so many excuses he could make for his friends in the force. "I know the police can be impatient. They have their job to do."

"I've no time for impatience," Omari replied.

Sidney realised he should leave while he still had this man's trust. "I cannot say that this will go no further, but I can promise that I will look after you in all eventualities. Inspector Keating is a good friend of mine and I am sure you had nothing to do with the theft of the painting."

"He did not, as God is his judge, nor did he know that girl," Francelle interrupted. "Parading around in all her glory like the day she was born. Has she no shame?"

"It seems not," said Sidney. "Omari, I feel I must ask you again to tell me this. Who was the man with the girl last Saturday?"

"I'm sorry, sir. It's hard for me to answer."

"Was it the director of the museum, Mr Anderson?"

"I can't tell no lie if you ask me flat out."

"So can I assume that I am correct without you telling me directly?"

Omari sat back in his chair. "Have you just been playing with me? Did you know the whole time?"

"I did not."

"Lord knows you did."

"Don't take the name of the Lord in vain, my brother."

"I don't mean to do that. Only I don't like to be played with."

Sidney apologised. "I meant you no harm. All I want is to understand the truth of this case and to protect you in all necessary ways."

"How did you know what I had seen?"

"It is the only explanation for your fear. I recognised that you were a man who was anxious about losing his job; and Mr Anderson is the one person who can take that away from you."

"Maybe I lost that job for sure now. But I want you to remember. I haven't told you nothing."

"You have been the soul of discretion, Omari, and I am grateful for your honesty and for the hospitality you and your sister have shown me. I will not forget that. I will leave you in peace. Please don't worry."

"We're always nervous. If it's not the bills or the job there's always the end of the world to worry us. These are the last days and I don't need this trouble."

"There won't be any more difficulty, I am sure. You have done nothing wrong."

"It won't be long until we reach the Kingdom, Reverend. The atomic bomb is telling us now. As Jesus said, we must keep awake for the time and the hour."

"Indeed he did. We must watch and pray. I am sorry to have troubled you." Sidney leant forward and laid his hand on his host's head. "God bless you, Omari."

After Inspector Keating had been given a full report of this encounter, the two men decided to visit the Director of the Fitzwilliam once more. Sidney worried that he had no proper pretext for joining his friend during the inquiry but Geordie told him to concentrate on his role as a witness and to keep asking the suspect, for that was what Graham Anderson was, a series of questions that would look as if he was simply checking that he had his own story straight.

The Director started by telling them that understanding a crime such as this one was a lengthy process and that it could often take years to solve a mystery and return an artwork. Provided the painting had not been stolen to order, in which case there was little hope of recovery, they just had to wait and keep a close eye on the auction houses, most of whom had already been asked to look out for a masterpiece on the cheap. It was even possible for the thief to pretend not to know that it was a Sickert in order to give the buyer a sense of superiority. The potential purchaser might then offer more in the mistaken enthusiasm that he was getting a bargain. An interim price in the case of this particular picture might be between four and five hundred pounds, giving the newfound accomplices a tidy profit if the work could be sold on a second time.

The other possibility, Graham Anderson continued, was to wait for a ransom demand, but he did not think that this was likely. The work was not sufficiently famous. He concluded that, in his opinion, there were only two motives: the theft to order or the quick, and hopefully thwarted, sale.

"It could also be an insurance scam," said Keating.

"In which case," the Director replied, "I think you are implying that I might be responsible."

"I'm not so much implying it as stating it," Keating began before Sidney gave him a "be patient" look.

"If I ever did such a thing I would be ruined, Inspector; and I am hardly likely to risk my livelihood for a minor work. I come from a family with three Rembrandts in our ancestral home. If I was a criminal I think I could do a good deal better than an unpretentious Sickert."

"Miss Kendall mentioned Jack the Ripper . . ."

"That is, I am afraid, a very fanciful theory. The man who is putting that story about came to see me a few years ago when he knew that we had something of a collection here. It's absolute nonsense. Sickert liked drama and scandal and gave dubious titles to his paintings, it is true; but he was also interested in the case of the Tichborne claimant, the Camden Town

Murder and in Dr Crippen's crimes. He could just as well have been involved in any or all of those. He may have lodged in the same boarding house once occupied by the Ripper, but he was on holiday in France at the time of the first four murders."

"In Dieppe?"

"No. At Saint Valéry-en-Caux."

Keating cut in. "I agree. This whole thing has got absolutely nothing to do with Jack the Ripper. There's a whole file at Scotland Yard and everyone there knows it was Aaron Kosminski and not a poor old painter."

"I keep wondering about the girl," said Sidney. "She had such confidence. She moved through the gallery as if she was in a dream. She did not pause at all but knew exactly what she was doing and where she had to go. Are you sure you have never seen her before, Mr Anderson?"

"I am."

"One of our witnesses is convinced that she was in the museum last Saturday."

"I do not work at weekends."

"The girl was in an animated conversation with a man he thought might have been you."

"Then he must have been mistaken."

"He said that she was talking to you in front of *The Trapeze*."

"I was on my way to the opera in London with my wife at the time. Have you been speaking to our security guard, Mr Baptiste, perhaps?"

"I can't say."

"If so, then you would do well to remember that he might simply be covering up for his failure to prevent a theft."

"If it wasn't you, and the girl was in the gallery, then I wonder who the man was?" Sidney asked. "Perhaps, like her, he was involved in the art world. If they were, then where do you think we could find them?"

"I've no idea. People come here from all over the world."

"In London, perhaps?"

"Or Paris. Or New York."

"I don't think she'll have got as far as New York," said Keating. "But Paris is interesting. She sang in French. Do you have contacts at the Louvre and the galleries over there, Mr Anderson?"

"It's part of my job," the Director replied. "I am considered to be something of an expert in French Impressionism."

"So you speak the language fluently?"

"I'm not too bad at it."

"Like the girl. You could even have spoken to her in French when you saw her then?"

"As I say, I didn't see her."

For the next day or two Sidney let his thoughts settle and did not involve himself in Inspector Keating's investigation. The staff at the railway station had been questioned, garages and workshops were searched and a reward announced, but the routine pattern of inquiry yielded no results. There was no sign of the painting and no ransom demand.

Sidney returned to his duties, attending school assemblies, taking his tutorials at Corpus, and visiting Mrs Maguire's ninety-year-old mother, a woman who had been bedridden for the past four years and was steadfastly refusing to die. He interviewed several candidates to replace Leonard Graham, none of whom came up to the mark; and he began to amass a rota of volunteers for the church fête. He even contemplated offering his services as a stand-in wicket keeper for the Grantchester cricket team.

His wife accompanied him on many of his walks through the village, by the river and across the meadows. The couple had begun to establish something of a routine that was their bastion against the criminality and violence that sometimes threatened to overwhelm them. Hildegard now ran regular coffee mornings and had secured a part-time teaching job at the Perse School. She also continued to give private piano lessons after school on three afternoons a week. It was still extraordinary, Sidney thought, to acknowledge the change she had brought to his life; her cheerfulness, her company, her music and the smell of baking in the vicarage. He sometimes stopped to wonder what it was that he loved most about her; the light in her eyes and the smile that was meant only for him. For he knew that she smiled differently when she was in his company; it was a particular look, a knowing confidence, a partially public yet elusive acknowledgement of the love that they shared.

He set to work on a series of meditations on the nature of Christmas, of which he was secretly rather proud, and he was able to listen to a little jazz while he did so, relaxing to Miles Davis's *Sketches of Spain*, and Art Blakey's *Mosaic*. He even found time to finish Iris Murdoch's latest novel, *An Unofficial Rose*, enjoying the irony and pathos of nine intertwined lives. This is what the life of a vicar should be like, he thought. At last he had the time to stop, listen, learn, pray, and be himself.

He also began to find out a little bit more about Sickert. It was not the small matter of people thinking, unconvincingly, that the painter had been Jack the Ripper, but his fascination with the female form, and his interest in the polar opposites of seediness and show business, that attracted our amateur sleuth. This was an artist who had reclaimed the figurative tradition from the mire of Victorian taste and prudery; who introduced narrative using shocking and topical subject matter, and who gave Post-Impressionism its bite and pathos. Like Sidney, Sickert was intrigued by the difference between the hidden and the revealed, public confidence and private misery, loneliness and companionship.

Sidney tried to think in a similar manner to the artist, looking for composition and compelling narrative in what he saw. He even considered how he might turn his life into a work of art. Could that be possible?

He thought of his parishioners and his friends, and how he could be a better husband to Hildegard. He wanted to tell her how much he loved both her soul and, if he had to be frank, her naked body, and how he only felt secure when he was in her arms.

He had just finished writing his sermon for the twenty-fifth Sunday after Trinity and was thinking of making his traditional late-night mug of cocoa when the telephone rang. It was Helena Randall. She told him that her friend Basil thought that he had found the girl.

"She's called Celine Bellecourt and, like the woman in the gallery, she's French."

"That sounds promising."

"She's been in London for the past year and is making a name for herself as a performance artist. Apparently she's also something of a musician although Basil can't be sure about that. She lives at the bottom of the King's Road with someone called Quentin Reveille."

"Is he French too?"

"I think not. Apparently, he's a rather loquacious socialist from Leeds."

"Yorkshiremen aren't generally known for their loquacity, are they?"

"Perhaps that's why he's pretending to be French. The two of them are becoming quite famous for their joint installations and their subversive use of text. Nothing is what it seems, apparently. It's all about different ways of seeing and a new art of looking."

"Then let's hope they can help us 'look' for the painting."

"Basil doesn't reckon they're thieves. He says they are too involved with their own narcissism; but he thinks that we should go to their show at the ICA. Would you like to join us?"

"I'm not sure that's wise. Perhaps I've done enough already . . ."

"Nonsense, Sidney. We know you'll want to come. It's called *The Festival of Misfits* so we should all feel at home. It's next Wednesday. Isn't that your day off? You could bring your wife if you like."

"I don't think the idea will go down very well."

"Tell her it's fun."

Helena gave him the details of the exhibition. It was being advertised as a "mixed-media Neo-Baroque happening" with no fixed beginning or end. It was all about flux. "Fun" was the last thing it sounded.

As she spoke, Sidney was already worrying how he was going to explain to Hildegard who had been on the telephone at such an ungodly hour. He asked Helena if she had also called Inspector Keating to brief him on her discoveries.

"God, no. I can't call Geordie because I am completely forbidden from ringing him at home. In any case, it might be a wild-goose chase and I don't want him getting cross with me. You know what he's like. The tiniest thing sets him off."

Sidney did not think flirtation, potential adultery, a series of murders and now a major art theft could be construed as "the tiniest thing" but decided not to pursue the matter. "I suppose it's always going to be easier to ring me if you want to speak to anyone out of hours. Vicars never sleep."

"Exactly! You are a clergyman, Sidney. That's what you always tell people. You are 'never off duty'. I've heard you often enough and now I'm taking you up on your offer."

Sidney wasn't aware that he had offered anything at all. "You can't exempt us journalists," Helena continued breezily. "We are your parishioners too. Besides, you're good at this kind of thing. And you were in the art gallery at the time. If we've got the right girl then you can tell Geordie and get all the glory."

"Whereas you . . ."

"I just get the story. And the first interview with the mystery blonde. I'll meet you there."

Sidney tried to think of an excuse for going. He was already keen to talk to Amanda and ask her a few questions about the London art scene. He supposed that it would at least give him the opportunity to see her again and to experience the "buzz" of creativity at first hand. He also thought he could justify his potential attendance at the 'happening' by arguing that he didn't want anyone to think that he had become a fuddy-duddy. It was 1962, for goodness sake. He needed to know what young people were thinking and doing. There was a freshness in their lives. He knew it, he had heard it and he had seen it in their fashions and the way they spoke. Now he wanted to understand all this new energy and be part of a groovy modern age that had had no experience of war.

On the other hand, Sidney didn't want to be one of those trendy vicars who were always getting their guitars out and going on television. God forbid, he warned himself.

He would have to strike a careful balance and find the right "vibe" — not that he would use the word "vibe" out loud or in company. But before he did any of these things he was going to have to get the idea past Hildegard. He would delay mentioning the word "Helena" for as long as possible, he told himself, and perhaps he might even get away without saying that anyone they knew, apart from Amanda, would be at this *Festival of Misfits* at all.

Hildegard was preparing for bed. Sidney hoped that if he worked for a bit longer and waited until she was asleep then he might be able to avoid any nocturnal inquisition and save their conversation for the relative calm of the following morning. But he had forgotten about the cocoa, and she would be expecting him to bring it.

He went into the kitchen, heated the milk and collected his thoughts. He looked at Dickens. The beloved Labrador had been lethargic of late and although his owner had put it down to ageing and arthritis rather than anything sinister, perhaps it *was* something more? Sidney really should make an appointment at the new surgery in Trumpington, he decided, remembering that it had been founded only recently because Grantchester's previous vet, Andrew Redmond, was in prison for murder.

"What are you doing down there?" Hildegard called down. "Who was on the telephone?"

"I'm just coming," her husband replied. He climbed the stairs with both mugs in one hand and opened the door. "Do you think modern painting is any good?" he asked. "I've just been doing some research into abstract expressionism and kinetic art and I'm not convinced. Figurative work may be old-fashioned but I still think there's a place for it in the modern world. People are fascinated by the human form. Here's your cocoa. What do you think, Hildegard? I'm not sure about all those blank white canvases and the 'monochrome propositions' of Yves Klein. I rather like Sickert and his nudes."

"You're not thinking of the art theft, are you?"

"I was just doodling and making some notes but I don't feel we know enough. I was thinking we could go to London on my day off and take in a few exhibitions. There's so much going on and I feel rather out of touch. There's a new Francis Bacon show, a Bridget Riley, and something called *The Festival of Misfits* at the Institute of Contemporary Arts in Dover Street. What do you think? Shall we go? It's just an idea."

"Will that girl be there?"

It had to be said that Hildegard did not miss a trick. "Which girl?"

"The naked one; from the museum."

"I don't know. Perhaps."

"I think that means yes."

"Well she may be part of the happening and if she were then I could probably find out a bit more about her. Perhaps I could ask a few informal questions that might lead us to the thief."

"You want to go all the way to London to identify a naked woman you saw very briefly three weeks ago?"

Sidney tried to make a joke about it. "Apparently she was not naked but nude."

"And what is the difference?"

"A naked person is someone like you or me in the bathroom. A nude is a work of art."

"Are you saying I am not a work of art and that this woman is?"

"I am not saying that at all, my darling."

"You always call me 'darling' when you know that you are in trouble. Why do you want to see this girl again?"

"That's not true."

"And you speak more firmly too. I remember your father saying . . ."

"Yes. I know. He is not always right about these things. I don't *want* to see this girl, Hildegard. I'm trying to help Geordie solve the case."

"And will he be coming with you?"

"No, not exactly."

"Then how do you know about her?"

Sidney hesitated. If he said the words "Helena Randall" at this point in the conversation then his cause would be compromised; perhaps fatally. "We've had a tip-off."

"From who?"

"Someone in the art world: a man called Basil Bonney."

"And do you know this bonny Basil?"

"It's Basil Bonney. Not Bonney Basil."

"I was trying to make a joke . . ."

"Oh, I see, very good." Sidney readjusted his approach. "I'm sorry, Hildegard, this is just an idea. I thought it might be fun if we both went to London. We don't have to go at all if you don't want to but I can't help feeling that we'll be missing out if we just stay in Grantchester. The girl is only a small part of the show. There's contemporary music, nuclear painting and a German outfit called Group Zero. I think there's also a man called Gustav Metzger who paints with acid."

For the first time in their conversation, Hildegard had the beginnings of a smile. "Rather than swallowing it, you mean?"

"Apparently. He throws coloured hydrochloric acid at nylon and metal which then corrodes and forms the image. It's called auto-destructive art. We should see it, Hildegard. It will be an adventure."

"That's what I'm worried about."

"But this will be fun; something to tell our friends about. We can be 'with it' at last."

"I don't know what that means. Are we 'without it' now?"

"Of course not. You are everything to me. And I don't want to go 'without' you."

"Then I'll come. Yes, of course, why not?" Hildegard answered. "We can go out for dinner afterwards. I have been told that there are many nice restaurants in Dover Street. Then I won't have to cook."

"Thank you, my darling. I will make it happy for you, I promise. We will have a wonderful time."

"Then I look forward to it."

"Marvellous." Sidney leant over and kissed his wife on the lips.

He had got away with it.

★ ★ ★

The following morning he preached his sermon on a text taken from the first epistle of Paul to the Thessalonians, Chapter 5 Verse 2: "For yourselves know perfectly that the day of the Lord so cometh as a thief in the night." He was pleased with this as it was a special service for Scouts and Girl Guides (motto: "Be prepared") and he could also double up on his thinking about death, opportunism and the end of days. He wondered if he should go and see Omari Baptiste again and check that he had not been blamed or made a scapegoat for the theft of the Sickert.

After an agreeable lunch of roast lamb and sherry trifle, spent in the company of Leonard Graham and his good friend Neville Meldrum from Corpus, Sidney thought he really should call in on Keating. He was not at all sure that it was a good idea to keep his visit to London a secret. If the girl turned out to have no connection with the events in the Fitzwilliam then he would not have wasted any police time; but if she did then he knew that his friend would accuse him of going behind his back and, worse, of betraying him by being in cahoots with Helena Randall. There really was no way in which he could please everybody all of the time, or be what people wanted him to be.

He decided to say nothing, hoping that it was the safer option, but he became more nervous as the day of the trip approached. It was hard to contain his anxiety, not least in the moments leading up to their departure. One of the parishioners had kindly offered the couple a lift to the railway station but Hildegard was still in her dressing gown when they should have been leaving. "I need to get ready," she said. "I will be ten minutes."

Sidney could tell that they were going to miss their train but he could not risk anything that might antagonise his wife or delay their departure.

"We are going to be late," he could not resist saying.

"Don't worry."

Hildegard's preparation time each morning, from the sounding of the alarm clock to departure by the front door, was an absolute minimum of one hour. Despite allowing for the morning cup of tea, a trip to the lavatory, and the transition from night-time drowsiness to daytime reality, it was physically impossible for his wife to move from dressing gown to departure in ten minutes. Even in a state of acknowledged urgency such as this, there would be the running of a bath, the checking of its temperature and the swearing about the failings of their heating system (a minimum of eight minutes). Then there would be the taking to the waters, the stepping out, the towelling dry, the application of talcum powder, and the cleaning of teeth (seven minutes). There could often be a further, unaccountable, two minutes after the bath and before the drying of hair. These first stages alone, therefore, constituted at least seventeen minutes, and they didn't include any further delay that might be caused by his wife's dreamy singing as she performed her ablutions.

From this moment on, Sidney thought, Hildegard was already late and she wasn't even dressed. There would then be the whole business of deciding what to wear, finding the right stockings and examining their

117

colour against the light (at least four more minutes) before putting on bra, blouse and skirt (three minutes), checking herself in the mirror and adding a brooch (two). If Hildegard was convinced that she had the right look (if not, and a change was necessary, that would mean a further ten minutes) there was still the small matter of adjusting the hair, putting on make-up, choosing a matching handkerchief and making sure that all the things she needed were in her handbag (eight minutes). And then, just as Sidney was convinced that Hildegard had completed her toilette, and he had already opened the front door in anticipation of their departure, his wife would announce, "I just need to do my lipstick. I won't be a minute."

You will be a minute, Sidney thought. *In fact you will be two minutes and forty seconds. We will miss our train.*

"We need to hurry up," he answered. *Thirty-seven minutes when you said ten.*

"Don't fuss, Sidney. You know how it slows me down."

Hildegard was right. Any argument would make her stop putting on her lipstick, start speaking and cause further delay.

Sidney was powerless. There really was no way of hurrying his wife along. "We are going to be late," he repeated.

"You are often late," his wife answered. "People almost expect it. But it is interesting that you are always on time for church."

118

Sidney knew that, even though he had been *extremely provoked*, it was wisest to say nothing. He patted his pockets to make sure he had everything.

Hildegard snapped her handbag shut and smiled. "Ready," she said. "Let's go. Come on, then. What are you waiting for?"

"I can't find my keys."

"Well, I'm ready."

From an initial position of lateness and vulnerability, Hildegard had managed to take the moral high ground. After a fluster of panicky searching round the house, Hildegard walked calmly to the table in the hall and picked up the keys.

"Here they are."

It was extraordinary that she could find lost objects in places where her husband was sure he had already looked.

They managed to catch their intended train down to London with three minutes to spare ("I told you not to make such a fuss, Sidney") and took the underground to Piccadilly Circus. Amanda had promised them a cup of tea in the Ritz and met them there before the excitements of the exhibition. After they had caught up on each other's news they then walked over to Dover Street for *The Festival of Misfits*.

Sidney could see Helena Randall in the doorway of the ICA with the man that he assumed was her "lovely friend Basil". Hildegard gave him a nudge. "I wonder if Inspector Keating is here after all."

"I wouldn't have thought so," said Sidney. "His wife keeps him on a tight leash these days."

"Then aren't you lucky to have me?"

Basil turned out to be a dapper Glaswegian who felt that it was his sole responsibility, as one of the dandiest men in town, to make sure that he knew everyone. He was dressed in a maroon smoking jacket, pink shirt with matching cravat, Black Watch trousers and winkle-picker shoes. He had left his home town after directing a disastrous production of *Goodnight Vienna* in Paisley which, he told Helena, had gone down about as well as a production of *Goodnight Paisley* would have been received in Vienna.

"You must be the famous detective who disguises himself as a clergyman," was his opening gambit.

"It's not as straightforward as that."

"I am sure it isn't. I don't go to church myself. Everyone's so badly dressed. Have you noticed?"

Helena giggled. "I don't think that's the point of going."

"I find it all so terribly ageing."

"There are young people who attend," Sidney answered in his defence. "And youth clubs. I've started a jazz night."

"Ah yes, very fifties. Helena tells me that you've got another string to your bow, or perhaps another reed to your saxophone? You can go in and out of jazz clubs almost unnoticed."

"I don't aim to be noticed," Sidney smiled hesitantly.

"Although he *does* like it when people recognise him," said Amanda. "There are very few clergyman who turn down attention."

"That is a little unfair," said Hildegard. "In Germany, the pastors . . ."

"Oh, *the Germans*," said Basil, "they always like to put on a show. Think of Nuremberg."

"Perhaps I forgot to mention," Helena said quickly. "Sidney's wife is originally from Leipzig."

"Well, I'm sure she's got a sense of humour," her friend replied. "Most of us are Saxon originally . . ."

"Or even Norman," said Amanda, moving away to talk to a group of women she thought she knew from the National Gallery. They appeared to be wearing dresses made of newspaper.

In Grantchester the villagers were tactful about Hildegard's nationality and she was spared the hostility that was more common in a city such as London where she met more strangers and had to defend herself more frequently. Most people knew that her father had been killed as a communist protestor in the early 1930s and that her family had never been members of the Nazi party. It was partly why she still liked living there. She never had to explain herself. But Basil continued his national stereotyping unabashed.

"The Germans have a stronger sense of the dramatic, don't you think? It's part of the Protestant tradition to go round smashing things up. All that *Sturm und Drang*. It's one of the themes of the happening tonight: auto-destruction. It's innately Teutonic." He looked at Hildegard. "Don't tell anyone, but I love Wagner."

He began to hum the leitmotif of "*The Ride of the Valkyries*". "Da-da-da *DA* da, da-da-da *DA* da . . ."

Hildegard realised that she was in the presence of a man who had never been taught about tact. "I prefer Bach," she replied.

"Well I'm afraid you won't be getting any of that tonight. This is all very avant-garde, I can assure you. No humourless *cantors* here. Let me make sure you've got something to drink."

After they had been introduced to the artist Ben Vautier, whose main contribution was to live and sleep in the window of the gallery as some kind of human installation, they were shown into a fun-making machine shop where a man called Terry Riley was explaining his *Ear Piece for Audience*. Every person in the room was to take up an object such as a piece of paper, cardboard or piece of plastic and place it over an ear. The idea was to make a series of sounds by rubbing, scratching, tapping or tearing it or simply dragging the object across their ears, or just holding it so that it could be placed in counterpoint with the other sound sources.

"This is John Cage all over again," said Amanda on her return to the conversation. "I'm all for percussion but I do think it's best within an orchestra." She started to talk to Hildegard about the bass drum in Stravinsky's *The Rite of Spring*, the crash cymbals in Mozart's *Seraglio* and the use of the xylophone in Gershwin's *Porgy and Bess*.

"What about the girl?" Helena asked Basil. "You promised she'd be here."

"We are moments away from seeing her. I only hope I'm right."

They walked through a labyrinthine blacked-out room to a large white space. Basil explained that the evening was a "monomorphic neo-haiku flux-event". Around the gallery were contrary slogans framed on the wall:

NOTHING   EVERYTHING

And then a triptych of words repeated

WHITE   NIGHT   LIGHT

Before

NIGHT   LIGHT   WHITE

"This is Quentin Reveille," Basil announced, producing the loquacious socialist from Leeds. He was dressed in a grey flannel suit with a black polo neck and prominent glasses, as if he were a cross between Yves Saint Laurent and Jean-Paul Sartre. The best art contained tension and opposition, he told Sidney. It was important to confound expectation, to lighten darkness and darken light.

"I'm interested in paradox. You know the kind of thing. *L'oeuvre d'art est bien une chose, chose amenée à sa finition, mais elle dit encore quelque chose d'autre que la chose qui n'est qu'une chose.*"

Sidney was impressed by Quentin's fluent French, even if it was delivered with a Yorkshire accent.

The artist then asked Sidney, Hildegard, Amanda, Helena and Basil to look through a "window into perception", and take a glimpse from the doorway of Celine Bellecourt naked in a glass case and covered in apples. It was, according to Reveille, a memory of paradise, a meditation on the Garden of Eden. The audience, who had to view the piece standing in a curled line, was collectively the serpent, waiting to prey on innocent beauty.

Sidney recognised the naked Celine immediately as Quentin explained the purpose of the installation. It was about encouraging people to look in different ways, to think about alternative methods of "framing reality".

"A naked woman, for example, becomes a nude in the presence of the artist," he told Hildegard.

"And if the artist leaves the room does she become naked again?"

"No, the artist has made his mark. The vision remains. It is about setting and context," Reveille continued. "Location is also important. A square foot of grass might look the same wherever it is but if it's the area in front of the batsman on a cricket field it is crucial; then again, if you put it in an art gallery it becomes something else. I am interested in working with context and how it changes meaning."

Sidney thought how the figure of the Cross was resistant to this kind of distinction. It remained a crucifix wherever it was and this, perhaps, explained its potency as an image. "And how do you decide what to frame?" he asked.

"As the mood takes me. It's like being a photographer. I pick my subject and then choose my frame. Sometimes, if I am lucky, the subject picks itself, and because I live with Celine I can always turn to her when I am stuck. She walks in beauty. She is, and will always be, a work of art. I am merely the person who shows the direction in which the viewer should look."

"And do you do your own framing, Mr Reveille?"

"I trained as a carpenter, Canon Chambers. Like the good Lord."

"But you can't do all that here, can you?"

"I have a separate workshop where I keep my tools. It's better to work with your hands, don't you think? It's important to touch, to know the material world. Although I suppose you're more interested in things spiritual."

"What's your favourite material?"

"Wood."

"Mine too," Sidney replied. "I remember learning to whittle at school. I wanted to make my own cricket bat."

"That's a very specialist skill. Even I couldn't challenge the work of Mr Gray and Mr Nicolls."

Sidney was impressed that Reveille knew the name of the firm that made Britain's best bats, but they were straying too far from the point of his inquiry. "Does your model perform in other shows?" he asked.

"She is a living work of art. We blur the line between performance and reality."

"I wonder if she has ever been to Cambridge?"

"Why do you ask?"

"I think she was there a few weeks ago. A painting was stolen on the same day. I think Miss Bellecourt

125

provided the distraction. She was the naked girl who caused a bit of a commotion."

"The nude, you mean."

"Of course. Do you know anything about what happened that day?"

"Celine never tells me where she is going. It's her statement of freedom. But I have spent months installing this exhibition. You can ask anyone. I have even slept here. In any case, why would I steal a Sickert? He's very old hat, you know."

"I didn't say that the stolen painting was a Sickert."

"I do read the papers, Canon Chambers. I won't be caught out. But Celine is perfectly innocent, I can assure you. I would have thought that a man in your position might appreciate the equation of nakedness with innocence?"

Amanda interrupted their conversation with news of the next happening: *Guitar Piece* by Robin Page. Wearing a shining silver crash helmet and holding his guitar ready to play, the artist waited a few moments before flinging it on to the stage and kicking it into the audience, along the aisle and down the steps into Dover Street. This was destruction, and it was, Basil told Sidney, a comment on the helplessness of the individual and the threat to world peace caused by the Kennedy — Kruschev confrontation over Cuba.

"I can't see how kicking a guitar is going to benefit world peace," Amanda observed. "I don't think that the leaders of the world are going to lose any sleep about a man in an art gallery with a crash helmet."

126

After this last "happening" Celine emerged from the back. She had got dressed but appeared to be wearing nothing except a man's white shirt with silver cufflinks. The top three buttons were undone. Sidney presumed she was wearing underwear but didn't dare look any closer.

"I have seen you before," he said, "although we have not met."

"I am used to being seen," Celine replied. "It is how I live." She lit up a cigarette and let it rest on her thick lower lip. Sidney wondered if the gesture was practised. How much came naturally and how much rehearsal went into this girl's public behaviour? Perhaps her French accent was put on and she wasn't French at all. It seemed too clichéd, this art-gallery version of Brigitte Bardot.

"Have you been in England long?" he asked.

"A few years."

"And do you like it here?"

"It is not France," Celine replied.

"I was just wondering," Sidney asked, "what you thought of Cambridge and if you had been to the Fitzwilliam Museum before?"

"I remember you now. I saw you and thought you might be shocked but you were not."

"I have seen most things."

"I am sure you have. It was the war, perhaps."

"And more."

"My mother died in the war."

"I am sorry."

"Don't be. Unless you killed her."

"Where was she?"

"Dieppe."

Sidney made his credentials clear. "I was in the Normandy landings."

"Then you know the town?"

"Is that where you are from?"

"For a little while, yes. Then Paris. It doesn't matter."

"You know there are paintings of Dieppe in the Fitzwilliam Museum?"

"Are there?" Celine asked.

"Did you not know?"

"Perhaps."

"Why did you go to Cambridge?"

"To see what it was like. Why do people go anywhere?"

"Were you alone?"

"I do not understand why you want to know this. You saw that I was."

"And what was the song you were singing?"

" 'The Rose and the Lilac.' It is about being left by a man."

"But you have Mr Reveille."

"I still know what it is like to be alone."

Sidney began to sweat a little. He was getting nowhere. "Why did you do it?" he asked.

"I wanted to be free. I want the public to think about what they see. Perhaps I shall go to every museum in the country. Every art gallery has its nudes. You start in the Renaissance and keep walking."

"You may be stopped."

Celine smiled. "No one ever stops me."

Sidney kept up his inquisition. "And how did you travel? Did you come up from London?"

"I was on the train."

"But where were your possessions, your money, your handbag?"

"When you are free you do not need possessions."

"But you must have had something?"

Celine exhaled cigarette smoke. "No, I am content with nothing."

"And you went back with nothing?"

"I had my fur coat. I left my shoes by the door of the museum. That was all I needed. As you saw for yourself, I had nothing to hide."

Sidney was at a loss. Why is this woman lying to me? he thought. And how can I get her to tell me the truth?

His frustration with his encounter at *The Festival of Misfits* only increased after he had made a full confession to Inspector Keating in the Eagle.

"You should have left it to us," his friend reprimanded. The game of backgammon lay unfinished between them. "Now they've got wind we're on to them, they may disappear."

"They don't strike me as the retiring type."

"I don't know why you didn't tell me straight away."

"I am telling you straight away. We only got back this morning."

"You could have made a telephone call. Now I'll have to get on to Inspector Williams at Scotland Yard. I might even have to ring him at home; and he never likes that. Presumably you think they're in it together?"

"I do. Although Reveille claims he has never left the ICA."

"And there's no sign of the Sickert?"

"I don't think they would put it on display . . ."

"An art gallery is as good a place to hide a painting as any other . . ."

"That's true. But Reveille did mention his workshop. I think it would be worth a search; although it won't be popular."

"They've probably moved it on by now."

"Amanda says that would be quite hard to do, unless it was at a knockdown price. She thinks it's more likely to have been stolen for sentimental reasons. The girl's from Dieppe, you know."

"But she can't have taken it. She was starkers and Reveille has an alibi."

"Unless he went to the Fitzwilliam in disguise?"

"That's possible. But witnesses say that the girl was alone on the train."

"He could have driven."

"Or the painting could still be in Cambridge."

"You suspect the Director too?"

"I don't like him, Sidney, but you can't suspect a man on those grounds. What about that Basil bloke, Helena's friend? I don't suppose he could be mixed up in it all?"

"I don't think so, Geordie. Although he can be tactless, Basil Bonney is, in fact, the same in name and nature. He's quite the dandy."

"A pansy, then."

"He is probably, as you put it, 'a pansy' but that is not illegal. Besides, it's not our policy in the Church of England to intrude in such matters. Everyone is entitled to a private life; homosexuals are no exception."

"You wouldn't catch me having a friend called Basil."

"He has been very good to us."

"So what's his game? What's in it for him?"

"He wants to be helpful and loved. It's a common enough failing."

"And Helena likes him?"

"She does."

"I presume you've told her she's got no chance."

"No, Geordie, you don't need to worry. You are still the only man for her."

"Don't start."

"I haven't. You did."

Keating drained his pint. "I'd better get on to Williams. We don't want those two doing a flit. I presume you'll come down to London with me?"

"You don't need me, do you?"

"I'd be glad of the company. Besides, it might give you a chance to see your new friend Basil again. And Zoot Sims is coming back to play Ronnie Scott's. You could listen to some jazz instead of watching people destroy their guitars."

"I'll have to talk to Hildegard."

"As long as it's just the two of us, she'll think we're safe."

"I'm afraid, Geordie, that's where you are wrong. As far as Hildegard is concerned, nothing is ever 'safe'. And if I tell her about the jazz she'll want to come too."

"Best leave her out of it, though; it could get messy."

"I don't like leaving her out of anything."

"You haven't been married long enough, Sidney, that's your trouble."

Before he was shown the warrant Quentin Reveille complained that the search was an attack on his civil liberties, artistic expression and personal freedom. He was then informed that his girlfriend's public nudity had been an attack on common decency and that they were lucky she was not on trial for a public-order offence.

The police looked through the ICA, Reveille's studio, the flat above it, and the lock-up workshop. This was packed with tools, woodwork and rolls of canvas that were all examined in turn. Nothing suspicious was found.

"I don't suppose you've painted over it?" Inspector Williams asked.

"Why would I do that?"

"As another one of your protests."

"I would have to have the painting in the first place."

"Where is it then?"

"You can look as much as you like. It's not here. Never has been and never will be."

"And where is Miss Bellecourt?"

"I think she's gone to the National Gallery. She felt like a walk."

"With or without her clothes?"

"It's a free country, Inspector. As we have always told you, we have nothing to hide."

As soon as Reveille mentioned the National Gallery, Sidney was alarmed. Perhaps he should warn Amanda that another theft was about to take place? He made his excuses to Inspector Keating and hastened to Trafalgar Square where he found his friend in one of the workshops. She was overseeing an inspection of Cranach's *Cupid Complaining to Venus* because the gallery was hoping to acquire it.

After he had checked that nothing was amiss, that no naked woman had appeared in the gallery and no painting had been stolen, he asked Amanda if she would like to go out for a cup of tea. There were things he needed to discuss with her, he said, not least because he felt that he had neglected her of late and wanted to catch up on her news.

Amanda did not believe him. She knew that Sidney was after information and said that he would have to wait a few minutes. She couldn't just drop everything as he did so often himself. She had an important job and she wasn't going to endanger it by leaving her post to consort with clergymen who appeared whenever they felt like it. If women were to be taken seriously in the workplace, she continued, then they had to work harder than men simply to keep their jobs, and she wasn't about to sacrifice her badly paid but hard-won career for the sake of a cup of tea and a flapjack with a vicar dabbling in detection.

Sidney was forced to wait and watched as Amanda examined the painting with a magnifying glass and then took the back off the frame to look at the condition of the canvas. As she did so, he had an idea. There were so many questions he needed to ask his friend, and they weren't about her love life. He hoped she would, at least, be relieved about that.

When he returned to Grantchester Sidney was dismayed to find that the Archdeacon had popped in unexpectedly earlier in the day. Caught on the hop, Hildegard had explained that her husband was in London, and Chantry Vine had immediately jumped to the conclusion that the visit was not ecclesiastical business.

Sidney was summoned to Ely to explain himself. He was going to have to reassure his boss yet again that his detective work was not in conflict with his parish duties. In his heart, he did not believe that was the case, but his loose interpretation of pastoral care could well be open to question. He worried that his recent resolution to be more discreet while avoiding any evasion or downright lying was going to be tested.

It was a dark day in mid November when he took the train up to the heart of the diocese and entered the cathedral precincts. It was rather like going back to his old school, he thought. He always feared that someone was going to tell him off.

The Archdeacon, however, was surprisingly cheerful, offering tea and Victoria sponge (his wife was a fête-winning baker), sharing news of the Chapter while eating with his mouth open. It was not an attractive sight, this small man who was perhaps trying to combat his deficit in height by hoping that his overeating would help him expand upwards rather than outwards.

"I hear you have been keeping yourself busy," he began. "How was London?"

"It was my day off, Archdeacon."

"There is no need to be defensive."

"I want to be clear that my parish duties always come first."

"And may I ask if the Fitzwilliam Museum is part of your parish?"

"Not exactly. But it is a University building and, as you know, I have responsibilities there."

"It is the subject of 'responsibility' that I want to discuss with you," the Archdeacon continued. "Isn't it time you were moving on from Grantchester?"

"I suppose it is."

"I imagine your wife might like a change?"

"Yes, I think she probably would."

The Archdeacon pressed on. "The Church needs bright men like you in its more prominent positions. I was thinking of a proper canonry, for example, or a big inner-city parish. The Bishop of Birmingham has been asking after you. Trevor Sheffield is on the look-out too."

"I was hoping for something in London."

"Ah yes, well, I'm afraid that you would not be alone in wanting such a thing. I have spoken to Bishop Geoffrey, and he has asked that there be some kind of condition attached to any preferment. He does not want to recommend someone whose commitment to the Church has been questioned."

"My dedication is wholehearted."

"Personally I do not doubt this, but you must acknowledge, Sidney, that there have been distractions, and I am not just talking about the blonde girl in the art gallery."

"The Harland murders were something of an exception."

"And everyone is grateful to you. But perhaps we should let the police get on with their business, while we continue with ours. I have been to see Inspector Keating."

"Really? What did he say?"

"He was surprisingly grumpy," the Archdeacon confessed.

"There's nothing surprising about that."

"He said that you were in the middle of a very difficult case which he could not solve without you and I should mind my own business. I pointed out that it was rather my business, and that I did not take kindly to distracted clergymen. I informed him, as I am telling you now, that I think it would be in your own best interests to abandon your gallivanting in search of stolen paintings and naked women."

"That is something of an exaggeration."

"You need to give it up, Sidney."

"I'm not sure I can promise to do so."

"May I then simply suggest that you reread the Parable of the Talents? It would be a pity if you didn't make full use of your spiritual potential . . ."

★   ★   ★

No one could accuse Sidney of being a negligent priest, but sometimes he would be so involved in one aspect of his work that he was unable to do anything else. Before he had Dickens, for example, he would frequently mistime visits to parishioners or fail to fulfil his daily duties because he was so preoccupied by the items on his desk. He would continue to work on a sunny day, for example, determined to complete his correspondence and his paperwork and get to the end of whatever he was doing. But once he had finished, it would either be dark and too late to go out, or the weather would have changed for the worse. Telling himself not to mind, and that he would not make the same mistake the following day, he would awake to gloom and thunder. Now, however, with his beloved Labrador, he had no choice but to get out of the house and walk regularly every day, never minding the conditions, where he found that the exercise cleared his head and improved his mood.

He was on one such walk, on the following Monday, when Inspector Keating intercepted him and said that he had had enough. He insisted that his friend come with him, dog or no dog, to the Fitzwilliam Museum immediately. "We need to search the whole ruddy thing."

"But if we start rummaging through the place Anderson will guess straight away that we suspect him of lying."

"He knows that already. They must have a painting store; and we know the canvas has been removed from the frame. It could have been rolled up in a cardboard tube and posted to France; or hidden in the attic of the Director's mother's house for all we know. They could even pretend to discover it having switched it with a fake, like that mad bloke did to the Holbein in Locket Hall before he kidnapped Miss Kendall. I hardly need to remind you of that."

"The Lost Holbein" had been one of Sidney's earliest forays into detection and had necessitated Amanda's rescue from a remote farmstead outside Ely. "I don't think we are dealing with anything as dangerous as that. The Fitzwilliam Director seems normal enough."

"By Cambridge standards, that is true. But you must have realised by now, Sidney, that this town contains nothing but madmen."

"Including us?"

"Especially us."

Once inside the museum they ignored all protest about the lack of an appointment and the appearance of a Labrador in the galleries and proceeded straight to the Director's office. There, Keating made his position clear. "We are going to go through the whole place and even close it down, if necessary, unless you start telling us the truth."

Graham Anderson remained behind his desk. "I don't think you will be able to do that. I have provided as much help as I feel I have been capable of giving."

The Inspector was adamant. "That is an evasive answer and it is not enough. You need to stop the nonsense. We have discovered the girl's name. It is

138

Celine Bellecourt. We know that you met her the Saturday before the work was stolen. There's no point denying it. How well do you know her and what did she want? Any more lies and I'll have you banged up right now."

"Please don't threaten me."

"Then answer our questions properly. You knew who that girl was, didn't you?"

"I met Celine Bellecourt for the first time last Saturday. She had been doing some research. She wrote to me and asked if she could come and see me. She had some questions."

"What kind of questions?"

"Well, to put it simply, she thought that *The Trapeze* was a portrait of her mother."

"And is it?"

"I'm not sure."

"I thought people like you were supposed to know that kind of thing?"

"Sometimes, Inspector, the answers are not so simple. You have to do a bit of detective work and trace the painting back to its origins."

"You don't need to lecture me about investigation, Mr Anderson."

"*Dr* Anderson. We acquired the painting as a bequest from a Lancashire mill owner called Frank Hindley Smith in 1939. It was framed in Paris by Paul Foinet but we don't know who first had it. Sometimes you have to use your experience and take these things on trust. An ideal provenance history would provide a documentary record of owners' names, dates of ownership and means of transference after inheritance. To be absolutely sure you have to trace all the past sales through dealers and auction houses; and know all the locations where the work was kept, from the time of its creation by the artist until the present day."

Dickens began to show signs of impatience. There was only so much sitting down in an art gallery he could take. Anderson rather touchingly tried to include him, clearly hoping that getting a Labrador onside might help matters.

"It's a bit like establishing the pedigree of a dog. But even this does not always identify the subject. There are similar presentation drawings that are titled *Mademoiselle Alexis*. So that is a clue. If the girl's mother was called Alexis that would be one link, but this could equally well be a stage name; especially because when the painting was exhibited at Agnew's in 1923 it was called *Mademoiselle Leagh*, possibly in homage to a work by Degas called *Mademoiselle La La at the Cirque Fernando*. So, you must understand that it's a complicated story and very easy to jump to the wrong conclusions where titles are concerned: hence all that Jack the Ripper nonsense."

"This may seem a ludicrously fanciful theory," Sidney began. "But, I wonder, is it at all feasible that Celine also thought Walter Sickert might be her father?"

"Why do you ask that?"

"She told me that she was an orphan, that both her parents were dead."

"I think that's unlikely. Sickert died in 1942. He was over eighty. Celine's only twenty-six."

"It's still technically possible," said Keating.

"I don't think so."

"Why not?"

"I just know it isn't." The Director did not return Sidney's questioning. He breathed heavily and was just about to speak when Sidney interrupted.

"I'm curious. You have just been very specific about Celine's age. You said she was twenty-six. That is very exact. How do you know? Did she tell you?"

"Yes."

"That is unusual. Women don't normally tell men their age the first time they meet them; unless of course you know more than you are saying?"

"I have told you all I can."

Keating banged on the table. "For God's sake, man, you've come out with enough lies. Let's get to the truth. How well do you know her? Is she your girlfriend? Don't let us make it unpleasant for you."

There was a silence. "I'm sorry," said Sidney, shocked by the outburst from his friend, the like of which he had never seen before. "Tell us."

Graham Anderson stared down at the floor and answered the question. "She is my daughter."

He had met Celine's mother, Alexis Ducroix, in Paris in the 1920s. It was the summer before he went to university and his father had paid for the trip, saying that it would make a man of him, and Graham

Anderson had assumed that one of the points of this extended holiday was to lose his virginity.

"I rented a studio in the Rue Descartes and went to all the nearby bars, cafés, cabarets and eventually the circus where I finally drank enough absinthe to summon the courage to ask Alexis if she'd like to go dancing at the hall in Rue Cardinal Lemoine. After that evening I went to see her on the trapeze every night. The show people had such stories. One of the older members claimed that he had even seen Blondin's great act of making an omelette while on a tightrope. I was thrilled by the excitement and the danger and yet, at the same time, I felt protective of Alexis. I wanted to be the one to catch her if she fell; I told her that I wanted to be her net, that I would always be able to support her. It was a ridiculous idea, really, since I had only just stopped being a schoolboy. But we were young and in love, walking hand in hand on the quays by the Seine, drinking Chambéry cassis in the Closerie des Lilas, sharing cassoulet at the Rotonde. But the timing was wrong, as any fool could have predicted . . ."

"So you came home."

"I had no more money and there was a university to go to. Alexis went on the road with the Cirque Rancy and eventually the letters stopped and we lost touch. We only met again in the 1930s by which time both of us were married to other people."

Sidney guessed that Celine had been the result of an all-too-temporary reunion.

"We can't be sure that the woman in the painting is the same Alexis," the Director continued. "She's seen from below and afar, her features are indistinct and it's a work of Impressionism."

"I can't believe you think that," Keating began. "You know it's her."

"It's true that Celine's mother trained at the Cirque d'Hiver in Paris and joined a troupe that toured Normandy and the Seine-Maritime every summer. She would have been about seventeen when Sickert was there and so it's possible that she is the subject. But I'm pretty sure she never saw the finished painting, and we never spoke about it . . ."

"That, too, seems strange."

"It was before we knew each other. But it's a pity, I'll admit. I'd like to have known what she made of him."

"She must have seen him at work?"

"Not necessarily. He could just have been sketching and worked up the painting later. Besides, you can't concentrate on anything else if you're doing a double somersault between two trapezes thirty feet in the air."

"She will have had a taste for the dramatic: like her daughter."

"I see what you are driving at, and yes, she was a show-woman. I used to think about her every time I passed the painting. I was never completely sure that it was she but I liked to pretend it was and that I could still see her every day. It's why I couldn't possibly have stolen it. Why take a painting that you can look at all the time? Then Celine arrived. She'd done the research, convinced herself that it was a portrait of her mother, and telephoned to make an appointment."

143

"Which was the Saturday before last?" Keating checked.

"That is correct. I am sorry I did not give you this information before."

"And you still didn't tell her the story?"

"I couldn't. I didn't want to have to go into all this."

"You could have saved us valuable time. So now, at least, we know why she would have wanted to steal the painting."

"If she genuinely thought it was of her mother then that is, of course, possible, but I don't want to incriminate my own child."

Inspector Keating cut in. "She's done quite a good job of incriminating herself."

"Why did you keep the fact that she is your daughter a secret?" Sidney asked.

"Cowardice, probably; or because the story of her past had been so clearly and tragically explained to her that I didn't want to confuse it further."

"Tragically?"

"Alexis was killed in Dieppe shortly after Operation Jubilee in 1942. Her husband had already died of drink. Celine was six years old when she was taken in by the owners of one of the hotels in Dieppe."

"Which one?" Sidney asked.

"The Hotel de la Plage."

"So she was born in 1936, which makes her twenty-six today. Did you ever meet her as a little girl?"

Inspector Keating interrupted. "How can you be sure that she's your daughter?"

"Her mother wrote to me at the beginning of the war, just after the German tanks took over Paris. She remembered that my parents lived in a stately home and sent the letter there. She didn't want money, she was very firm about that, but she wanted to tell me the truth just in case anything happened. Which it did."

"How did you know she had died?"

"I didn't at first. I tried to find her after the war. My wife and I weren't getting on well and I found it difficult to adjust to peacetime. I went to the circus and one of the old boys told me everything."

"And you weren't tempted to find your daughter?"

"I went to the hotel in Dieppe. I didn't stay there but I waited in the Café des Tribunaux. It was 1948. Celine was twelve years old. I saw her coming home from school. It was the briefest of moments. Her hair was in a ponytail and she was carrying a music case. I wondered what instrument she played and if she was happy. She looked it. And I didn't want to do anything to disturb that contentment so I said nothing and left the next day. Seeing her was, perhaps, enough. And then I recognised her as soon as she arrived in the museum."

"I still can't believe you didn't tell her," said Keating. "It's unfair to keep her in the dark."

"She has her adopted parents."

"But not the true ones."

"They're still alive?" Sidney asked.

"And at the same hotel. They know the truth but Alexis told me that she had made them swear not to tell

145

our daughter. She wanted her to think well of the man she had said was her father. She was loyal that way."

"And you really haven't seen Celine since her stunt in the art gallery?"

"I wish I had, and that I could have done more for her. Perhaps if I had told her then she wouldn't have involved herself in all this drama."

"And you have never met her friend Quentin Reveille?"

"I don't involve myself in conceptual art."

"I'm not sure I believe you."

"I think I've told you enough truth for one day."

Sidney could see that the Director was desperate for the conversation to end.

"You don't suppose there's any possibility that Celine has nothing to do with this? That someone saw what was going on and just seized the moment?"

"To take that particular painting at that specific time?" Keating replied. "No chance."

Shortly after this encounter the two friends agreed to meet at the unusually early hour of opening time in order to talk about what to do next. The Inspector thought that, despite the Director's late confession, he was unlikely to be involved. "I can't believe a man would make his daughter walk naked through a gallery in order to steal a painting."

"That is because you are a father yourself. I still think it's possible."

"As likely as Reveille?"

"Who has an alibi."

"I don't believe that it holds water."

"There are witnesses," Sidney reminded him.

"Yet he is also an expert in making people look where he wants them. He could have had an assistant take his place in the studio, or created some other sleight of hand while he made his way to Cambridge."

"You mean people assumed he was working because there was such a lot of banging about; whereas it doesn't mean that he was the one doing the banging?"

"But he would have had to leave London for four or five hours and no one we talked to in the museum has given us anything like his description. You're quite sure no one looked anything like him, Sidney?"

"I am."

"Unless he dressed as a security guard."

"I suppose that's possible. Like the postman in that G.K. Chesterton story. No one notices a postman."

"I don't suppose they could all be in it together. Celine, Reveille and Anderson?"

"All three?" Sidney asked. "I don't think so."

"What about poor old Omari Baptiste? Are you still sure it can't have been him?"

"I keep thinking that it could be the girl acting on her own."

"But how, Sidney? She had no clothes on."

"But what if she stole the painting *before* her dramatic act of nudity?"

"Then why go to all that trouble? It seems very far-fetched."

"It's a good way of showing she had nothing to hide. I wouldn't mind looking at her fur coat."

"It would take some nerve."

"But that's just what she's got."

"I'll telephone Williams. I hope they are still in London."

"And I'll get on to the museum. I just wonder if anyone left a change of clothes in the Ladies'."

"Are you sure about this, Sidney?"

"Of course not, Geordie, but the girl has by far the best motive. We must *cherchez la femme fatale*."

The following evening Sidney's mother telephoned to complain that she had heard from Amanda that her son had been in London so why hadn't he paid a visit? Did he now consider himself too busy to see his own family? His father was recovering from flu, his sister Jennifer had finally agreed to marry her boyfriend and his brother Matt was becoming increasingly active in the CND movement. She only hoped that her other son had no such plans as she couldn't abide the sight of vicars trying to make themselves modern in this world when they should be concentrating on the next. When was he next in London, was he involving himself in any criminal activity (she had heard rumours) and what were his plans for Christmas? If the family were to have a gathering in London on Boxing Day she needed to know now so that she could make a start on the cake and the pudding.

It all seemed a very long way away and Sidney had only just put down the receiver when Inspector Keating telephoned to say that no change of clothes had been found in the Ladies' at the Fitzwilliam Museum and that when Inspector Williams turned up to interview Celine and Reveille he had found no one at home. The couple had vanished.

"Where the hell do you think they've gone?"

"Well," Sidney answered. "If I was a young girl, and I wasn't sure of my mother's appearance, and if I had no picture of her but discovered a painting, then I'd take it over to France and ask my adopted parents. All we have to do is check in at the Hotel de la Plage, Dieppe."

"Then what are we waiting for? Let's get over there."

"I have a wife and a job and I'm not sure that I can afford the trip."

"You could bring Hildegard too; combine it with a little holiday."

"She has her teaching which she takes very seriously. She will also need some convincing that I will have any proper time with her. She knows me rather too well."

"And that is a blessing."

"Indeed it is."

"Then ask her. And if she doesn't want to come, tell her it will only be one or two nights and that I can't go without you. You'll then have to promise her something by way of compensation: an exotic holiday to Rome or the south of France; something like that."

"That might be rather costly."

"Not if you get the promotion the Archdeacon was telling me about."

"There are conditions, Geordie . . ."

"Why are rules made if not to be broken?"

Sidney smiled. "And you a police officer . . ."

* * *

Amanda was amused by her friend's news when they met at the Savoy a few days later. She insisted that they drank Churchills, a lethal concoction that the barman had created in honour of the great statesman, mixing whisky with lime juice, vermouth and Cointreau. A first would take the edge off the day, a second would ease the nerves and a third would surely make any man, let alone a clergyman, inarticulate. Sidney was determined on restraint.

"What is interesting is why you have to go to France at all?" Amanda asked. "It is surely the business of the British and the French police. If anyone else were to be involved it should surely be someone from the Fitzwilliam. Mr Anderson, for example . . ."

"He is considered too partial."

"You mean he is still a suspect?"

"You suggested it, remember?"

"I can't be expected to recall everything I have said, Sidney, no matter how perceptive or witty. It's all off the top of my head. I suppose you think they must have spirited the painting out of the country."

Sidney explained his theory and Amanda asked, "Are the police paying you for this? Isn't it going to be rather expensive?"

"I fear so."

"Do you need a loan?"

"No, I don't think so."

"Or a gift? Do you think ten or twenty pounds would do it?"

"I think the ferry is about three pounds, and then there's the hotel, food and petrol."

150

"Keating will surely pay for most of that. I'm not sure I'm prepared to subsidise the police. I pay my taxes, after all."

"I think ten pounds would be fine."

"I'll give you twenty."

"That's too much."

"I don't want you going short and I do accept change. The only thing I insist upon is that you buy Hildegard a proper Christmas present with some of the money."

"That seems rather indulgent."

"Believe me. It will be a wise thing to do. I only have your own interests at heart."

Sidney tried not to show his concern. "We've had to be rather thrifty recently, Amanda. I don't want her to think that I've been throwing money about."

"I'm not talking about extravagance. I was just making a suggestion. Some nice French perfume would do, for a start."

"I can never remember which one she likes."

"It's Shalimar, Sidney. Even I know that. I'll write it down for you so you don't forget. Another cocktail?"

"It will be the death of me."

"No, Sidney, it won't. Something else, probably something rather criminal, will be the death of you. This will only cheer you up and it is my treat. Besides, what could be nicer than cocktails in the Savoy with your oldest friend? All you have to do in return is listen to me tell you about the most divine man I've just met . . ."

The two men travelled to Newhaven and caught the night ferry to Dieppe. Keating had formulated a cover story to explain their visit to France. He and Sidney were to be brothers, both of whom had taken part in the Normandy landings, and they were on a tour of the region for old times' sake. They could not stay long as they would need to be on the road to Caen the next day.

As the ferry approached Dieppe at first light Sidney felt sick. It wasn't from the journey, but memory. He remembered waiting in the great belly of a Landing Ship Tank in the war, making its way to Juno Beach in the middle of the night with a heavy sea running. He had been on the right flank of a convoy of ships many of which had barrage balloons tethered above that soared skywards, then dropped out of sight as the flat-bottomed LST rolled and pitched over the waves. The coastline had been fortified by the occupying Germans and bristled with guns, concrete emplacements, pillboxes, fields of barbed wire and mines.

Before the infantry landed on the beach, the artillery launched a saturation barrage against the enemy defences.

When the ramps lowered he had disembarked and waded ashore. He was then engaged in the most haphazard and deadliest run of his life. It was impossible to know if he was making the right decisions or not. He had to put what trust he had in God and chance, working his way through obstacles and around minefields before facing the German guns. His

152

comrades raced across the beaches through the curtain of machine-gun fire, rushed the pillboxes and eliminated the German strong-points with Sten guns, small-arms fire and grenades as a truck with petrol-filled jerricans exploded nearby.

It could hardly have been a greater contrast to see the same coastline by daylight and in peacetime. Anyone approaching might have thought that there had been no war. The two men checked in at the Hotel de la Plage and decided on an early lunch.

The hotel patron was a tall man with a faint air of Monsieur Hulot about him. He had thick high eyebrows, a surprised expression and a prominent Adam's apple that looked like a forgotten gobstopper still waiting to go down. His wife was far smaller, well preserved, and in a simple black dress that had seen better days.

Guy and Delphine Girard were solicitous in their provision of lunch, insisting that the two men tried a little *cidre bouché* before they partook of the Coquilles Saint Jacques, Veau à la Dieppoise, Petit Suisse cheese from Gournay-en-Bay and a slice of tarte aux pommes.

Inspector Keating remarked that after a lunch like that it was amazing the French ever got any work done. He finished his cider and reminded himself as much as Sidney that they should concentrate. "Don't give the game away too soon. We don't want them getting suspicious."

"I must be allowed to pose a few questions, Geordie."

"I understand that."

"I have been using this lunch as a means of preparing the ground. I'll ask how the town has changed since the war and if there is anything particular I should look in on. I'll tell them I'm interested in art and see what happens."

"Don't make the asking about art too obvious."

"It will only be enough to get an answer."

"Well, I'm off to the gendarmerie."

It did not take Sidney long to establish that Celine had indeed returned to Dieppe and that a friend had organised an event at the Château Musée. She had been planning her visit with Reveille for three months and was staying until Christmas.

He left the hotel and walked through the gardens skirting the beach. It was half past three in the afternoon, the kite flyers were beginning to pack up, and lights were coming on all over the town. It was, Sidney thought, a French seaside version of Grantchester. He looked at the church of St Jacques with its fifteenth-century tower and made his way back through the town, passing the Café des Tribunaux that Sickert had painted, where Oscar Wilde had written *The Ballad of Reading Gaol*, and where Graham Anderson had waited for his daughter Celine. Sidney thought of that twelve-year-old girl coming home from school, unaware of the man in the café, and how different her life might have been had Anderson spoken directly to Guy and Delphine Girard or told his daughter the truth.

Sidney passed the castle off the Rue de la Barre, and began his ascent to the Château Musée. He tried not to think how embarrassing it would be if they found nothing. Although his hunch had already proved correct and he had established that the couple were in town, there was still a long way to go if they were to recover the Sickert.

He approached the museum. Quentin Reveille's word paintings were already displayed in the window. This time they were in French:

L'OBSCURITÉ	LUMIÈRE
HAUT	BAS
CACHÉ	RÉVÉLÉ

Inside the château, they had been hung in opposition to their meaning so that the dark paintings were brightly lit, the hidden painting was the easiest to spot, and the high painting was placed low down against the floor.

Sidney was just inspecting the backs of the pictures displayed in the window when Celine appeared. She was wearing a short white dress and long white boots with hearts under their indented tops.

She gave Sidney a weary smile. "I suppose I should say that I am surprised to see you, but I am not. Have you come alone? Are you in love with me?"

"No, I'm afraid not, I just wanted to have a look round . . ."

"I didn't realise that you were so interested in art. Perhaps you will buy something. Quentin takes commissions. You could have paintings for your church. Light and Darkness, the Hidden and the Revealed. Whatever you want."

"Yes, I can imagine. *Haut. Bas.* We look up to the heavens and then down to the ground beneath our feet. You were in the Fitzwilliam Museum a week before the theft, were you not?"

"I see that you have still not recovered from my performance."

"I would be grateful if you would answer my question."

"I do not see why. You are not my confessor."

"Then you have a confession to make?"

"There is always something."

"Please tell me."

"It doesn't matter."

"I think it does. The day you walked through the gallery was not your first trip to the Fitzwilliam, was it? The guard saw you on the previous Saturday, even though you had your hair pinned up and looked like a boy."

"So?"

"You were looking at the Sickert painting. And you took a particular interest in it."

"Perhaps I did."

"And why was that?"

"I think you must know why. Otherwise you would not have come all this way."

"The Trapeze Artist is your mother."

"Perhaps. We cannot be sure. I told Quentin about my past life and he remembered the painting. He had once had a girlfriend in Cambridge. So I went to see for myself. Then the Director helped me. I wanted to know about my origins; you understand?"

"It must have been a strange feeling, seeing the painting for the first time."

"I cannot know for sure."

"And so you took it."

"But how would I do that? I had no clothes."

They were interrupted by the return of Quentin Reveille. Inspector Keating was with him, and announced their arrival by saying, "Look who I've found."

"This is a complete waste of time," the artist answered. "The exhibition opens tonight. We have a lot of people coming and although we are used to unpredictability in our happenings they don't normally include the police."

"Well it doesn't have to if you hand over the painting."

"We don't have it. I wish you would give up your fruitless pursuit."

"I wondered if we could have a closer look at *Haut*?" Sidney asked.

Reveille was surprised. "Why that particular picture?"

"Don't," said Celine.

"I would be grateful if you would oblige me."

"I suppose there's no harm."

An assistant removed the painting from the wall. Sidney took it from him. "I'd also like to see the way in which it's been framed. I know how you take pride in these matters." He turned the picture round. "Does the back come off?"

"Not easily."

"But simply enough to conceal another painting inside, I would have thought. A substantially smaller image of, say, of, twenty-five inches by thirty-one inches?"

"You are mad, Canon Chambers."

"No, I think I am merely persistent." He carried the painting over to a nearby trestle table. "You don't mind if I pull off the masking tape, do you? It will be easy enough to put back. I presume you have a screwdriver?"

"Of course," said Reveille. "And I presume you will pay for any damage."

"I will be careful. Amanda showed me how to do this."

"So that is why you insisted on seeing her last week?" said Keating. "That was very devious of you."

"There are reasons for everything," Sidney replied. I will just lift the top away. Of course I may be wrong but this is quite fresh. The paint still has some tackiness to it."

"That is because the exhibition opens tonight."

"I think we'll decide on that," said Keating.

Reveille was unrepentant. "You realise that you have no jurisdiction here?"

"That's not entirely true. It is why I brought my colleagues from the gendarmerie. They are intrigued; not least by our clerical friend. And they want to impress their superiors at Interpol. I've promised them the credit."

"Then I presume you'll take the blame when this has proved to be a wild-goose chase?"

Sidney slid the wooden back off the frame. Then he carefully pulled out an old canvas and turned it over. It was *The Trapeze*.

"I had no idea that it was there . . ."

Keating looked inside the frame. "Perhaps you would like to explain, Miss Bellecourt?"

"There is nothing to say."

"I think there is."

"I wanted to take it. It should have been mine. And I thought of a way."

"It was before you took off your fur coat," said Sidney.

"It was."

"But no change of clothes has ever been found," Keating continued.

"That is because the dress Miss Bellecourt travelled in was made of paper," Sidney answered.

"I've never heard of such a thing."

"Neither had I, but Amanda pointed out how flimsy her dress was after *The Festival of Misfits* and how she had seen other women in paper outfits; they were the first examples of immediately disposable clothing." He turned to Celine. "You wore such a costume to Cambridge under your fur coat, and then threw it away in the Ladies'."

"What about the knife to cut away the canvas?" Keating asked.

"Hidden in the paper dress in the wastepaper basket. Omari Baptiste was responsible for three rooms. You waited until he had left the gallery containing the Sickert and seized your opportunity. Then you went to

159

the Ladies', rolled up the painting and hid it in the sleeve of your fur coat. The display was calculated to show that you had nothing to hide, but you had it all the time and left by the front door."

Reveille tried to deny the obvious truth. "An ingenious theory. So you're saying she travelled all the way back to London in nothing but a fur coat."

"It was large enough. Miss Bellecourt then went to your workshop. Perhaps, Mr Reveille, you really did know nothing. But it seems unlikely. We have already established that you do your own framing."

"Celine is just as capable."

"Then you are distancing yourself from her?"

Celine interrupted. "How did you know it was there?"

"A guess, I'm afraid. But it would be too obvious to conceal it in a painting called *Caché* or *Révélé*. Much better to acknowledge the subject matter: the height of the trapeze and the chasm below. You were also hesitant when we discussed the titles. I just needed to check the picture was newly framed with the back sealed tightly."

"I didn't realise that you were such an expert in picture framing?" Reveille asked.

"I'm not. But I have a friend at the National Gallery and I tested my theory on her. She was intrigued and we tried it out. There's often plenty of room between the canvas and the frame. She told me that in the war people sometimes varnished the canvas of a masterpiece and then painted over it; an amateur daub that could be removed later. But you wouldn't want to stoop so low as to appear amateur, would you?"

"I don't see why either of us should tell you anything."

"Of course you can remain silent. But you will have to speak to others."

Keating explained. "The gendarmes are waiting at the door."

"Will I go to prison?" Celine asked.

"Probably."

"How did you know it was me?"

"I think, first of all, it was the way you walked," Sidney replied. "You were unaware of the audience but glided through the room, looking straight ahead at all times, as if you were sleepwalking or thinking of something entirely different. And you never looked down. Your mother would have been proud of you."

That night Sidney and Geordie decided to have a celebratory drink at a bar in the harbour, in a venue similar to one Sickert had referred to as "the kind of place a European prince visits just after he has been ruined". They watched the boats bobbing and ringing under a chain of evening lights before enjoying a seafood stew. Sidney imagined Sickert painting the scene before going on to the circus, Graham Anderson as a young man in love, and Mademoiselle Alexis on the trapeze, waiting to jump, each character in the story unaware of their future or their fate, swinging briefly over the abyss.

There was paperwork to attend to the following morning, and Sidney managed to persuade the Chief of

Police to let him see the prisoner once more, if only to say goodbye.

Celine was dressed in a pale blue slip, with no shoes or shoelaces or trousers with a drawstring, but was, in a curiously French way, still allowed to smoke. It wouldn't take her long, Sidney thought, either to escape or to persuade everyone to let her off completely.

He began by apologising; for intruding into her detective work about her mother and for "spoiling the party".

"It wasn't much of a party. But it's over now."

"Perhaps it would have been easier to bring your foster parents over to Cambridge than take the painting to them. Have they seen it yet?"

"They came last night."

"They didn't tell us that."

"They are proud. And they think you are tourists."

"And do they think the painting is of your mother?"

"They understand that I wanted to believe it. So they said it was. But we cannot know for sure."

"Perhaps it is better in the imagination."

"It is almost the same as memory, don't you think?"

"You need imagination to remember."

"I just wanted to think of a time when my mother was happy," Celine began. "I can picture her standing on the trapeze, holding the attention of the crowd below and then taking that leap into thin air, flying, even if it was only for seconds. I don't want to think of her being hit by my drunken father or shot when the Germans took over the town. I want to imagine her there; *la balance, la jetée, la liberté.* That moment of flying and floating and being free. That is why I wanted the painting. It's like watching your mother with her future still in front of her, the air unknown even though it surrounds her: all that it requires is the bravery to make the leap into who we are and will be."

"Did you ever plan to give the painting back?"

"It was a stupid thing to do. But I hope she would understand. I too needed to do something rash and sudden; a great jump over everything that does not matter. We all have to do this at some point in our lives. Perhaps you have done this too?"

"People talk about the leap of faith," Sidney began. "You have to dedicate yourself. Then, once you are committed, it's almost impossible to go back. You take the risk that what you are doing and what you believe is true."

"And what is life without risk, Canon Chambers? It is no life at all."

"I think it was Kierkegaard who said that 'without risk there is no faith, and the greater the risk, the greater the faith'."

Celine smiled. "You must love flying more than the fear of falling. Have you read Anaïs Nin? *'La vie se rétracte ou se dilate à proportion de notre courage'.*"

As she spoke, Sidney could see why Reveille had loved her. "I'll be taking the painting back to the Fitzwilliam."

"Mr Anderson will be pleased."

Sidney did not know how much to say. "Do you have any message for him?"

"You can tell him that I am sorry. I didn't mean to cause trouble. I wasn't thinking."

"It is his favourite painting."

"I wonder why?"

"I think you should ask him that."

"That may be a long time away. I shall be in prison."

"I will ask him to come and see you."

"Why would he want to do that?" Celine asked.

"Because the heart has its reasons," Sidney replied.

Even though the trip had only lasted a few days, England appeared different on their return; darker, colder and ready for Christmas. Lights had been put up in the Cambridge town centre, trees both real and artificial were on sale in the marketplace, the window displays in the shops were frosted and silver, and tinsel tipped over the tops of shopping baskets as parents tried to restrain the excitement of their children. The Fitzwilliam Museum had put on an exhibition of nativity paintings, and Sidney found Graham Anderson in a swirl of Ghirlandaios, Correggios and Parmigianinos, with all the fat babies, obedient angels and improbable weather that comprised those stilled romanticised versions of what must have been a more difficult birth and a harsher truth. The Director drew his attention to a Dürer engraving of the Nativity and an Altdorfer of the Adoration of Kings, saying that if ever Hildegard wanted to come and look at the museum's German holdings she would be welcome. "But I can't imagine that's why you're here."

"No. We have obtained the Sickert, as I think you know. It was your daughter, after all, who stole it."

"And what will happen to her?"

"Prison, I am afraid. Keating thinks it will be a minimum of three and a maximum of eight years. It depends on how the trial goes."

"Should I say something?"

"I think you should see her. You don't have to tell her everything but you could start with her mother."

"I know that it's wrong for a child not to know her own father."

"And I think," Sidney continued, "that it might not be the shock you are expecting. Celine is used to doubt, secrecy and uncertainty. She knows of her own tragic past. Perhaps you can give her hope. The man she thought was her father is dead and you are alive. What can be more joyous than that?"

"I wish I could have been better for her."

"There is still a future."

"I'm not sure if I know how to be a good father or what it means at all."

"I am not sure anyone does. I don't have children myself but my own father seems to regard the whole business of parenting as a benevolent accident that has little to do with him."

"Perhaps it's all to do with the confidence of a happy marriage?"

"I am sure that helps."

"And will you have children, Canon Chambers?"

No one had ever asked Sidney this question so directly, and so he had never prepared an answer and he found himself saying, to his immense surprise,

"Actually, I do hope so, however unlikely it may be. I think I'd like to be a father."

As instructed by Amanda, Sidney had managed to bring back a souvenir from Dieppe as a thank you to his wife for letting him go in the first place. Despite being a little too pleased with himself with the purchase, he knew that he still had to be careful because Hildegard was cautious about their finances, especially just before Christmas. In fact, they had already agreed upon a rather unusual money-saving scheme involving the presents they gave to each other. Instead of buying anything new they had decided, as an experiment, to wrap up possessions *that they already had* and had forgotten about. The idea was that this would make them appreciate the things they took for granted, and rediscover objects that Sidney thought had either been lost to the vagaries of his behaviour or the eccentricity of Mrs Maguire's cleaning. Thus, his grandfather's leather pouch that he had kept for change, a newly cleaned jumper that had been something of an old favourite, and a silver matchbox case were all about to be given to him as if for the first time; a metaphor, if ever there was one, for the need for light and rebirth in the darkness of winter.

"You have broken the rules." Hildegard looked at him with mock seriousness as she unwrapped her present. "And you remembered."

Sidney had got it right. It was, indeed, her favourite perfume. Shalimar.

"There are some things in life which are too important to forget," he replied, as truthfully as he could.

Later that night, after he had confessed to all his adventures, and while he was going through the correspondence that he had missed while being away, his wife called down to say that she wanted to ask him a question and it was important that he come upstairs without delay.

Sidney climbed the stairs with trepidation. The light on the upstairs landing had been turned off and the bedroom was lit by candles. Hildegard had also brought up the two-bar fire from the living-room.

As he walked through the door Sidney could only just discern the figure of his wife, unclothed on top of the bed and surrounded by apples.

"What do you think?" she asked. "Am I naked or nude? Be very careful how you answer."

Death by Water

Sidney was uneasy. He knew that it was one of his principal duties as a priest to keep cheerful at all times and he liked to think that he was content with his lot in life, but the copy of *The Times* that he was reading one late April morning in 1963 carried a biblical quotation at the top of the Personal Columns that gave him pause.

"Woe unto you, when all men shall speak well of you."

Sidney smashed the top of his boiled egg. What on earth was wrong with being liked? he mused. Did such a verse from the scriptures suggest that being popular was an attempt to curry favour and the deliberate result of flattery and hypocrisy? Why should one suffer for being loved?

Hildegard recognised the familiar signs of anxiety, tidied away her own breakfast and went off to practise the piano, leaving her husband alone with a vexatious newspaper and an overcooked egg.

This was one of those darker moments when Sidney wondered if his life since the war had been a mistake and that he should, perhaps, never have become a priest at all. It would certainly have been easier for his family, and now, indeed, his wife. He could have been a teacher or an academic, or trained himself up for something to do with the law. His mother and father, liberal North London agnostics both, had hinted at other possibilities while being generous in their acknowledgement of Sidney's gathering clerical momentum, but there was no family history of holiness, and their son suspected that he would have filled their hearts with more pride had his willingness to work for the greater good been diverted into medicine or politics. Now, however, as he turned the pages of *The Times*, and looked idly into "Situations Vacant", it was clear that he was ill-suited for any position other than that of a priest in the Church of England. He was too old to be a "brand executive" at Lyons Maid ice cream and only just young enough to apply for a job as an agronomist promoting the use of boron in crop nutrition. He read that he could more than double his salary by becoming an electrical engineer in Nigeria (at £1,800-£2,200 per annum), or work perhaps in Canberra, in the Commonwealth of Australia, in "three-dimensional site planning" (if he could ever find out what either of these posts involved). As he turned the pages of the newspaper he thought fancifully what it might be like to up sticks and live with Hildegard in Germany, and *The Times* helpfully advised him that Deutsche Edelstahlwerke AG needed a Managing Director for their works in Krefeld (wherever that was), but Sidney knew he had as much chance of acquiring *that* job as he had of becoming the local blacksmith.

Such idling over the idea of an alternative career had become more persistent after he had been persuaded to take a small part in a low-budget film directed by an old army friend, Nigel Binns. The forthcoming presentation, *The Nine Tailors*, was an ecclesiastical thriller based on the novel by Dorothy L. Sayers. It was set in the fictional village of Fenchurch St Paul and combined crime with campanology as the villain of the piece, a jewel thief, suffered divine retribution in a case of death by bell-ringing.

Grantchester was, in being both rural and relatively close to London, a convenient location for the film and Sidney had been persuaded to play a fictional clergyman, the Reverend Theodore Venables. This was the character who rescues Lord Peter Wimsey from his broken-down Daimler at the beginning of the story, puts him up at the rectory and then asks the great detective to take part in a nine-hour bell-ringing session to see in the new year.

The part of the vicar was, Nigel Binns told him, the "engine of the entire drama", but when Sidney checked the script against the novel he found his character described in more satirical terms, as "a man who seldom allowed anybody else to finish a sentence".

He was surely too young for the part. Venables had thin grey hair and a long nose; his hearing was not as good as it had been and he was always misplacing things (the only thing both actor and character had in common). He was a comic figure and despite the affection Dorothy L. Sayers undoubtedly had for the

170

Church of England, Sidney worried that he would be playing the part of a buffoon.

Nigel Binns reassured him that he had no intention of poking fun and viewed his potential casting as a masterstroke. To have the character of Theodore Venables played by a living, breathing clergyman would give the role depth and authenticity. The film was going to be made like a documentary, he told his old army colleague. What Nigel wanted was the essential truth of things. Neither acting nor costume was required. All Sidney had to do was to learn his lines.

He offered a fee of £50 and Sidney initially thought that he would give the honorarium to charity until Hildegard reminded him that they did actually need the money. She also managed to persuade the director to throw in driving lessons since Theodore Venables had to give Wimsey a lift at the start of the film and her husband still could not drive a car convincingly. It was high time he learned, she said, and this would be the perfect opportunity to get going.

Nigel Binns agreed to the lessons on one extra condition; that Sidney's Labrador could also be cast in the film. His presence by the water in a final tragic drowning scene would add extra sympathy to the tearjerker he had in mind.

This was slightly worrying because Dickens was not on top form and had recently begun to show signs of arthritis. There were walks on which he could not find his ball or appeared disinterested in any form of play. However, the film was an opportunity and, taking a longer-term view, there was always the thought that his beloved dog would be preserved on celluloid after he had made his final journey to that great kennel in the sky, and so all was agreed.

Sidney had a month to learn how to drive well enough to be filmed motoring up and down a private lane in a Morris Oxford "Bullnose". He took instruction from Fergus Maclean, a lugubrious undertaker with a penchant for quoting Thomas Hardy, and then, on one memorable occasion, from Amanda who thought it would be a "lark" to see how her friend coped with the double declutching required.

"I really don't know how you have got away without driving for so long, Sidney. I thought you learned all that stuff in the army," she teased.

"I never got round to taking my test."

"You had your mind on other things, no doubt," Amanda replied before screaming "*Concentrate*" as they approached an oncoming tractor on the wrong side of the road.

Sidney's driving was, it had to be said, erratic. He stalled at junctions, proved reluctant to turn right, and was often unsure of the width of the car the film crew had lent him, veering away from the verges into the middle of the road before swerving back into his lane to brush the branches of the hedgerows.

"I used to think driving revealed the character of a man," Amanda observed, "but now I am not so sure. You have an alarming ability to alternate between confidence and absentmindedness. You must pay more attention."

"I am trying my best."

"Still, I suppose it will be good for the part. You'll look like a typical vicar."

"There is no correlation between vicars and bad driving. That is most unfair."

"RED LIGHT," Amanda shouted as they made their way back into Cambridge. "STOP."

Sidney hit the brakes and stalled.

His friend looked straight ahead. "I rest my case," she said.

The weather was far from promising on the day the crew arrived and Sidney knew that he should get Dickens's morning walk out of the way before the rain came on. Nigel Binns had told him that they were filming at this time of year because they wanted a look of "March winds and April showers" but Sidney did not feel it necessary to experience these things before production began. He therefore set off across the meadows with his beloved Labrador before the weather turned for the worse. Daffodils, crocuses and even a few fritillaries were popping up amidst fresh grass, and he noticed that these signs of spring gave the people of Grantchester renewed confidence. As they looked up to greet each other rather than down to their uncertain footsteps on frosty pavements, smiling a little more often, bicycling with renewed speed, their hearts, perhaps, more hopeful now the weather was warmer. The first cricketing schoolboys had even set up an impromptu game, and Sidney remembered that he had tickets for the forthcoming visit of the West Indies and would be able to see Gary Sobers bat at last.

Both dog and owner settled on a gentle amble across the grass, a look at the river, and a quiet return home so that Sidney could concentrate on his Easter sermon. His mood began to lift as he thought of his dog's exemplary companionship and how much his canine friend had taught him over the last ten years.

As the morning progressed the film crew began to take over the village. Sidney had been told that it was a low-budget affair, but the presence of camera crew, designers, costumiers, wig-makers, make-up artists, drivers and no fewer than three assistant directors made the film look far from cheap. Every spare room in the village had been commandeered, with the stars staying in a range of Cambridge hotels and the crew overnighting in Grantchester. Mrs Maguire had even been persuaded to take in one of the dressers. The village school became the production office, and most of the High Street was made impassably narrow by the presence of camera and sound vans, three different lighting trucks, as well as caravans for design, costume, make-up and special effects: not to mention an enormous catering vehicle that was dispensing bacon rolls and cups of tea to the crew.

Nigel Binns had an authority on set that he had never enjoyed in the army. He wore a range of eccentric hats, and had a preference for pin-striped suits, colourful socks, brogues, braces and tiepins, and he carried a silver-topped cane. He also sported an oddly styled beard which tufted outwards from the chin.

Nigel had originally said "you won't notice we're there", but as Sidney watched the growing encampment of people he realised that this perhaps was only the first of the many evasive exaggerations that film people go in for. The unit was staying for three weeks.

Sidney was first introduced to the three main actors with whom he was to play the majority of his scenes. Roger de la Tour, a former matinée idol with luxuriant hair and a romantic history that was as chequered as his trousers, had been cast as Lord Peter Wimsey, while Melvyn Robertson was his manservant Bunter, a pale, bald man with a beard and a prominent mouth-shaped wrinkle across his brow which made him look as if his head had been put on upside down.

Sidney was more than intrigued by the actress who was to play his wife. This was Veronica Manners, an ageing red-haired woman in a cerise shot-silk dressing gown who knew how to make herself look considerably younger than she was. Only her smoker's mouth gave her age away. Veronica began by complaining that her glory days were behind her and that she would soon have to age-up rather than down and go for parts normally taken by character actors if she wanted the work. There were so few decent roles for women between the ages of Juliet and her Nurse, she added, and most of them involved crying. At least she wouldn't have to do so in this film but, as far as she was concerned, a small part as the vicar's wife was the thin end of the wedge. Sidney asked her why she had accepted the role.

"The money, darling; and Robert wanted a bit of company."

"Robert?"

"My husband. Surely you know him? He was the Hamlet of his generation and the toast of the Old Vic; but you're probably too young to have seen it."

"I don't get to the theatre as often as I should."

"Busy working, I suppose. You're lucky."

"Yes, I suppose I am."

"Robert's confidence has taken a knock recently and he's not getting the work he should. Nigel's cast him as a favour, I think. He's got a tiny part as the sluice-keeper. It's only a couple of scenes but it involves drowning, so at least he's got something to do."

"Do you often act together?"

"We were in rep at Bristol Old Vic for centuries: Chekhov one week, Rattigan the next, and a panto at Christmas. You know the kind of thing. I prefer being apart because it's so exhausting to work together. Robert doesn't. He likes our companionship and says we need each other but that's not always easy in the business, as I'm sure you know. Other actors are uncomfortable around married couples. They don't feel they can say anything and that you're in a little exclusive club of your own."

"Have you been married long?"

"Nearly thirty years. That gives my age away but I'm past caring. The days of wine and roses will soon be over. Is your wife in the biz?"

"No. She's a musician."

"I don't think we've worked together before, have we?" Veronica continued. "You weren't in *The Seagull* at the Theatre Royal in Bath a few years ago? You have a hint of Trigorin about you."

"Alas not."

"So what have you been in recently?"

Sidney could not think how to reply. "Church, mostly."

The penny dropped. "You're not a bloody parson in real life, are you?"

Sidney admitted that this was, indeed, the case.

Veronica was appalled. "I thought there was something iffy about you. There are moments, no, I mean weeks on end in point of fact, when Nigel really does *prenez la biscuite*. He keeps going on about all this documentary realism and the need to be 'authentic', whatever that means, but any drama has to be a *story*. It's all *made up*. It involves *acting*. That's why we're called *actors*. Real life is *boring*. That's why no one puts it on the stage. People need *entertainment*. They want a bit of a show. The last thing we require is bloody amateurs who think they can get by in the biz by being 'authentic'. There aren't enough parts for us actors as it is without pulling in the parsons to make up the numbers. I don't know how Nigel's swung it with Equity."

Sidney began to plan his escape. "I'm sorry if I offend you."

Veronica shook her red curls emphatically. "It's not your fault, darling."

"Perhaps I should step down?" Sidney looked hopeful.

"Please don't. It's almost amusing. But I would ask, if we have any of these little tête-à-têtes in the future, that we stick to the subject of *acting*. It's the only thing I know about and it will confuse me if you want to talk about religion instead. Please don't think you can get round me on the sly and ask what I think about Christianity. Since I am hardly the shiniest decoration on the Christmas tree I would also be grateful if you didn't ask me about my sins."

"I can't imagine there are many of those."

"They are *legion*, darling. If we started on them we'd be here for *weeks*."

"I thought you *were* here for weeks," Sidney replied rather glumly.

The rest of the cast were sitting around reading the papers and playing cards, as if they were waiting for the departure of a delayed train. Sidney was lost. Everyone appeared to know what they were doing except him. After his second cup of tea, the third assistant director told him that it was time for make-up.

Sidney did not think that he would need much, particularly as he was due to play an extended version of himself, and he was not anticipating anything too exciting when he entered the relevant truck.

He was wrong.

The make-up artist was a small blonde woman in a sleeveless white dress, and even with a beehive hairdo she was scarcely five feet tall. She had piercing sapphire

178

eyes, long dark eyelashes, high cheekbones and delicate earlobes, which contained two perfect pearls.

"Just pop your bum on my magic chair and we'll see what we can do with you, darling," she began.

Daisy Playfair spoke in a husky voice that sounded like a sore throat, and with her tongue forward in the mouth, as if she was about to offer an all-too-alluring kiss. Her lipstick was glossily pink, her skin was tanned and her cleavage was pleasingly visible. Sidney tried not to stare and composed himself by looking down to the floor and concentrating on her white slingbacks; only to discover that Daisy also possessed the most erotic feet he had ever seen.

"You're more handsome than I expected, Vicar. We'll have a challenge making you look old."

"What do you mean?" Sidney squeaked.

"You're supposed to be in your sixties," Daisy said firmly.

"I thought I could be myself."

"Not with Veronica Manners as your wife. She's twenty years older than you if she's a day. One of our best-known character actresses."

"I understood she was a leading lady?"

"No such luck," Daisy answered as she busied herself before fluffing up Sidney's hair, touching his cheek and deciding what make-up to use. "She never got that far. Now it's too late. You can look ten years younger on stage but once you're on film there's only so much a girl like me can do. She's a difficult woman."

"I've noticed."

Daisy put both her hands on her client's shoulders. "You can't look younger than her or she'll go mad, my darling." She winked and put a finger to her lips.

"So I'm to be an old duffer?" Sidney asked.

"That's what's in the script."

"But Nigel said . . ."

"I wouldn't take any notice of him," Daisy interrupted as she set out the necessary make-up. "He'll say anything to get his way. Now let me powder you down. At least your hair's quite thin. It shouldn't take too long to grey that up. There's quite a bit of fade in there already."

Sidney felt ten years older and it wasn't even lunchtime. Was it too late to bottle out? he wondered.

Daisy chatted away. She had seen everything in the business, she said, even though she was only twenty-five. Actors came in to make-up and started confessing all sorts of things. It was a bit like being a clergyman, she imagined, people coming out with stuff whether she asked for it or not.

"Yes, I can imagine people wanting to tell you all about themselves."

Daisy picked up a brush and enquired if Sidney had used foundation before. He remembered the hymn, "The Church's One Foundation" and thought he would try and make a joke about it. He could use it the next time he saw the local doctor, a man who was always pleased with a pun. (As it was, the title of the novel on which the film was based, *The Nine Tailors*, was also a play on words. The largest bell in the story was "Tailor Paul", a letter crucial to the plot was addressed to "Paul Taylor", and Dorothy L. Sayers had used a man called "Taylor" as her ecclesiastical adviser during her research.)

Daisy's ministrations were completed all too soon. "There, that's you done."

"I could stay here for ever," Sidney replied, surprising her and indeed himself by saying this out loud, when he had intended only to think it.

"No, no, no, Vicar. No chance of that! We've all got work to do. You get on that set. And remember your lines!"

Despite the vast number of people around when Sidney emerged from the consoling reverie of Daisy Playfair's attentions, nothing much seemed to be happening. He asked what everyone was holding out for and was told that it was "the light". Nigel Binns explained that most of his life was spent waiting: for transport, crew, actors, design, costume, make-up, but mainly for good light.

"You know it's called 'waiting for God?'" he remarked. "However, in this case it's a bit different. Now we want bad weather. I'm after dark brooding clouds." He held an eclipse glass up to the sun to look at the movement of the greying skies. "So it's the opposite of cricket," he joked. "Rain *starts* play."

It was just as well that Sidney had brought his copy of *The Times*. He settled down to read near the catering truck but found that he could not relax. He was worried about his performance and why he had agreed to all this. He should really be doing something less frivolous and more consistent with the needs of the

Church and he felt guilty that he had not joined the Aldermaston march his brother had asked him to go on. Plenty of clergy were taking part, Matt had told him.

Sidney had not been sure. After the terrors of war, he now believed in deterrence. He was not at all convinced that the clergy on such a march, despite their good intentions, really knew about the horrors of conflict and in any case, he had told his brother, there were the duties of Easter to attend to. The clergy should be in church not marching up and down the country in duffel coats trying to be "relevant".

As he leafed through the pages of the newspaper he became increasingly disenchanted by the members of his profession.

There was a murder trial in London, for example, at which the evidence of Father Keogh at the Court of Criminal Appeal had been deemed "wholly inadmissible". The Reverend Edward Ronald Broadbent, age thirty-nine, vicar of St Mark's, Bradbury, Cheshire had been sentenced to six months' imprisonment for several charges of indecent assault on three boys, aged eleven to thirteen; and the Archbishop of York was proposing the removal of the word "hell" from the prayer book psalter; presumably because it scared people.

That was, of course, the point, Sidney thought irritably.

There was also a review of the Bishop of Woolwich's new book *Honest to God*. According to the anonymous critic, John A.T. Robinson had undermined the very idea of an omniscient and benevolent creator. Instead of being a supernatural Being or Person with whom men can nevertheless be in relationship, God had become, for the Bishop, something he referred to as "ultimate reality" which was only revealed in the life of Christ. He had then argued that the doctrine of the Incarnation was mythological rather than literal; and he had dismissed the traditional understanding of the divine presence, fatally, Sidney thought, as "God dressed up like Father Christmas". According to the Bishop and his critic, it appeared that Our Father was not in heaven, there were no angels or archangels, and eternity was empty of inhabitants.

Sidney's personal theology was dependent on the promises of Christ and it certainly included the idea of life after death. Otherwise, surely, there was no meaning in the resurrection. This was the foundation of faith and it didn't help matters that a bishop, no less, appeared to be playing for the opposing team.

"Blimey, blimey, blimey," he muttered to himself as he read more of Robinson's credo. " 'Ultimate reality.' This is all we need."

He was reminded of Benjamin Jowett's remark to Margot Asquith: "My dear child, you must believe in God in spite of what the clergy tell you."

He was interrupted from his reading and his reverie by the first assistant director who came over and told Sidney that he would be required in fifteen minutes' time. He needed a "final check" in make-up and should make sure he knew his lines. "Nigel hates actors fluffing," he was warned.

Perhaps he could do some good after all, Sidney thought. He would play the part of the Reverend Theodore Venables seriously and with decency, as a steady and reliable man of God, not foolish or soft but holy, principled and well-intentioned.

He decided that, in taking on the role, he was, in effect, going in to bat for nothing less than the reputation of the Church of England.

Sidney's first sustained piece of acting was to show Peter Wimsey round the fictional church of Fenchurch St Peter and take him up to the bell tower.

He had already explained that this scene might be compromised since Grantchester had only three bells: one of which was medieval, the others dated 1610 and 1677; but Nigel explained that they would find other bells for the close-ups and the important thing was to make use, of Grantchester's "atmosphere". The fact that they had fewer than the eight bells called for in the script did not seem to worry him.

"I thought the novel was set in Upwell, Norfolk, at the church of St. Peter and St. Paul?"

"It's all made up, Sidney. Besides, the vicar there wanted too much money and you can't get back to London so easily in a day. I like getting home to see Anne whenever I can and that's not so easy when you're with a film crew in the middle of nowhere."

"I'm sure the people of Norfolk don't see it like that. There's a vicar in Emwell who would have been of service. He's obsessed with railways."

"I met him, but I thought it would be much more congenial to work with you, Sidney. You've always liked a bit of drama."

"Rather too much, I'm afraid."

"Well, now your moment has come."

Sidney had been asked to learn a complex speech that explained the point of the story; how Dorothy Sayers took her title from the number of times a bell will toll to mark the passing of a man: nine strokes ("ringing the nine tailors"), followed by a pause, then the slow tolling of single strokes at half-minute intervals to match the age of the deceased.

The ringing scene was filmed at dusk with Peter Wimsey joining a motley collection of Grantchester's "authentic" bell-ringers led by Stan Headley, the local blacksmith. Although the interior of the church was lit, the exteriors were to be shot in the "magic hour", when everyone needed to work at speed before the darkness fell. Nigel told Sidney that he was relying on him to bring out his "inner clergyman" and that he was going to need to act with complete conviction. They only had time for a maximum of two, possibly three, takes to get the scene in the can.

It was straightforward enough. All Sidney had to do was to walk into the church, but the breeze blew his clerical cloak up high and obscured Wimsey's face so that a dresser was asked to secure it. "The costume's getting in the way," Nigel complained. "Keep it down. And look up at the tower when you go in, Roger. I want to anticipate the sound of the bells."

In the end, it took four takes to film a simple shot of the two men walking into the church and a further three hours to cover the first bell-ringing scene. Sidney could not understand how anything could take so long but was assured that what they were doing was fast. Some directors spent a day on a single sequence; others were "no good after lunch". It was always a drawn-out process, he was told. Now the electricians began to talk about overtime and a properly union-negotiated break that would mean a late start the following morning. Sidney noticed that the first assistant was deep in conversation with the director and thought he heard the word "re-cast". He hoped they were not referring to him.

That night he confided his fears to his wife, telling Hildegard once they were in bed that he was worried that, when it came to acting, he had made an unconvincing clergyman.

"I'm sure you've done very well. You always convince me."

"And yet, when I am on the set, no one seems to behave as if they believe me."

"But they do in real life."

"I hope so. You know, Hildegard, it's sometimes hard to keep cheerful in the midst of things. I'm sorry if I've been a bit down."

"It's been a long winter. But the spring is coming. And we can go on holiday with the money from this film work. Fifty pounds! You've earned it."

"I should pay back Amanda the twenty she gave me to go to France."

"As you wish. That still leaves thirty. Perhaps we could go to New York?"

"Good heavens, that's miles away."

"Which makes it all the more exciting. I've always wanted to go there."

"We can't count our chickens, Hildegard. I haven't finished my scenes yet. I might even be sacked."

"I'm sure they wouldn't do that."

"Or re-voiced. I've heard it done. They say you can't tell how the whole thing's gone until you see the final film. What you feel and what comes out can be very different things. That's why actors can never be sure. They are not in control of the script, the direction, or the edit. Their performance can be changed again and again; made better, made worse."

"I would not want to give up so much of my life to the decisions of others," Hildegard answered.

"Well, acting seems a very parlous profession, I must say," her husband continued. "I was also thinking that I am spreading myself rather too thin. Three jobs are far too many. I am a professional priest, an amateur detective and now an actor. Some people might think that was greedy."

Hildegard nudged her husband and he spilt his cocoa. "What was that for?" he asked.

"There is also your employment as a husband," she said.

"That is not a job, my darling." Sidney was surprised that his wife could doubt him. "That's my life."

Hildegard turned out the light and held on to her husband's hand.

Still, he worried. "I don't know," he mused. "I hope Dickens makes a better fist of being a dog then I have done as a clergyman."

The rushes were sent down to London at the end of each day, processed overnight and viewed before filming began the next morning, just in case any pick-ups were needed. Sidney was invited to the screening room so Nigel could show his friend how a scene was constructed, and he introduced him to Warwick Lyons, the film editor who was working at a Steenbeck on a first assembly. It was seven in the morning. Warwick told Sidney about the importance of pace, mood and atmosphere, how the real art was in letting the audience imagine more than was shown. This was Hitchcock's great technique, the editor explained. If you looked at the shower scene in *Psycho* frame by frame, you realise that the knife never touches the woman's body.

Nigel agreed. "We're constantly playing with a gap in the imagination. The actors don't know what's going to happen to them. They have to be unaware; or they have to expect one thing and get something else. You have to put the audience in the same position as the protagonist. If he wants something then the audience will too. You can't give the direction of the scene away. There has to be a space between what is happening and what is understood: a sense of mystery. That's why you mustn't overact, Sidney."

"I wasn't aware that I was."

"Less is more. Look at Veronica Manners. She knows where the light is and lets the camera find her. She hardly does anything at all. It's all in the turn, the eyes and the cheekbones. She doesn't hurry. She doesn't try too hard. She knows the audience will watch her. You're doing too much bustling about, just like her husband does. He thinks he's still in the theatre. He's not."

"Does this mean I'll have to do it again?"

"No, we'll play it on the reverse."

"So you won't see me?"

"Not at the beginning of this scene. It'll be from behind and over your shoulder."

"So my performance is going to end up on the cutting-room floor?"

"You'd better get used to that, Sidney. There's no place for sentiment in this business."

"You could have got anyone to play this part."

Warwick could see that Sidney was put out. "That's not true. The audience will wonder who you are. We'll create mystery around your character. Then we'll see the wind in the trees, the rooks alighting, the church tower in silhouette (this cameraman always under-exposes) and add some music. It's all in the cutting. People often find the rushes disappointing, but there's so much you can do, provided you've got the coverage. Nigel's an old pro so he gives me what I need: establishing shots (most of which I cut, by the way), long takes and plenty of angles. It means we overshoot and go over on cost but no one ever went to see a movie because they heard it was under-budget."

"I imagine it is rather like being a magician," Sidney mused.

"I certainly show people where to look. Then the idea is to surprise them. They have to know enough of what is going on so that they are not confused, but not so much that they can be sure what will come next. They may have ideas, but our job is to give them what they could not have anticipated or imagined. Then, when we have made them think of every possibility, I finally show them what really happened and how we did it."

"It's like a detective story . . ."

"In many ways."

"The same rules apply."

"It's not only about suspending disbelief. It's about tension. If the audience can anticipate the story then there's no point in them coming to the cinema. The narrative sets off and something has to go wrong. Then there are obstacles, unpredictabilities, unforeseen circumstances, random moments of chance until, at last, it's resolved; either happily in a romantic comedy or tragically in a thriller. My job is to keep the audience there for the ride."

"And do you think this film will have enough suspense?"

"Do you mean on or off the set?" Warwick asked with a smile and a sardonic glance at Nigel.

"I meant the finished article that you create here in the cutting room."

"I'm sure our director hopes that any shocks or surprises will be confined to the screen, Canon Chambers."

*   *   *

Sidney took his morning communion and was called shortly afterwards. He was involved in a short scene with an actor called Andy Balfour, a man known for his good looks, strong jawline, high cheekbones and thick dark hair. Sidney's first glimpse of him was when he was lying down and in a bedroom, playing the part of a farmer with flu. Daisy Playfair was already applying false sweat to his forehead. The scene was crucial, Nigel said, because it established the character's alibi, while his brother went about his business. On rereading the novel Sidney did think it a bit obvious to have two brothers, each believing the other was responsible for the murder and then involving themselves in a mutual cover-up, but then, he mused, perhaps these stories weren't so much about the intricacies of plot but atmosphere, character and morality.

Once the scene had been set up Sidney was asked to step outside and take advantage of a new shower of rain and involve himself in a quick exterior shot. This meant him doing nothing more than walking along the street, a straightforward course of action made unusually complex by the demands of the director.

"Scuttle, Sidney," Nigel Binns had advised. "I want it to look like the rain is getting the better of you."

"I don't scuttle."

"Put your hand to your hat. Then, just after you have checked it's on safely, let it blow off in the wind and chase after it. It will be a little moment of colour."

"I don't want to look like a comedy clergyman."

"You won't. It'll make the audience fond of you."

"You told me yesterday I was doing too much bustling about. Now you want me to 'scuttle' and lose my hat."

"It's raining. You are in a hurry. You need shelter. I don't think I can explain it more clearly."

"I'm not sure it's me."

"You are playing a part, Sidney. It's not you. Theodore Venables is the man we need to understand."

"But I don't want him to look like he's frightened of a bit of rain. He'd be used to it. I don't want him to be weedy. It doesn't ring true."

"Cinema is all lies, Sidney. You have to lie if you want to tell the truth."

"Even when you're trying to be real?"

"Especially then. Once you know how to fake sincerity then you've made it. Now get on with it. Stand by, everyone."

The first assistant called for final checks, Daisy Playfair came in to adjust Sidney's hair under his hat and Nigel Binns gave his last-minute instructions.

"You know what to do, Sidney?"

"I think so."

"You do what I say. When I ask you to 'scuttle' you 'scuttle'. There is no negotiation. On this set, I am God."

"Then I can't wait to get off it and talk to the one who is real and lives in the form of Jesus our Lord and Master," Sidney muttered to himself, half hoping that he might be heard.

Back in make-up he told Daisy Playfair that he didn't think he was cut out to be an actor and that he should never have agreed to take part in the film.

She removed his foundation, rinsed out the grey from his hair and, as she patted it dry gently with a towel, she explained, "Professionals often think that too. I wouldn't worry about it."

"Is that true?"

"Everyone's so insecure. We're all frightened. My job is not just about make-up. It's to make people feel safe. I have to look after everyone, make them feel a little better, and not rush. Everyone gets tense. That's why there's so much hanky-panky on location. People feel they need to reward themselves after all the tension on the set."

"And is there a lot of that kind of thing? Hanky-panky?"

"Well, there's so much waiting about: and if you're in a love story people often get a bit carried away. They're not at home, there's plenty to drink, and so there's always a bit of corridor creep in the hotel. You have to remember that the business does tend to employ good-looking people, they tell great anecdotes, and they are very highly strung. It's got to come out in the wash some time or another."

"I see."

"DCOL."

"I'm sorry?"

" 'Doesn't count on location.' You learn to put it behind you. As long as you don't make the mistake of actually falling in love. And you just mustn't take any gossip off the set. Like the crew say: 'what's said in the van stays in the van'. It's the same in make-up. This room's like a confessional, as I've told you. Don't ask

193

me why people tell me things. They just do. Every secret comes here in the end. I just have to make sure it never goes any further."

"I'm sure there's nothing like that going on at the moment."

"Well, that's where you're wrong, Vicar. You don't think Veronica Manners is here to support her husband in a couple of scenes? Why would she do that?"

"Loyalty?"

"That's a bit naive, if you don't mind my saying so."

Sidney did mind but said nothing.

"She's had what some people might call a horizontal career. I know I can't talk but I've always stuck to the camera crew myself. But Miss Manners likes a bit of stardust. Now she's realised that her husband isn't going to make it she's got her sights on what's up and coming; and you don't get much more promising than Andy Balfour, I can tell you. He's always on the look-out too. A very dangerous man."

"I think I can see that. The set is full of temptation, Daisy."

"I used to sometimes have a go myself but I've got Darren back at home now and I'm too busy for any of that kind of carry-on. Some nights I don't finish until ten and then I'm back in at five. I can't go exhausting myself in the night as well. But it's easier for the actors. They're not on set all the time and only have to turn up when they're called. Otherwise they're just resting; and you know what that means."

"I'm sure that's not the case with all of them."

"I'm not saying it is but there's a lot of it goes on and Miss Manners puts it about with the best of them. At first I thought she was hired as the DF, but she's getting on a bit and Nigel's never been a wanderer. His interests lie at home. I don't know how he keeps his hands to himself with all the actresses that come his way but he's got a very nice wife. She's Catholic, although in my experience they can be the worst offenders because all they have to do is confess and start again."

"DF?" Sidney asked. "Is that another film term?"

"Not exactly," Daisy Playfair explained. "It means 'Director's fancy-woman', if you'd like me to put it politely. One of the perks . . . like the casting couch, if you get the idea."

Sidney was certainly beginning to get the idea. It was another world, he thought, as Daisy finished drying his hair.

His next scene in *The Nine Tailors* was the discovery of the mutilated body of Deacon the jewel thief in the graveyard, disguised as a casual motor mechanic named "Driver", who had come back to the village in order to find an emerald necklace that had been stolen and then hidden. Sidney had three lines:

"*A man's corpse! What do you mean? Is it in a coffin?*"

Followed by:

"*Who is this man? Do you know him?*"

And:

"This is a very terrible thing. I suppose there will have to be an inquest."

Sidney thought that this was well within abilities. He only hoped that he wouldn't have to do too many reaction shots during which he might be accused of over-acting. He still didn't quite understand what Nigel wanted in terms of the subtleties of performance. Apparently it was all about being seen to be listening but whenever he raised a quizzical eyebrow and tried to look interested, leaning forward with his hand under his chin, he was told that he was "mugging" and should cut it out. When he took a muffin and bit into it with vigour Nigel said that he should hardly touch it, but just make it look as if he was eating it, as he didn't want to be filmed saying any lines with his mouth full.

"I never speak with my mouth full," he complained.

"Just appreciate it with your eyes," Nigel counselled. "The muffin is your prop. Use it. Don't let it control you."

"I won't."

"Dominate the muffin."

Sidney was sure that he was either being teased or being asked for the impossible. The business of acting was more complicated than he had imagined.

The next day, Daisy Playfair explained that the discovery of the dead body in someone else's grave was her biggest challenge. The corpse in the script was said to be unrecognisable, but the audience had to guess that it might also be Andy Balfour's brother. There could, she had suggested to Costume, be some

196

similarity in the clothing, just to give the audience a clue, but Nigel Binns was insistent that this discovery should be as mysterious and brutal as possible.

Daisy told Sidney that the director had "done his nut" over the way the corpse should look, and asked her, "ever so rudely", if she had seen Edgar J. Ulmer's famous film *The Black Cat*? Or the nailed-down face in *The Mask of the Demon*?

" 'What do you take me for?' I said to him. 'Some kind of mad person?' "

The part of Deacon was played by an actor called Lawrence Riding. Daisy Playfair described him as an ageing Peter Pan with halitosis. "You don't want to kiss him after a party, even if you have had a few, but unlucky for me it's my job to be all over him, mutilating his face with all kinds of gunk to make him look like he's been battered with a blunt instrument."

She had already dyed his hair grey and matted it with dirt, throwing in a fake worm that made him look like a latter-day Medusa. She put rope burn marks on his wrists and feet to suggest that the victim had been tied up. She applied skin wax over the left eye, brushing in blood-red colouring, then black and yellow for bruising, easing the edges with her fingers. Lastly, she added more skin wax and fake blood to a split on the edge of the mouth as if the victim had been punched, brushed in darkness round the lips, patted it in, and contemplated a slit-throat effect on the neck.

"Have you seen any actual murder victims?" Sidney asked.

"I went to a mortuary just before I did a production of *Titus Andronicus* at Stratford. I wouldn't want to do that again in a hurry, I can tell you. But even though Nigel Binns goes on about his documentary realism I reckon you want to go for a natural but really dramatic effect. Whenever I do this kind of job, what I need to know is first if it's in black and white or colour and then how shocking to make it. Do you want an eye out, a smashed-in nose, or an ear off? People always need something done to the eyes. It's what people are most afraid of. That and their genitals, but I've never had to do them. Well, only on the outside."

Sidney remembered the dead that he had seen all too recently: Philip Agnew, Isaiah Shaw and Jimmy Benson. He heard their names as if he was in church, praying for the recently departed, and thought about the gap between the illusion of cinema and the reality of death. There was nothing sensational about reality. It went on. Cinema was entirely different; a lie, a fable, a fiction that might presume to tell the truth through allegory but was as far from it as any other story. Sometimes you had to look at life and death without colour or drama but with a cold eye. *Horseman, pass by!*

Sidney decided to view the rushes again the next morning. He wanted to see whether his performance had got any better and how to appear natural. How did someone "act" naturally?

Warwick Lyons said that he had something to show him; the difference between being on and off camera. "This might be of interest to you," the editor began. "It demonstrates how people should never be off-guard. Perhaps the camera never lies after all."

Nigel Binns had wanted a distant shot of Andy Balfour during the discovery of the dead body. Now, as the cameras were rolling but before the director had called "Action!" Sidney could see that he was joined on set by the distinctive figure of Veronica Manners, holding on to his arm and arranging what looked like a later assignation, while a dresser stood by, carrying an umbrella and waiting to put on the actor's raincoat.

As the cameraman checked focus, suddenly and in shot, Veronica Manners touched Andy Balfour on the cheek; a simple gesture that revealed their intimacy. It was meant to be discreet, but on screen it was nothing of the kind. It was picked up by the camera and no doubt by the dresser as well. Were secrets in the film business always so badly kept, Sidney wondered, and did anyone care about their discovery?

He tried to imagine what Veronica's husband Robert would have thought had he seen such a gesture. Would he make a public fuss or let it go? Would he give his wife the benefit of the doubt, pretend not to know, or confront her later?

"How do these film-star marriages ever survive?" he asked himself, as his mind moved on to ponder the nature of romantic relationships, the meaning of fidelity and the rise and fall of passion.

It was time to get back to Hildegard.

There was a delay in filming the drowning scene later that day because Nigel Binns wanted a sombre light with heavy clouds even though he was behind on his shooting schedule. Producers had arrived from London to tell him to get on with it but he was unwilling to engage them in any serious conversation, and looked busy even when he was not. Sidney rather envied his ability to evade the blandishments of people whom he did not want to speak to; it was not something a canon in the Church of England was able to do in *his* work.

Sidney and Dickens waited patiently in Daisy's make-up truck for the light to change. The Labrador was basking in adoration from the extras and costume assistants and Sidney felt a surge of renewed affection for his loyal and patient companion. He thought, not for the first time, how much he could learn from Dickens's dignity and quiet acceptance of all that life brought him.

Finally the light was deemed adequate, the crew moved to the sluice gate near the Silver Street Bridge and preparations were made for the moment that was set to be Dickens's finest hour.

His big break had come through personal recommendation from Mandy Cartwright, the dog wrangler on the film. Just over two years earlier, she had avoided becoming the victim of bigamy when her husband had attempted to marry Amanda Kendall for financial gain. Sidney had foiled the plot by going to King's Lynn and seeking her out; after which the Norfolk breeder had promised to repay Sidney's vigilance in whatever form he chose. Now that moment had come, and Mandy, having advocated Dickens being part of the film, was determined to do her best for the dog, ensuring his warmth, safety and suitable recompense.

"He's not getting any younger, is he?" she remarked on their reacquaintance. "But he's a fine-looking Lab."

"He is extremely good-natured," Sidney replied. "And he bears no grudges. He looks on each day as an opportunity for happiness. I have never known any creature so glad to be alive."

Mandy was a small thin woman in a bulky red jumper, jeans and a well-worn waterproof. "I'm so grateful for what you did when we had that trouble with Anthony. All that quantum physics went to his head, thinking he could be in two places at the same time. What a liar."

"And is he well?"

Mandy looked surprised that Sidney should ask after the man. "He's a good deal chastened. I've got him trained now. He's not likely to go running off into the hedgerows with young women who should know better than to go after married men. But he's slowed down a bit, in any case. He can look but he can't touch. Age has some compensations."

"I am glad things have improved."

"We've both settled down. Sometimes people can have too many expectations about marriage and the future and what they can really achieve, don't you think, Canon Chambers? You see it all the time in the film business, of course. I'm not saying we should accept second best."

"No . . ."

"But sometimes that's better than third, fourth or fifth. Not everyone gets the gold medal when it comes to marriage, do they?"

"I suppose not."

"And how is that wife of yours?"

"She's very well, Mandy, I must say."

"A gold medal then, eh?"

"Quite. And now if you'll see to Dickens . . ."

"Of course. I didn't mean to be personal. She's German, isn't she? They're always in the medals when the Olympics comes around; there's that Armin Hary, Jutta Heine and that well-built girl Gisela Birkemeyer. I went to Rome to see them."

"I think there is a difference between a good sportswoman and a wife, Mandy."

"Canon Chambers, everyone who has met Hildegard can see that you are a very lucky man. But you took a risk in marrying when people still remember the war . . ."

"Perhaps love is always a risk."

"I bet you were supposed to marry a Harriet or a Belinda . . ."

"I think some people were surprised that I married at all. Shall we head off to the set?" Sidney asked, determined not to develop the conversation further. "I am sure they'll be wanting Dickens by now."

Once they arrived, Nigel Binns explained the set-up. "It's really all on the reaction shots but we need to get the basics right. I've heard that Hitchcock's doing a drowning scene with Sean Connery later in the year so I have to get in first."

"That's right, Nigel. Show him how it's done, eh?" Mandy encouraged.

"There's the drowning in *Vertigo* when Madeleine tries to commit suicide under the Golden Gate Bridge, and there are three in *Lifeboat*, but this is my chance for some showreel direction."

He gave Sidney the storyboard for the sequence. The scene would start with an establishing shot of the weir, the sluice-gates and the keeper's cottage and then cut to a close-up of the raging torrent.

"We're on the bridge. We pick up the gate-keeper on Laundress Green."

"Ah, yes, he's played by Robert Vaizey, isn't he? Veronica's husband."

"Yeah, of course. To be honest, he wouldn't be my first choice. We only cast him so that we could get his wife in the film. So . . . he's walking with his dog to inspect the sluice-gates. We have a quick close-up of the dog and then cut back to the water. The dog barks . . ."

"I'm not sure about Dickens doing that. He's a reticent barker, aren't you, old man?" Sidney suddenly felt protective of his Labrador standing patiently by his side, his eyes never leaving his master's face.

"Don't worry then. We can dub that on later. The sluice-keeper leans over. We pick him up on a second camera from a boat on the water, the gate gives way, we're underneath him now, he loses his balance and topples past camera. We use a dummy for the actual fall (it will be in silhouette) and then pick up the real actor in a safer bit of water downriver."

"Nigel, you're a wonder," said Mandy.

"Special effects are on the bank with the bubble machine for the final drowning. We cut back to the dog, we see the dummy in the danger area on a long shot and then we pick up Andy on the bridge camera. He runs along the bank, and we reshoot that hand-held, so the audience feel they're with him."

"It's going to be so exciting. I can't wait to see it, Nigel."

"He jumps into the river and then we see him grapple with Robert; the boat camera captures the men turning over twice in the water as they pass through frame, we cut back to a close-up of the broken sluice-gate, the bubble machine does its stuff and then the two dead bodies float off into the distance, with a final close-up, perhaps, of the distraught dog."

"Dickens isn't usually a distraught kind of dog, I'm glad to say." Sidney gave his Labrador a consoling hug. "Think you can do that, old man?"

"We'll have the sound of the water up high, mix in the music, end on the water and there you go: next stop the Oscars."

"I only hope Dickens is up to the job."

"All he has to do is stand there," Mandy reassured.

"Can he look frightened?" Nigel asked.

"He can look startled and he can pace up and down, especially if someone is in the water. He might even jump in."

"We don't want that. The audience will worry more about the dog than the actors. He'll take all the sympathy."

"We could tie him to the bridge?" Mandy suggested.

"No, that's too tame. Let's risk it. We'll do his reaction shots with the dummy first. Then we can see where the water takes it."

"But won't the dummy be wet?"

"We won't dress it for the dog shot. We'll only put the replica costume on when the time comes."

"Do you only have one go at this?" Sidney asked.

"We'll try to get the fall in one take. It keeps everyone on their toes. But it's only a dummy. You've got to be more careful with the actors in the water."

"It sounds dangerous."

"It only looks that way. They've rehearsed in a pool. Both men are good swimmers. In fact they're probably better swimmers than they are actors."

"I wouldn't let them hear that." Mandy laughed. Nigel caught her wink and returned it.

Goodness me, thought Sidney, what is it about film directors and women? He knelt down to talk to Dickens. "It'll be all right, old chap, you'll be the star of the show."

The first assistant asked for positions and final checks, and stationed special effects close to the dummy. "Clear the set," he called. "Sidney, you're in shot."

"Sorry." Sidney gave Dickens a last reassuring look, and turned away.

"Get behind the camera. Quickly. Roll sound."

"Sound rolling."

"Roll camera."

"Set."

205

"Mark it."

"137. Take One."

"Action."

The dummy was thrown into the water and Dickens leant forward. He then began pacing up and down the bridge. The dummy turned in the weir below but appeared to have caught on something. Dickens was confused. The cameraman abandoned the tripod and moved in for a hand-held close-up. He knelt down so that he could be at the same level as the Labrador. The movement upset Dickens and made his performance as a distraught dog all the more convincing. Nigel Binns was just about to call "cut" when the Labrador suddenly jumped into the river.

"Help!" Sidney called. "Get him out of there."

"Keep rolling," the director called. The cameraman stood up and adjusted focus on the scene below.

"Cut," shouted Sidney.

"KEEP ROLLING," Nigel Binns screamed. "Only I can say 'Cut'. He'll be all right. Let's have five seconds."

"You said you didn't want this," Sidney snapped.

"Never mind that. It might work."

"But Dickens could die. Get him out!" Sidney shouted.

"It's OK," said the boom-swinger. "He's making for the bank!"

"What's happened to the dummy?" Nigel asked.

"Never mind the bloody dummy," Sidney answered. "Save my Labrador."

Mandy had already run round with a towel. She hauled Dickens over on to the bank. The dummy had sunk but the dog was safe.

Confused, wet, cold and betrayed, but safe.

"Don't ever do that again," Sidney said to the director.

"We had it covered."

"I'm not sure you did."

Mandy dried Dickens and wrapped him in a rug. Sidney fed him biscuits and the first assistant arranged for a car home.

The crew now moved to the waters around Byron's Pool for the moment of drowning. Robert Vaizey waited on the opposite side of the river with Ray, his dresser, while the crew made their final checks. The director showed him the exact patch of water that was best for the light, and his dresser belted up the actor's raincoat and gave him a trilby.

The idea was that the cameras would roll, and Robert Vaizey would thrash and call out for up to a minute so that they could get a range of shots. Then Andy Balfour would dive in, they would do the double-turnover stunt they had practised before both men played dead and let the waters float them out of shot.

"Are we ready?" the first assistant called.

"As ready as I'll ever be," Robert Vaizey replied. "To think I once played Hamlet. Now look at me. A glorified extra."

"There are no small parts, darling," his wife consoled him. "Only small actors."

"Clear the shot please, Miss Manners," the director asked.

"I'm going, don't panic!" Veronica answered. "I do not want to ruin my husband's greatest cinematic moment."

"You too, Ray."

The dresser stepped back into the trees.

"You've ruined enough of my life as it is," Robert Vaizey muttered as Veronica walked away.

Camera and sound began to roll, the clapper-loader marked the scene, and the actor jumped into the water and made for the lit area he had been shown. He turned twice to give the effect of being buffeted and sank convincingly, resurfacing without his hat, his hair already matted, and called out for help.

"More desperate," Nigel Binns called. "Go in close," he said to the cameraman before issuing further instructions to the actor. "Let your mouth fill with water, spit it out, go under again, come up and look around then go underneath. Stand by, Andy. Sink down once more. And — cue, Andy. Action!"

Robert Vaizey spent longer each time he was underwater, the idea being that he should only surface three times and then he would be gone. Andy dived in and approached him from behind, anticipating a life-saving manoeuvre, and the two men turned over twice.

"Good," the director called. "Keep it going. Pull him away, Andy. Go under yourself. Stay on the surface, Robert. Start to float. Don't go under again. The camera's on Andy. Now back to Robert. That's good,

Robert. Hold your breath. Don't sink. What are you doing? I said don't sink. Get back up. Where's your damn trilby? Andy, your turn. Play dead. Hold your breath. Let the water take you out of shot. Hold it there, everyone. Good. Lovely, lovely. Close on the waters. Keep it close. Hold it there. Hold it there. Five more seconds. That's it. Lovely, lovely and CUT."

Andy Balfour swam to the side of the river, pulled himself out of the water and collapsed on the bank.

"Is he all right?" Veronica Manners asked, as she ran to be near him. "My God, my God, Andy? Andy?"

At the same time her husband's body was sinking deeper into the waters. "I said: 'Cut,'" Nigel Binns shouted. The assistant director, special effects and the dresser ran to the rescue but it was too late. Robert Vaizey had sunk for the last time; his trilby sailed on downstream while his body found its way to the dark weeds on the river bed.

An ambulance was called and filming was suspended. It had been a tragic accident, although some of the crew began to mutter that it had been too dangerous a stunt and there should have been divers in the water. The production had cut corners on safety and this was the result. Andy Balfour also blamed himself. Perhaps he had pulled Robert Vaizey down too strongly, or he had caught on something underwater, and he should have realised that his fellow actor was in trouble.

Veronica Manners took to her hotel bed and refused to come out, calling on room service for food, drink and cigarettes. She was going to sleep for a week, she said. Sidney made his visit and tried to offer consolation but was sent away. He spoke to Inspector Keating who took a dim view of the production. "A very slipshod operation, if you ask me."

"It is such a tragic accident. And now the whole project may have to be abandoned."

"There's too much money invested to do that. I'm told there are only a few days left to go. Let them have the funeral, finish the job and clear off."

"Has the coroner seen the body?"

"The corpse is with Jarvis now. I think it's a pretty clear-cut case of accidental drowning. There were plenty of witnesses."

"Yes, I've heard . . ."

"And you weren't one of them."

"No."

"Then why have you got that look on your face, Sidney?"

"What look?"

"The one I don't like."

"It's nothing, really."

"Out with it, man."

Sidney swallowed. "You know that Andy Balfour was having an affair with the victim's wife?"

"You don't think he drowned him deliberately?"

"No, I'm not saying that, quite yet."

"Then what are you saying?"

"I'm not sure. It's a bit convenient, isn't it? Perhaps they were trying to drown each other."

"I'm not buying that, Sidney. It was acting, pure and simple, and then an accident. Both Balfour and Miss

Manners are distraught. Prostrate with grief, I'm told. I know they're both actors but if you're saying they're putting that on they're the best I've ever seen."

"I'd like to think about this a little more."

"Sidney, sometimes these things are what they are. Accidents. I know God may move in mysterious ways but this really would be something; a murder in full view that's also caught on film? I don't think so."

"No, I don't think so either, Geordie. But I wouldn't mind having a look at the rushes."

As expected, Jarvis the coroner decided that Robert Vaizey's demise had been an accident and recorded a verdict of "death by misadventure". His widow sent word that she would like Sidney to take a small family funeral in Grantchester and that there would then be a full memorial at the Actors' Church in Covent Garden in a few months' time.

She also suggested that he preach a sermon based on the text "Many waters cannot quench love" but he gently dissuaded her of this idea. He felt that the mourners should not be distressed by memories of the drowning. In truth, he was not sure about the idea of "love" on that film set. "Lust", he thought, would probably be more accurate, but he did not say so.

Veronica was dressed completely in black when they finally met for a late-afternoon tea at the Garden House Hotel to discuss the service. Once they had decided on the anthem, the hymns and the readings, Andy Balfour joined them. Although he was well turned out, in a navy blazer and grey flannel trousers, the neatness of his appearance could not disguise the collapse of his confidence. He was tentative in his approach and careful not to interrupt but said quietly that he had only come to make sure Veronica was coping and to see if either of them would like the first snifter of the evening. It had been such a terrible time, he said, and there were only a few ways of getting through it all. Alcohol was one of them.

Sidney allowed himself the teeniest whisky while Robert Vaizey's widow ordered champagne. She wanted to toast the memory of her husband. While Balfour saw to the drinks Sidney wondered how open the adulterous couple would be to any inquiry about the death. He would certainly have to proceed with caution.

"Perhaps it's just as well you're a real vicar after all," Veronica Manners continued. "I'm sorry I was so abrasive when we first met. I expect you take a dim view of the whole situation."

"It's always tragic when life is lost like this. I try not to judge anyone."

"Actors are always being assessed. We are used to criticism. And we don't mind talking about the things that matter."

"I wouldn't want to intrude."

"Everyone else does," said Andy as he returned from the bar. "I suppose some people might even think I drowned Robert myself so that I could be with Veronica."

"Did he know about you both?"

212

The actress smiled, almost impressed by Sidney's strange directness. "We were very discreet. But Robert always understood about my need for additional entertainment."

"He turned a blind eye?"

"As I did to him. Once the gilt goes off the sexual gingerbread you tend to take your meals elsewhere."

"You had what I think is called 'an open marriage'?"

"Not exactly. It was, perhaps, a bit more complicated. But I suppose I should ask if you had guessed that my husband liked boys as well as girls?"

Balfour interrupted. "Oh, Vonnie darling, I don't think Canon Chambers needs to know about all that."

"I did not."

"Robert wasn't aware of it when we were first married. It was something we both came to realise eventually and we talked about it quite openly together and then, when the crunch came, we decided that it did not necessarily mean an end to our companionship. We were a good team after all, and we couldn't imagine actually living with anyone else or, indeed, anybody else putting up with us. And so we decided to remain as a couple and enjoy the odd diversion. As long as we treated each other with respect and were kind, that was all that mattered. We had to keep our dignity above everything else."

"And you were aware of this arrangement, Mr Balfour?"

"Not entirely, if I am honest. But I didn't have any expectations that anything with Veronica was ever going to last. It was just a fling."

"Was?" Sidney asked.

"Oh, it's all over," Veronica cut in. "We're just friends now. You can't expect us to go on as before after all that's happened."

"No, I suppose not," Sidney replied. He had no idea what the rules were in these situations. Did actors just make it all up as they went along?

"The guilt is bad enough."

"And the loss," Andy said. "Everything stops after a death like that."

"I was wondering about the accident itself," Sidney asked. "Was there anything different when you came to film from the way in which the scene had been rehearsed?"

"Quite a lot," Andy explained. "We practised in a tank and not in our real costumes. I think we were both surprised by two things: the current in the river and how much heavier our clothes became than we had been expecting. Obviously I can't speak for Robert but it was hard work. Nigel Binns's quest for authenticity nearly killed us both."

"And did Mr Vaizey panic at the time?"

"He certainly did. He swore when we were going at it together. I thought it was acting and he was just getting cross with me, but then it turned into something darker. He was angry and frightened. Then he clung on for longer than he should have done and I told him to get off. In the end I had to kick him away."

Veronica Manners interrupted. "You didn't tell me that before, darling."

"The kick didn't kill him."

"Then what did?"

"The current. It was so fierce. We were in the wrong bit of river at the wrong time. I only survived because I'm younger and stronger. Poor Robert didn't have a chance."

"Will you sue?" Sidney asked.

"Oh God, I don't know," Veronica Manners replied. "These things are always so hard to prove; and I'd rather not have a court case. All sorts of things will get out. I don't mind so much about myself, you'll no doubt be surprised to hear that, but Andy is at the start of his career and he doesn't want to be branded as 'trouble'. Also there are bound to be insinuations about Robert's sexual preferences, however coded it appears, and I'd like his reputation to be unsullied. That reminds me, I have made a few extra background notes for your sermon at the funeral; the parts he played, the kind of man he was, his generosity."

"That would be very helpful. I don't think it will be too difficult to work in a reference to Hamlet. I know you said he would have liked that."

"He would. I did love him. I may not have been the best of wives but I was always true to him in my fashion. You have to understand that."

"I'll do my best," said Sidney.

"Please," Andy Balfour added. "Don't think badly of us. I know we have not behaved well. Forgive us."

"If you are truly penitent, then you will have forgiveness; that is God's promise. Forgiveness is not mine to give."

"I'm more than penitent," Veronica Manners responded. "I'm broken."

At the funeral, Sidney spoke about time and chance and the need to understand the truth of things, concentrating on what mattered in a life; the difference between outward appearances and the abundant truth of what is real. The task of the actor was to find that inner truth and disclose it to the world.

After the ceremony, Robert Vaizey's dresser thanked him for his words. Sidney had met him only briefly on the set. He expressed his condolences and, finding the man both reticent and oddly distracted, made polite conversation by praising his exceptionally well-cut suit.

"I'm glad you noticed," Ray Delfino replied. "It's important to dress well for a funeral."

He was a small man with a thin face, light blue eyes and gracefully expressive hands. "My father's a tailor," he explained.

"That's rather appropriate given the title of this film. Weren't you tempted to join his trade?"

"He hoped I would. He made costumes for all the stars and suits for their public appearances; ladies too. I met Miss Manners when she came for a fitting and we got on so well she found me a job on a film set. I've always loved the cinema. Dad wasn't keen but I've given him plenty of star contacts since then and the money's good. But when you earn it, you spend it. That's what Veronica always says."

"Were you often her husband's dresser?"

"He always asked for me."

"So you must be devastated by his loss."

"I can't stop thinking about it. We were so close. I blame the director. I don't care who knows it and even if we have been in church. He was reckless. And Andy Balfour wasn't much better, kicking out at him like that. I know what I saw."

"It was a terrible accident."

"Oh yes, everyone says that; but there's no doubt Andy Balfour would have liked Mr Vaizey out of the way."

"That's a bold claim. Did you tell the police?"

"I'm not saying it was deliberate and I wasn't asked to make a statement. But it's convenient, don't you think?"

"But there is no means of proving that, Mr Delfino, and the coroner has already given his verdict. I think you should be careful what you say."

"You know what the film industry is like. People will talk."

"I thought that you lot were all rather discreet about that kind of thing."

"It's ironic, don't you think? That actors are so bad at pretending when it comes to real life."

"I wouldn't know about that," Sidney answered. "Most of us spend at least some of our time performing in one way or another. We all play a part of some kind."

"Some more effectively than others."

"I'm sure you are a better judge of that than I am, Mr Delfino. Will I be seeing you on the set before filming comes to an end?"

"I won't leave Miss Manners," the dresser replied. "She's never calm when she's working. And I wouldn't like anything else to happen to her."

"What do you mean?"

"She's suffered enough. She needs protecting."

"Really?" Sidney asked. "I would have thought that she was more than capable of looking after herself."

"Well that's just where you might be wrong, Canon Chambers."

Sidney felt distinctly uneasy when he returned to the vicarage. That had not been a satisfactory conversation at all. He felt that although people were telling him things, they weren't telling him the *right* things. Everything was happening in front of his nose, but nothing was clear. Perhaps he was reading too much into the situation but he could not help but feel that Robert Vaizey's death had been staged in some way. It had been too melodramatic, and too obvious.

He had just poured himself a whisky and was about to settle in his favourite armchair when he remembered that Dickens had failed to greet him on his homecoming. This was out of character. Sidney's fears were confirmed when he returned to the kitchen and saw his beloved Labrador in his basket, shivering under his blanket.

Sidney crouched down and stroked his back and then the fur at the scruff of his neck.

"What's wrong, old boy? Have you got a chill?"

Dickens gave him a mournful look but would not meet his eye. "Why are you putting me through this?" he seemed to be asking. "What have I done wrong? I have been good and true and faithful and now I don't know what is happening to me, or why I am suffering, or how long this will last."

Hildegard walked into the kitchen and saw Sidney kneeling beside his dog. "Robert Vaizey may not be the only victim of this sorry situation," she said.

She told her husband that she had already telephoned Mandy Cartwright to ask for her advice and that the prospects were not good. They should prepare for the worst.

Filming resumed a few days later. There were just a few scenes left to cover but each one took an age. Although the local publicans were happy with the increase in revenue, Sidney wished the crew would just leave and let the people of Grantchester get on with their lives.

The next scene was supposed to be a straightforward interior, where Roger de la Tour, as Lord Peter Wimsey, had to bring in the cipher that would lead to the discovery of the emerald necklace in the church rafters. Theodore Venables then had to explain to him that the cryptogram was related to change ringing and the Book of Psalms.

Sidney's lines were tricky and he kept fluffing his longest speech:

"It's composed of verses from three psalms. Most singular. 'He sitteth between the cherubims'; that's Psalm 94 Verse 1. Then 'The isles may be glad thereof.' That's Psalm 97. Both those psalms begin alike: '*Dominus regnavit*', 'The Lord is King.' And then we get 'as the rivers in the south'. That's Psalm 126 Verse

219

5. '*In convertendo*', 'When the Lord turned the captivity of Sion'. This is a case of *obscurum per obscuriora* — the interpretation is even more perplexing than the cipher."

How was Sidney supposed to remember all of this? The language was almost deliberately obtuse in its construction. He kept thinking of his dear old dog until he was so distracted that he could hardly concentrate.

After this last scene with Veronica Manners he took the opportunity to say farewell. "Will you be going back to London?" he asked.

"I don't think I can return to our house. It won't be the same without Robert. Thank you again for the funeral."

"I'm happy to have been of service."

"And I'm glad that you're a better priest than you are an actor."

"Ah. So are you saying I'm not a very good actor?"

"No, I'm saying you're an excellent priest. Just don't let it go to your head."

"I don't think there's much chance of that."

"There's no room for complacency, Sidney. Once you've got a taste for an audience, you find that you want one all the time. It's how we actors keep going."

"It's been brave of you to stay."

"You know what they say. 'The show must go on.' Besides, what have I got to go home to now?"

"Your husband's dresser told me that he has plans to look after you."

"Ray Delfino? I don't think that's a possibility."

"He was very close to your husband."

"Not in any physical way, if that's what you're getting at."

"No, I didn't mean that. He's very concerned about you. Particularly protective, I should say."

"Well that's very kind of him, I'm sure. But I think I can do without a dresser in my own home."

"I'm sure you can."

"Do let me know if you're ever in London, Sidney. Come and see me in a show. I think I might be doing a bit of Ibsen."

"Won't that be rather gloomy, Miss Manners?"

"Exactly. I've just had the perfect preparation."

Later that day, Roger de la Tour popped out of his dressing-room. He was still in his costume. "Coming for a drink, Sidney old boy?" He spoke as if he was still playing the part of Peter Wimsey and the elision between illusion and reality continued some half an hour later in the Eagle when the two men bumped into Geordie Keating.

"This is too much for my brain to comprehend," the Inspector railed. "I now have a clergyman who helps me in my inquiries, and an actor who plays an amateur sleuth. That's two of you doing my job. I want it acknowledged that I am the real detective round here."

Roger de la Tour consoled him. "Don't worry, Inspector, we are all off duty now."

Sidney and Geordie looked at each other and replied simultaneously: "We are never off duty."

They settled by the fire with their pints. "Poor old Balfour," Roger began. "People are saying he should have done more. He could have pulled Robert to safety."

"I don't think he saw where he'd got to in the water," said Keating.

"He confesses to having kicked him," Sidney answered.

"That's not quite the same as bumping him off, though, is it?"

"I don't see why he had to do that," Roger de la Tour continued. "He hardly needed the husband out of the way to carry on with the wife but people are ascribing all sorts of base motives. It'll be difficult for him to get decent work. Even though he's got those dark matinée-idol looks and that great sweep of hair, he'll always be known as the actor who was in an accident with Robert Vaizey. It'll be the first thing people say about him. 'He's the one that drowned that actor while carrying on with his wife.' No one's going to cast a chap like that any more. And it isn't even his fault."

"Well," said Keating. "I would have to say that I think he's responsible for the bit about the wife."

"That's why I've always found that it's best to stay faithful. Once you start messing around everything spirals out of control," Roger replied. "I don't suppose you two men have ever been tempted by other women?"

The lull in the filming had given Warwick Lyons plenty of time to work on his assembly but when Sidney called to see him he confessed that he was finding the editing of the drowning scene difficult. It was upsetting to keep seeing a man repeatedly die on camera and he still could not distinguish the moment when the performance became reality.

"It looks like he's acting all the time," he told Sidney. "I wonder when he knew."

"Perhaps he never did."

"The last time he comes up for air he seems to be saying something different. The word isn't 'help' but I can't quite see what it is. The shot's too wide at that point and the camera goes in to refocus just after. It might be 'help', of course, and we can try projecting it but his mouth closes twice so I think the word in question has two syllables."

"Do you think his foot could have caught on something?"

"It doesn't look like that."

"Or that Andy Balfour could have punched him in the stomach on the turn?"

"Like Houdini drowning, you mean?"

"I think that's a myth but you get the idea. I am not saying that the punch would have been on purpose. That too could have been accidental."

"Let me play it again. We can check the trim bins as well. It's all here," Warwick Lyons continued. "Take hold of the controller. You can stop the film whenever you want. This is neutral. Right to play, left to rewind, you can zip forwards and backwards as well. Think of it as the gearbox to your car."

"I hope I'm better at this than I am at driving," Sidney answered, and he began to play through the

223

scene. This included Dickens waiting by the weir, the fall of the dummy, a surge of water, Andy Balfour diving in and the two men struggling. Sidney stopped the Steenbeck just after the actors had separated from each other.

"We can watch frame by frame."

"Show me," said Sidney.

They advanced through the images. "Vaizey falls away to his left. Do you think that's the current?"

"It could be."

"And then he appears to get sucked down. Do you think the word could be 'Heavy'?"

"But why doesn't he ask to be rescued?"

"Perhaps because he doesn't yet know he's drowning."

"You would expect the coat to flare out as well, wouldn't you? The tails should be floating on the surface of the water."

"I think it was quite tightly belted."

"I wonder why that was? Do you think it could have been deliberate? Is there any sign of him trying to get the coat off?"

They played on and saw that one arm had become free of its sleeve. Robert Vaizey was, indeed, trying to remove his outer clothing as he drowned.

"I think I need to find that coat," said Sidney.

It was now late April and the film had over-run by two weeks. If there was to be any further investigation they didn't have much time. As soon as the crew moved out of the village, scattering themselves across the country to their next jobs, the memory of events would fade and it would be harder to get to the truth. Sidney therefore asked Daisy Playfair if she could do him an urgent but secret favour.

"What kind are you after?" she asked, slipping her arm through his companionably. "Nothing too kinky, I hope?" She was wearing a low-cut white blouse and a black and white mini-skirt.

"No, really, Daisy, this is quite straightforward."

"That's a pity."

Sidney explained his need for the coat without giving away his suspicions. The fewer people who knew he was conducting his own unofficial inquiry, the better.

"It's funny you should ask for that," Daisy went on, suddenly serious. "I heard one of the wardrobe girls complaining that the coat had gone missing. It was due to be returned to the hire company."

"Perhaps it was lost in the aftermath of the tragedy?"

"Or it could have been ruined and Wardrobe decided to throw it out."

"Who would have been the last person to have it?"

"The dresser, I suppose."

"Ray Delfino?"

"That's right."

"I wonder if his father supplied the coat?"

"I can find that out for you easily enough. But what do you want to do about it? You're not going to stir up any trouble, are you? I wouldn't want anything bad happening to the girls in Wardrobe. They're decent and they need the work."

225

"I'm sure that's true."

"Although not as nice as me." She dazzled Sidney with her smile.

"No, Daisy, that would be impossible."

Sidney returned home to find that Dickens was still poorly and Mandy Cartwright was with him. The Labrador's chill had developed into a kidney infection and she believed, sorrowfully, that he did not have long to live.

"Do you think his time in the water during filming is to blame?" Sidney asked.

"It did not help. But you know he was getting older and he was a little frail. I shouldn't have asked you to let him be involved."

"I'd like to say that I enjoyed it all but that would be a lie. And Dickens hated it, I know."

"It's been a tragic few days. Poor Dickens. And I'm sorry for Robert Vaizey. It's hard to believe it was an accident, isn't it?"

"Why do you say that, Mandy?"

"Because film people are generally so organised. They plan for every eventuality. You would have thought it more likely that someone had meant it to happen."

"And who would that someone be, do you think?"

"I know people think it was Andy Balfour. He had a motive, the perfect opportunity and an excuse. He could have rehearsed a few extra moves and disguised his attack underwater. But he's a gentleman. I'm sure he wouldn't do such a thing."

226

Sidney remembered Cardinal Newman's definition of a gentleman as "one who inflicts no pain". Now it was possible that they were dealing with the exact opposite.

"Then who do you think would?" Sidney asked.

"Someone who had other reasons. Someone who wanted, perhaps, to ruin Andy Balfour's career."

They took it in turns to stroke Dickens's back and massage his legs, placing warm blankets around him. He had given up wanting food and water and was waiting to die. Sidney felt that all he could do now was to stay by the side of his loyal old friend for as long as he needed him.

The doorbell rang and Sidney assumed it might be the vet but the visitor was none other than Daisy Playfair. She was dropping off the coat Sidney had asked about.

"That is not my husband's," Hildegard was saying.

"It's the one he asked for."

Sidney emerged from the kitchen. "It's all right, Hildegard. Daisy and I . . . we have . . ." and with Hildegard's gaze upon him he felt temporarily unable to express what it was they actually did have.

"I've been looking after him," Daisy explained. "Making sure he doesn't get into any trouble."

"Would you like a cup of tea?" Hildegard asked calmly.

"That's very kind but I can't stop. I'm always on the go. Your husband just wanted the coat."

"You're a dear," said Sidney, letting the coat drop from his hand. "It's lighter than I expected. I thought it would be heavier. Are you sure it's the right one?"

"It's labelled with the actor's name. We always do that."

"You couldn't have made a mistake?"

"We don't make mistakes, Sidney." She knelt down to pick up the coat. "Look."

"Curious."

"I need it before we go, mind, or the girls will have to pay for it. It's due back at Angels on Monday."

"I'll come and find you."

"You know where I am," Daisy smiled.

Sidney closed the door to meet the quizzical gaze of his wife. "That was entertaining. First that woman in the art gallery and now this . . ."

"I like to think of them as my reward for all the elderly spinsters I visit."

"You haven't seen many of *them* lately, Sidney. What are you up to?"

Derek Jarvis had been the Cambridge coroner for over ten years. Sidney had not liked the man at first, principally because he had a slightly awkward manner and put efficiency before charm, telling him that a clergyman had no place in the world of criminal investigation. He had suggested that Sidney should confine himself to providing consolation after death rather than enquiring why it had happened in the first place.

However, after a few initial problems, the two men had become firm friends through a mutual love of cricket and fine wine. They also trusted each other's judgement and Derek Jarvis had made it clear to

Sidney that he no longer considered his semi-professional visits a waste of time.

"You are, however, pushing me on this one, Sidney. The case is considered closed."

"I know, Derek, but what's an overcoat between friends?"

"And you'd like my colleagues to take a close look at it without telling anyone else?"

"That is correct."

"Not even Keating?"

"I am more afraid of him than I am of you."

"That is a lie, Sidney. You just trouble him more frequently."

The coroner listened to a further account of the priest's suspicions and asked if he was to check for evidence of lead weights or any other heavy substance in the lining.

"It looks like the coat has been mended recently, perhaps since the drowning."

"Well then, this really is a job for Keating's boys. I would guess a good many people have handled it since the accident."

"I'd like you to take a look inside," Sidney asked, "where perhaps only one person has looked before. Because I believe that this coat is nothing less than the murder weapon itself."

"Unless, of course, we are dealing with an elaborate case of suicide," Derek Jarvis answered.

Sidney was perplexed. "I hadn't thought of that."

The next few days were awful. Dickens was immobile, his face a mask of canine despair. Sidney and Hildegard took it in turns to massage his legs every few hours but he was pitifully lethargic, his paws were deathly cold, and he had difficulty breathing.

The vet made a further visit and confirmed that Dickens had had a stroke. There was no hope. He had been a jolly good dog, but he'd had his innings. The kindest thing was to put him to sleep.

Sidney took time to pause. He remembered his Labrador's first arrival as a puppy ten years previously, scampering between Mrs Maguire's legs, confused by the stairs, with the *Church Times* littered across the kitchen floor in case of accidents, and his new basket by the stove. After his owner's initial misgivings Sidney had come to depend on this splendid animal; grateful, appreciative and seldom tired, eager for activity, always enthusiastic for the next adventure. Dickens had been Sidney's daily companion on walks through the town, along the river and across the meadows. He had eaten cake at every fête, been made drunk on beer by mischievous students on Guy Fawkes Night, and once he had somehow managed to drape a bra over his head. On another occasion he had stolen an entire Cheddar from Hildegard's Women's Institute picnic; and, on a different summer afternoon, he had run off with a cricket ball as it rolled across the boundary rope to end the match. He had discovered crucial evidence, been a silent presence at murder scenes, had nearly been poisoned and, most recently, almost drowned. His amber eyes were the windows of expectation, his waving tail eternally optimistic. Most importantly he had been Sidney's friend, teaching him more about loyalty, fidelity, patience and trust than any human being he had known.

Now it was over.

The vet positioned the syringe over the dog's leg and slid the needle into the vein. Sidney stroked his beloved Labrador for that last moment, easing him into the next world.

"Farewell, old man," said Sidney. "No one could have given more than you have done. What a joy you have been."

Hildegard laid a hand on Sidney's shoulder and wept with him. "He changed your life, my darling, and he made me welcome too."

Sidney wondered where in the garden to dig the grave and if the earth would be warmer now that spring was here.

He recalled Kipling's lines:

> Brothers and sisters, I bid you beware
> Of giving your heart for a dog to tear.

For the next few days, Sidney's sorrow could not be alleviated; either by compassionate friends, cheerful company or the warmer change in the weather. His return to daily duties did nothing to improve his mood and the sympathy of his parishioners only made him feel his grief for the loss of Dickens more keenly. Despite the undoubted love of his wife, and his popularity in the village, Sidney felt lonely and restless.

He returned to the Coroner's Office and Derek Jarvis confirmed that the remains of several hydrating crystals had been discovered in the lining of the coat worn by Robert Vaizey.

Sidney asked, "You mean there's a way of making the coat suddenly heavy in the water?"

"Very heavy, yes," Derek agreed.

Sidney remembered the film sequence in the river and Robert Vaizey calling out.

"The active agent in those crystals is an absorbent polyacrylamide; a polymer that expands when in contact with water."

"How does it work?"

"It's called sodium bentonite: it swells up to eighteen times its dry size when saturated."

"And it could have been stitched into Vaizey's coat?"

"Quite possibly."

"How quickly does it work?"

"With that amount of water it would have been a matter of moments. As long as the man was wearing that coat he didn't have a chance. It would be relevant to know who supplied the coat, who last had it, and why the actor needed to wear it."

"May I then suggest that this coat is, in fact, a murder weapon?"

"You may."

"And is it easy to get hold of these crystals?"

"It's used as a sealant in the building trade to absorb damp; and gardeners are starting to use hydrogels that swell to many times their original size in order to retain moisture which is then slowly released. It works particularly well in hot weather, not that we have very much of that round here at the moment."

"And so anyone with connections to the building or gardening trades would be able to access these chemicals?"

"Exactly. But not anyone in the film business. Unless, of course, they took a particular interest, or had relations in those trades."

"So a special-effects man might know about it?"

"It's possible. Or a farmer. Didn't one of your actors play a rustic?"

"I don't think his research would have gone as far as investigating bentonite."

"There are different kinds, of course. Calcium bentonite is an active ingredient in Fuller's earth. It's also used as a solvent purifier in the dry-cleaning industry."

"Dry cleaning! Ray Delfino's father is a tailor."

"Sidney, I think you may be pushing things a bit, even by your standards."

"But surely tailors know all about dry cleaning?"

"I thought they disapproved. A gentleman never has his suit cleaned; only aired and brushed. Those dry-cleaning agents damage the fabric."

"But Delfino could have done some research? And he would be able to access the chemicals."

"I'm not sure, Sidney. You'd better talk to Keating about this. It's a long shot but the way you're going you certainly seem on form. I would never have thought to look at the clothing rather than the man. I presume you are thinking that the murderer removed the swollen crystals from the coat after the deed had been done and re-stitched the lining."

"Yes, and thank goodness Daisy found it."

"And who is 'Daisy', might I ask?"

"A very nice make-up artist."

Derek Jarvis smiled. "Really, Sidney, you are incorrigible. By 'nice' I presume you mean attractive?"

"Extraordinarily so, but please don't tell my wife I said that."

"The sooner you get out of this film business, the better. You know how fast those people can be."

"The situation is under control, Derek. Daisy is almost young enough to be my daughter. She is simply an invaluable aid who will be leaving the vicinity in the very near future."

"And I assume Hildegard has not met her?"

"Oh but yes! She has indeed. Although it was not a success."

"You surprise me, Sidney," the coroner answered drily. "As you always do."

For once Geordie Keating needed little persuasion to act and Sidney joined him when they confronted Ray Delfino at his lodgings in Mrs Maguire's house. The facts of the case were presented to him along with the raincoat.

"We know your father runs a business in the tailoring, altering and maintenance of high-quality clothing," Keating began. "We have checked and discovered that he also deals in dry-cleaning techniques. I assume that you yourself know about the chemicals involved and traces of bentonite have been found in

Mrs Maguire's house where you have been lodging for the past month."

"Then surely she must be the person who acquired them and used them for her own purposes, I would think."

"The traces were found in your room."

"You should have got a warrant. It is my room."

"It is not. You are merely renting it. We did not need a warrant. Mrs Maguire was happy to allow the search."

"You are linking the discovery of bentonite with Robert Vaizey's death?"

"The same chemical that was found in the raincoat involved in the drowning."

"Then why was it not heavy afterwards?"

"Because you removed the bentonite from the lining and sewed it back up again. Only a few traces remained."

"But enough for you to come up with this ludicrous theory, I imagine."

"You admit that you supplied the coat."

"It came from Angels. And I did not murder Robert Vaizey."

Faced with this outright denial, Keating paused in his questioning. Sidney had been watching in silence but now found himself asking: "Why should we believe you?"

"Let me tell you another version of the story. It's about an unhappy man who takes his own life. He knows his wife is about to leave him and he can't bear to live without her. He hates her lover. And so he arranged his own death in such a way that her lover would be blamed. He dies knowing that Andy Balfour will be found culpable and will spend the rest of his life in prison. This is his revenge; to remove both men from the life of Veronica Manners and leave her with her fading beauty and her failing career."

"There is no evidence that Robert Vaizey was unhappy," Sidney said.

"He was an actor. How can you tell? Actors can deceive most people; even you, Canon Chambers."

"His wife says she loved him," Sidney replied.

"And you believe her?"

"I do. She may once have been a great beauty but I don't think she's ever been a good liar. I do believe her, as a matter of fact; and I don't believe you, Mr Delfino."

Ray Delfino turned to Keating. "I don't know how you are going to prove anything at all."

A few hours after they had left, and after a lengthy consultation, Veronica Manners found her way to the very same lodgings in Barnton Road. She asked Mrs Maguire if she could talk to the dresser.

Ray Delfino was surprised by the visit. "I thought you had gone back to London. We have wrapped."

Veronica spoke with a determined calmness of tone. "I am aware of that but I just hoped to go over a few things. I know you were close to Robert and I wanted to thank you for all that you have done for him."

"It has been a terrible tragedy."

"It has indeed, Ray. What are your plans for the future?"

"I was thinking that I might work for you."

"That might be possible but I would like to know why. There are so many up-and-coming actors and actresses you could work for instead of me. Talent with the future all before them. You don't want to hitch your wagon to a falling star."

"You will never fade, Miss Manners; and you will always be a star."

"That's very kind."

"It's what I believe."

"And I am grateful. But something puzzles me, Mr Delfino."

"And what is that?"

"It's about my husband's coat."

"What about it?"

"You removed it after his death."

"I returned it to Wardrobe, as was my duty."

"But there was a delay . . ."

"No more than usual."

"But I have a problem, Mr Delfino, and it's a very grave one."

"And what is that?"

"I think that coat may have killed my husband."

"I don't know how you can say such a thing."

"It was all arranged to look like an accident."

"I don't see how."

"And it could have been someone like you that did it: someone who treated the coat and weighed it down."

237

Veronica Manners held her gaze and waited for Ray Delfino's reply.

"If I did such a thing, and I am not saying that I did, then it was for you, Miss Manners."

"And why would anyone do that?"

"Because you were not, and are not, happy."

Veronica bristled. "Who are you to tell me whether I am content or not?"

"You were having an affair. That means your marriage was unhappy."

"Having an affair and being in a happy marriage are not necessarily contradictory, Mr Delfino. A woman can be merely bored or lonely."

"You didn't love Mr Balfour?"

"Of course not. Although it's no business of yours."

"I saw the way that you looked at each other."

"You are a very naive young man. Passion generally dwindles. Some of it is fantasy and that, too, goes all too quickly. Mr Balfour made me feel alive at one transient moment in time; he let me believe that I had retained my *allure*. It never meant that I wanted to leave my husband."

"But by your actions . . ."

"What are actions, Mr Delfino? What do you think we mean by the word? It is mostly impulse. I'm sick of the word 'action'."

"I thought you could be free."

"From my husband as well as Mr Balfour? Don't tell me you intended to kill them both?"

"I'm not saying anything at all."

"What on earth is the matter with you, Mr Delfino? I loved my husband."

"It didn't look like you did."

"It doesn't matter what things look like. It is how they are. You must have been in this business long enough to know not to trust appearances?"

"I wanted you to be free; to protect you and to look after you."

"You don't even know me," Veronica Manners replied.

"I do. I have watched you for years."

"That is not the same thing. You have no idea what I think."

"I saw you with Mr Balfour."

"And so? Who is to say that I didn't tell Robert everything? He was my best friend."

"He neglected you. Then you sought comfort elsewhere. Your husband was not good enough for you; and neither was Mr Balfour. I could offer a better constancy in their place. I would never leave you or let you down."

"Why are you telling me all this?"

"I think you know," Delfino answered.

"What have you done?"

"My only crime has been to love you."

"But we hardly know each other."

"We do; and I adore you."

"Love and adoration are not the same thing."

Ray Delfino sat down at last. "I think you are wrong."

Veronica picked up her gloves and prepared to leave. "I don't know whatever gave you the idea that anything could ever be possible between us. If you have always felt this way then you should have come and told me. Why didn't you do that?"

Delfino leant back in his chair. "Because I did not want to lose hope. If I had asked and you had said no, then I would have known it was not to be and I couldn't have lived with myself. But if you were alive and on your own then I could wait until you loved me. I could have waited for ever but there would always be the possibility that you would come to me eventually."

"I don't understand. You murdered my husband and framed my lover. How is that going to make me love you?"

"No one knows that is the case. It's for the police to prove. And I don't believe they can. I'll deny everything. There's no evidence."

"Yet you admit it to me?"

"And only to you."

"Or not," said Inspector Keating as he entered the room, followed by two police officers and a priest.

Inspector Keating was in a surprisingly mellow mood the next time the two friends met for their regular backgammon game in the RAF bar of the Eagle after the trauma of the case had settled. The sun shone, there were hyacinths and daffodils on village windowsills, and the world had righted itself, if only temporarily, at last.

"Sometimes, I don't know why I bother, Sidney. I should leave it all to you. But then if we had to swap roles I know that I would be useless at being a priest."

"I'm not so sure. You have the capacity to get to the heart of things, Geordie. And you have the confidence of your convictions."

"Even if I am wrong?"

"People like certainty."

"Isn't that what the Christian faith is supposed to give?"

"Hope. I think that's different from certainty. A home for love and a future after death."

"In heaven, you mean?"

"Whatever one chooses to call it."

Inspector Keating became thoughtful. "I see that one of those bishops of yours has been getting into a spot of bother lately."

Sidney raised a metaphorical eyebrow at the implied criticism. "And which one might that be?"

"I don't know his name. The Bishop of Arsenal or somewhere. The one that says that God is like Father Christmas and there's no such thing as heaven."

"Ah yes. You mean Woolwich . . ."

"What's his game then? Once you start saying you're not so sure about bits of Christianity you're in a minefield. You can't pick'n'mix with faith. You've got to stay true to the whole thing like the Catholics do . . ."

"I am aware of their position."

"And what is yours then?"

"The Anglican tradition is one of tolerance . . ."

"Come on, man, spit it out!"

"I try to give people hope in faith and trust in the promises of Christ. That then means I can have uncertainties in other parts of my life."

"Even if it leads you into trouble?"

"Even so."

The Inspector laid out the board for their game of backgammon. It had been a long time since he had claimed a victory. "I'm surprised you pursued this case, Sidney. Many people would have preferred to think it was an accident and kept their mouths shut. It was all done and dusted. Least said, soonest mended."

"I know. But when one has doubts . . ."

"Sometimes I think you substitute your religious doubts for those about other people's motivations . . ."

"Be careful, Inspector."

"You're not offended, are you?"

"On the contrary. I am worried you are too close to the truth."

"I am sorry, Sidney. There's no need to be cagey. I know you're on edge so I'm going to let you win this game . . ."

"There's no need to do that, Geordie. I'll fight you fair and square. But to be honest, it's just good to be with you. Life has been a little discombobulating of late."

"You're telling me."

"The accident that turned out to be murder. The end of an affair and the death of a marriage. Hopeless, misguided infatuations . . ."

"And don't forget the make-up artist."

"I don't mean her."

"Only teasing, Sidney."

The Inspector, who knew how to stop Sidney's philosophical pondering, had already gone to the pub's jukebox and put on Elvis Presley's "Old Shep".

"All these things stop you in your tracks, Geordie. Not to mention the loss of dear old Dickens."

"I'm sorry about your Labrador," Geordie began as the jukebox played. "He was a lovely dog. I think this might be appropriate." He joined in with the chorus, vowing that Dickens, just like Old Shep, would have his own place in heaven.

Sidney listened to the song and thought, fervently, what a dreadful dirge it was but, despite his misgivings, it proved the resilience of the human heart and a steady belief in its future; and, as he swallowed down his second pint of the evening, he avowed that it was certainly going to take a lot more than a book by that upstart suffragan Bishop of Woolwich, the so-called John A.T. Robinson, to demolish the idea of an optimistic future in heaven for our greatest loves.

The première of the film was, to everyone's surprise, a Royal Gala Performance in the presence of Princess Margaret at the Odeon Leicester Square. Nigel Binns sent a car for Sidney and Hildegard bought a new black cocktail dress with some of the fee they had received. She told her husband that she had put on a little weight recently and wanted something with a bit of "give" in it that, at the same time, would not make her seem dowdy among the starry throng. Amanda lent her a string of pearls to complete the look.

The film had gained enormous pre-publicity from the recent trial for murder of Ray Delfino and Leicester Square was packed when they arrived. Daisy Playfair bounced up to Sidney and gave him "a proper smooch". Roger de la Tour and Nigel Binns signed autographs, while Veronica Manners posed for the photographers, remarking bitterly that nothing sold a film better than a dead husband.

Once inside the cinema they took their seats in the grand circle, and then stood up for the National Anthem and the arrival of Princess Margaret. ("She's *tiny*," Hildegard remarked, "but what a tiara!")

At last the film began with opening credits, an establishing shot of Grantchester at dusk, the street sign of Fenchurch St Paul, and Lord Peter Wimsey's car coming off the road. He then sought shelter at the Wheatsheaf pub and the audience had its first sight of Sidney.

People tittered at his driving which was made to look even more uncertain than it had been, and laughed out loud; first when he ate a muffin with too much eager relish and then when his hat blew off in the wind. It was worse than Sidney had ever imagined it might be. He had portrayed a comedy clergyman after all, and the situation was not improved by the editor's choice of reversals and reaction shots that made him seem distinctly eccentric. The idea that the glamorous Veronica Manners could realistically be his wife was absurd, and the gloom of watching the film was only relieved by a first sign of Dickens looking elderly but endearingly loyal, the embodiment of patience and good temper.

"Dear old Dickens," Hildegard whispered. "You can tell he's fading a bit even there."

"So lovely to see the old boy again. Look, he's trying so hard to keep up."

"He was old and ill. Oh look, it's you again . . ."

"I cannot bear to watch."

"You look like your father."

"I think this film is terrible," her husband replied.

"No, it's good."

"It's awful."

"Think of the money."

"Reputation matters more than money."

"I don't think people are here to see you, *meine Liebe*," Hildegard whispered before being shushed by film fans behind them.

She was proved right when, in the royal line-up after the screening, Princess Margaret failed to recognise Sidney from the film but, having noticed his clerical garb, asked if he was there because he had allowed them to use his church.

Sidney was somewhat mortified by this oversight but his wife reminded him that he could not have it both ways. If people did not know it *was* him in the film then he could go about his business anonymously. However, if he *was* recognised, then he might be expected to chase after his hat every time the wind blew or perform comedy pratfalls on a daily basis. "We don't want people thinking you are Norman Wisdom."

Sidney was aghast. "No one thinks I look like him, do they?"

"You must learn to be teased, my darling," Hildegard smiled. "You may like to do so yourself but you are not so good when you are on the receiving end."

The reception party was as dauntingly glamorous as they had feared, and they felt so like country bumpkins in the presence of the Duchess of Devonshire, Viscount Astor, Diana Dors, Hattie Jacques and Max Bygraves that it was a relief to get back into their chauffeur-driven Daimler and return to Grantchester. After murmuring that it might be nice to travel like this all the time, Hildegard fell asleep on her husband's lap and Sidney mused on the events of a long day and how out of place he had felt. Amanda would have known how to waft through the entire première with her airy beauty but he was not married to Amanda and this was not his world. Instead, he really would have to get better at being a priest. There had been enough frivolity and distraction already this year and he knew that he would be in further trouble with the Archdeacon when the film secured its general release. He sighed, and stroked his wife's golden hair as she slept.

It was almost midnight when they arrived home. Sidney offered to make the cocoa before bed.

Hildegard took off her coat wearily and left it on the sofa rather than hanging it up. "That would be nice."

"You don't seem to be yourself."

"I'm tired, that's all."

"You had a good sleep in the car."

"I know, but . . ."

"Was it the film? The terrible drowning? The sight of dear old Dickens again? What?"

"That *was* sad, but . . ."

"Then what is it, my darling?"

Hildegard turned to face her husband. "Hold me."

Sidney was suddenly frightened. "What's wrong?"

"It's all right, *meine Liebe*. Just hold me. I have something to say."

"Of course."

Sidney wondered if he had done anything wrong. She couldn't be harbouring a grievance about his slightly over-enthusiastic reunion with Daisy Playfair, could she?

"It's important but I haven't told you. I think I was worried. I'm sorry. I should have confessed. And now it's late at night and I don't want to alarm you."

"Tell me, my darling. I am here."

"I'm pregnant," Hildegard replied.

Sidney kept hold of his wife. Then he took his head from her shoulder and looked into her eyes. He started to cry. His heart was full. He had never known anything so wonderful and he had never felt so responsible or been so scared. "Why didn't you tell me before?" he asked.

"You've been distracted."

"I'm always distracted."

"I know."

"But not so much that I can't take in momentous news."

Hildegard tugged his arm. "I hope you're pleased?"

"There are no words."

"None?"

"Nothing that can do justice to this moment."

Sidney's wife took a little step backwards and then gave him a playful punch on his right shoulder. "So that is yes?"

"I never thought it possible. I don't know what to say."

She smiled. "'Thank you' would be a good idea perhaps? Or 'Well done'. Or 'Aren't we lucky?'"

"It's more than any of those. It's more than anything I can say."

"Then, hold me."

"I owe you the world."

"I don't need the world, Sidney," Hildegard replied. "I just need you."

Christmas, 1963

In late November, Sidney attended the funeral of C.S. Lewis at Holy Trinity Church, Oxford. The great Christian thinker had died four days earlier, but the news of his death had been overshadowed by the assassination of President Kennedy on the same day.

Sidney had brought a copy of *Surprised by Joy* to read on the train and his thoughts were much possessed by death. He sat next to a former tutor who was disturbed that so many of his friends and former colleagues were dying. The old don was finding it hard to live in Christian hope and the general trajectory of his thoughts was retrospective rather than anticipatory. He had recently met his first wife in a pub for a drink and he had expected, foolishly and romantically, that they might speak about the love that they had once shared and what might have been had they stayed together, but instead they had talked about growing deaf, their arthritis, and how much time they had left on earth.

"Old age strips life of its poetry," the man said.

Sidney wondered how much that was true. The transience of life had always made him determined to enjoy the youth he still had left in him; appreciating each day as it came and counter-balancing the future threat of death by living as vigorously and cheerfully as he could.

Soon it would be Christmas, and this year it would not only be a celebration of Christ's arrival into the pain and darkness of the world, but the moment when Sidney's first child was to be born. This advent he was going to find it so much easier to imagine himself into the nativity scene at Bethlehem; the night on which the Christ child stood for all children and all humanity, when the word of God became flesh and dwelt among us.

He had no doubts about Hildegard's talents as a mother but was anxious about his own paternal potential. He wanted to talk to his father about it and remembered his own childhood as he thought about the questions he might ask his parents and the advice he might seek. He called to mind the natural authority they had displayed in their provision of a home. It was a place in which there may have been anxiety about health, money and, above all, war, but where love had been unconditional.

How had his parents achieved this? He wondered.

They had been exemplary. Sidney had never seen his father drunk or heard him swear. He had always answered his telephone calls cheerfully no matter how busy he was ("Ah, Sidney, how good to hear your voice!") and they had ease in each other's company, particularly when watching cricket. Now, Sidney thought, he had to step up to the wicket himself. He had to play with a straight bat, cover the field, anticipating danger and alert to unpredictability, ready for the first and most important delivery of his life.

Duty had called him to the funeral of C.S. Lewis but he made only the briefest of appearances at the wake. Although the baby was not due for a few more weeks, Sidney didn't like leaving Hildegard alone for any period of time and certainly not overnight. He looked out of the train window at the encroaching winter darkness and told himself firmly that he had been absent from home, pursuing ridiculous crimes, for long enough. All he wanted was the safe haven of the vicarage and the consolation of his wife's company.

Preparations had been made for Advent Sunday and Hildegard had decorated their home in the German tradition. She insisted that Sidney fill his shoes with hay and carrots for the coming of St Nicholas. She placed a wreath on the table with four red candles, and made sure that each morning they opened the Advent Calendar her mother had sent: a snowy German street scene dusted with glitter.

Hildegard cooked with determined enthusiasm throughout her late pregnancy, perhaps hoping that all that energy spent standing, mixing and stirring would encourage the baby to arrive in good time for Christmas, perfectly formed and beautiful, just like the *Stollenbröd* and gingerbread men she made or the Hansel and Gretel cake with white icing which she studded with Smarties for the Sunday School party.

She baked frosted biscuits in the shapes of stars and half-moons which she hung from the Christmas tree

251

with red ribbon. Sidney loved coming home to see his wife's industrial organisation as she kneaded the dough for the *Vanillekipferl*, beat egg whites until they were glossy, and mixed in hazelnuts, cinnamon and zest for the *Zimtsterne*. She made loaves of sweetbread, filled cakes with candied fruits, warmed brown sugar, honey, molasses and butter for her *Lebkuchen*, and created gingerbread snowmen as treats for the children's concert. Despite the rain and the daytime darkness, the vicarage kitchen was warm, light and filled with the smell of baking. This was his own home at last, Sidney thought. He was no longer a child who needed to return to his mother to feel safe at Christmas. He and his wife were creating something new, a sanctuary ready to welcome its new addition.

Hildegard sang as she prepared their meals; German folk songs, carols, snatches of Bach. She showed few signs of stress. Only occasionally did she lose her composure: when Sidney dithered around her, for example, half-heartedly offering to help while plainly hoping to be let off any household chores; or when, it seemed, he was almost deliberately getting in the way; or at other times when lady parishioners of a certain age made unannounced visits and implied that they had a special, private, understanding with the vicar that Hildegard, as a foreigner, could not hope to appreciate. She became especially on edge when the Archdeacon called in for sherry after evensong and pointed out that their Christmas tree wasn't straight. Sidney had to move swiftly to her defence.

"I think you'll find that it's not crooked if you are in the main body of the room," Sidney explained patiently. "It's rather like life. It all depends on the way in which you look at it."

Then the fairy lights would fuse, and Hildegard would almost snap, saying that all she wanted was for everything to *work*, and for her husband to replace the faulty bulbs when they broke and not wait for God magically to turn them on again.

Consequently Sidney would get down on his hands and knees and sort out the lights and try and straighten the tree without knocking it over and quietly retire to his study until the next meal.

He made Hildegard cups of tea first thing in the morning and mugs of cocoa before they went to bed. He kissed her on the back of the neck unexpectedly when she was at the piano or in the kitchen. He gave her as much affection as he could, and he told her frequently that he loved her. The couple privately acknowledged that they were more anxious about the baby than they were prepared to say out loud, as if admitting their fears might jinx the birth.

The grandmothers-to-be had both been knitting for their respective countries. Hildegard's mother, Sibilla Leber, had sent a package of cardigans, mittens, booties and baby outfits from the DDR in socialist red, thereby avoiding the pink or blue conundrum. Iris Chambers had bought a second-hand Moses basket and lined it in tactfully chosen lemon-yellow sprigged muslin with a prodigious number of ribbons and bows. She had also crocheted a reversible shell blanket in innocent white.

253

The due date was 15th December, and Sidney had been careful not to say anything about the additional Christmas parish duties he would have to attend, knowing that first babies could often be late, hoping and, truth be told, praying, for the safety of a Boxing Day arrival.

Hildegard diligently attended antenatal classes and saw her doctor more regularly than other mothers-to-be might do because, now in her late thirties, she was considerably older than young parishioners like Abigail Redmond (a mere stripling at twenty-two who was also pregnant and proud). It was felt that Hildegard needed closer monitoring and a little extra attention.

As they waited, the couple enjoyed talking about what their child might be called. Sidney favoured the name of an apostle for a boy (Mark, Luke and James) and a Shakespearean heroine for a girl (Rosalind, Viola, Imogen or Miranda). Hildegard held out for Christian names that would work equally well in German (Frank, Paul, Max, Thomas; Anna, Julie, Stephanie, Sophie) but was prepared to compromise with James or Imogen. She would know exactly which name would be the right one immediately she saw the child, she said.

Hildegard was worried about hers being unflatteringly termed a "geriatric pregnancy" but some of the younger mums-to-be were so insouciant about their impending births she found their lack of nerves rubbed off on her and gave her confidence. Abigail Redmond was particularly sympathetic, and when her baby boy was born prematurely, weighing in at just over five pounds, Sidney made a point of going to see her in hospital: both as a pastoral visit to thank her for her kindness to his wife and to get an idea of what lay in store for him in the all-too-immediate future.

He had an uneasy relationship with the Redmond family. Agatha Redmond, the matriarch, organised the flowers in the church and was a well-respected dog breeder who had supplied him with his beloved, and now much lamented, Labrador. For some reason that had never been explained, most of the female members of the family had names beginning with the letter "A". Abigail, the new mother, was Agatha's daughter with a colourful past which had involved a liaison with a photographer who had burned down his own studio, and then a brief affair with the local garage mechanic who had failed in his attempt to become a pop star. She was currently the paramour of Colin Sampson, the wayward son of the local solicitor.

Abigail was sitting up in bed in Addenbrooke's Hospital, her mother was by her side holding the baby, while the new father seized the opportunity provided by Sidney's visit to take a fag break. They bumped into one another in the corridor leading to the ward. "You don't mind me nipping off now you're here, do you, Vicar? This isn't really the best place for blokes and I'm meeting some mates in the pub to wet the baby's head. Just as well the little nipper came at the weekend. I can't miss work."

Sidney touched the man's arm in a gesture of solidarity. "You must be very proud," he said.

255

"Well, Vicar, it was an accident, to tell you the truth. We got carried away; and with a girl like Abi, well, once you start you don't want to stop."

"I think I can imagine."

"I'm sure you can, Vicar. She told me you were keen on her yourself once. Is that true?"

"No, it is not," Sidney replied firmly.

"Not that it matters. She's my girl now. I hear your old woman's up the duff and all."

"She's not old."

"Abi made us laugh when she told us about her being pregnant . . . said she's about old enough to be her mum."

Even Colin saw that the conversation was not going well and adjusted accordingly. "But she was very kind to our Abi at the antenatal class, I'll say that for her. How long are you stopping?"

"I thought I'd just offer a prayer and a bit of support."

"I'm not sure she needs that, really. Although people have got a bit panicky, to tell you the truth. I think it's because he was premature. The nurses keep taking him away for tests but he looks all right to me. That's why I'm off; I won't be long." Colin did not wait for an answer.

Sidney entered the ward and looked at the small, red-faced baby in Mrs Redmond's arms. "Isn't he beautiful?" she said. "Look at his tiny toes and fingers."

He inspected the roseate figure in detail, putting his finger gently in the child's palm, and was immediately touched and moved when the small fist trustingly clenched around it. He smiled and turned to the new mother. "You must be very relieved, Abigail. Are you very tired?"

"Yes I am, Canon Chambers, and they're keeping me in for another week."

"I suppose they need to make sure everything is in order."

"It hurt to buggery."

Her mother was aghast. "Abigail . . ."

"He's not shocked, Mum. He was in the army. You can say anything to Canon Chambers."

"Not quite anything," Sidney answered carefully. "But I am glad that all is well."

"It wasn't what I was expecting, to be honest, but I suppose if doctors told us the truth most of us wouldn't bother going through with it all. At least it's over now."

"Although with a child I don't think anything is really over. You are at the beginning of something wonderful."

"It doesn't feel like it."

"But it's why we live," Sidney continued. "This child is the meaning of why we are here; the creation of new life that will continue when we are no more."

"It didn't feel like that at the time, I can tell you. I thought I was going to die."

"I was wondering if I could say a little prayer?" Sidney suggested.

"Can't do any harm," Abigail replied.

"Shall we wait for Colin?" Agatha Redmond asked.

Abigail looked to Sidney. "He'll be off to the pub on the corner for a good couple of hours. You do what you

257

have to do, Canon Chambers. You're going to be a dad yourself soon enough. I bet you'll be there properly right the way through it."

"I think it's customary for men to wait outside."

"But a clergyman like you can go anywhere in a hospital, can't he? They'll let you watch if you like."

"I'm not sure that I want to do that."

"Coward."

Sidney smiled. "I probably am, Abigail, I probably am."

"We're the ones that have to go through with it," the new mother continued. "That's what men keep forgetting about. Watching is nothing. Perhaps if more blokes were to see what it was like then they wouldn't be so keen on the old how's your father in the first place."

"You may well be right; but until modern medicine makes male pregnancy available, I'm afraid we'll have to be content with the status quo." Sidney opened his *Book of Common Prayer.* "Have you decided on a name?"

"I thought of calling him after my dad, but I don't like the name Harding. I think I prefer John; like John Lennon in the Beatles."

"I hear they are quite the thing."

"I don't suppose you've been to see them? I did. Screamed my bleedin' heart out."

"I haven't had the pleasure of seeing them on stage. But John is a very good name," Sidney continued. "The last, but by no means the least, of the evangelists."

"I don't know about that."

258

"You will, Abigail. One day, I am sure. Once we get your boy into Sunday School."

"You like to catch them early, I suppose."

"I believe it is my duty to look after them throughout their lives; from the cradle to the grave."

"That'll keep you busy then."

"Let us pray," Sidney began. " 'They brought young children to Christ, that he should touch them: and his disciples rebuked those that brought them. But when Jesus saw it, he was much displeased, and said unto them, suffer the little children to come unto me, and forbid them not: for such is the kingdom of God. Verily I say unto you, whosoever shall not receive the kingdom of God as a little child, he shall not enter therein. And he took them up in his arms, put his hands upon them, and blessed them.' "

He leant forward and kissed the baby on the forehead. "God bless you and keep you, John. May He keep you safe from all evil. May you walk in His glory."

Sidney stepped back and prepared to leave the hospital. Even though there was a newborn baby before his very eyes, he still could not possibly anticipate or imagine what it might be like if that child was his.

Hildegard's mother Sibilla had already decided that her daughter needed help and that she would come both for Christmas and the birth of her third grandchild. Sidney was not at all sure that this would help (her mother's judgemental presence always made Hildegard anxious) but once the suggestion had been aired there was no stopping it. Frau Leber was a proud woman

259

who frequently liked to remind people that she was the widow of an East German communist hero. She was in her late sixties and, despite a minor stroke two years earlier and a lifetime addiction to cigarettes, she was far sturdier than she let on. Furthermore, because she was over the pension age she had no trouble travelling to the West as her country's government was eager to divest itself of the responsibility of looking after an ageing population.

Frau Leber was to be spending a few days in London on her arrival and Hildegard had arranged a trip to the National Gallery where Amanda was to make sure that she proved to her mother that the greatest European art was not Italian but German.

She telephoned the vicarage to say that she would be happy to see Frau Leber on to her train up to Cambridge and that she had even organised a replacement for Dickens. The Labrador would be ready for collection just before Christmas.

The last thing on earth Sidney needed was a puppy; and he had already done his duty by the Redmond family and their new arrival. He didn't really want to have to go out to their farm.

"Don't be ridiculous, Sidney. The puppy is simply adorable. I've already given him a name."

"Oh no, Amanda, really."

"It's very literary. You have to guess."

"Crab," said Sidney. "After the dog in *The Two Gentlemen of Verona*."

"That's too clever of you by half. It's another writer."

"Please don't tell me you have called my new puppy Dostoevsky?"

"Of course not. He's 'Byron'. Don't you think that's a wonderful name?"

"You've called him after a great — but scandalous — poet who died at the age of thirty-six?"

"Mad, bad and dangerous to know. He's a bit like us."

"Amanda . . ."

"And I'm sure I don't need to remind you that Byron also wrote the lines about how a dog is 'in life the firmest friend, the first to welcome, foremost to defend'? Isn't that appropriate? He's just the ticket."

"Life is a little bit difficult at the moment," Sidney muttered. "To have a baby and a puppy at the same time is crackers."

A few days later, and a week after the funeral of C.S. Lewis in Oxford, Sidney met Geordie Keating for their regular session of drinks and backgammon in the RAF bar of the Eagle. He had promised his wife that he would not stay long but it was clear that the Inspector needed cheering up. He was tired and unusually bolshy, partly because he had had to escort a drunk home the previous evening only to discover that the man was too inebriated to remember where he lived.

"You only had to look into his eyes to see that he couldn't have many years left in him," Geordie complained. "Still, it's Christmas. You have to forgive and begin again. That's the message of the season, is it not, Sidney? Peace and goodwill to all men. The baby

261

that saves us all. Soon you'll be having a little chap of your own."

"We can't be sure it's a boy."

"That's true. Cathy had three girls and we thought each of them in turn was going to be a boy. Now we've just about given up, certainly as far as I, and my bank manager, are concerned. Besides, any more children are bound to be girls."

"You mean you could still add to the family?"

"I don't know, Sidney. It's all a mystery. They seem to keep popping up unexpectedly. At least with Hildegard you've probably only got one shot at it. Is she keeping well?"

"Remarkably. I think pregnancy suits her."

"You'll be interested to observe it all happening as the baby gets older."

"I think I will be doing more than observing . . ."

"No, you will be a father. But the women do most of the work. You'll still be able to be out and about. You will only be told to mind the child when the wife is under pressure. Otherwise she won't really trust you . . ."

"Oh, I think with Hildegard . . ."

"No, Sidney, she won't. If ever a woman knew what she wanted, it is your wife. You can rely on her for anything. I'd trust her with my life, I don't mind telling you. She's an admirable woman."

"She is indeed."

"You'll probably have to change a nappy or two."

"Really?"

"Yes, I am afraid the modern man is expected to do that."

"I don't think my father ever changed a nappy in his life."

"These are the 1960s, Sidney. Times have changed."

"So nappies are no longer a woman's responsibility alone . . ."

"Exactly. Then you will have to pick the child up and walk the baby in the middle of the night. It's tiring. But when they begin to sit up it gets interesting. You start to see yourself in them. They look at everything around them, pick up things and ask, 'What is this? How does it work? Can I eat it?' When they're tiny you'll be worried when they are asleep that they aren't breathing and when they're awake you'll worry that something awful might happen to them."

"I never thought you'd want to spend our time together in the pub talking about babies like this."

Inspector Keating gave his friend one of his knowing looks. "Well, there is a reason for this, Sidney."

"Aside from my wife's situation?"

"I am afraid so. You know Abigail Redmond?"

"Of course I do. She is a pretty memorable young woman."

"Someone has stolen her child."

"What?" Sidney was aghast.

"From the hospital," the Inspector continued. "He's only a week old."

"And he was premature. That's utterly terrible. What happened?"

"A straight snatch, we think, in the middle of the evening. No one saw anything. We're going house to house tonight, but it's a very delicate business and it's upsetting when you find yourself questioning and suspecting married couples who don't have children. It's a difficult subject, obviously, and we aren't getting anywhere. I shouldn't really be here with you. I should be out on the case."

"And why aren't you?"

"Because I'm talking to you."

"Why waste your time doing that?"

"I'm not wasting my time and I think you can guess why."

"Don't tell me . . ."

"You know the Redmond family."

"Not that well."

"Well enough. I want you to talk to them. Find out who they know."

"But it's most likely to be a complete stranger, isn't it? Do you have any suspects?"

"Anyone could have done it."

"But you must have some ideas."

"One of the nurses, Sister Bland I think she's called, said she saw a woman with a scarf and a dark coat holding a bundle that might have been Abigail's child. In all odds it's a woman. I don't think men go in for stealing babies."

"I don't think we can rule anyone out at this stage, surely? Do you think it was someone who knew Abigail, or an opportunist impulse by someone who might, for example, have just lost their own child?"

"That's often the case. I've asked the ward sister to have a think. One woman died in labour recently, and the baby didn't survive."

"I suppose it could be her husband."

"Not a chance. We've already been to see him. That was no picnic, I can tell you."

"Any others?"

"Two other losses. Then there's the possibility of abortions. People feeling guilty; having second thoughts. It's a grim business, Sidney. We need your tact."

"I'll talk to Abigail. Stealing a baby seems so much more despicable than taking a painting or staging a bank robbery, doesn't it?"

"It is desperate. But we hope it is a woman who knows how to look after him and wants to care for him. Then we have more of a chance of finding the baby alive."

"I do hope so. Isn't that what usually happens?"

Keating pushed his pint to one side. "I'm afraid not. Sometimes they are just abandoned."

"I must talk to Hildegard. I don't want her to hear this from someone else."

"I wouldn't do that, Sidney." Keating was unusually firm. "She'll be worried the same thing might happen to her."

"She's tough enough, Geordie, and I can't keep things from her any more. I have to tell her everything."

"She's got you trained then?"

"I hope and pray she will be a match for anyone who tries to steal *our* baby."

"I am sure she is. You must do what you think best. I just don't want her getting anxious about it. Of course you need to look after her, but I also need you to help me to solve this case. We have to secure the return of Abigail Redmond's child."

It did not help Sidney's mood that Helena Randall was already out and about. She stopped him outside Corpus to ask how much he knew about the baby snatch, as it was a story she was going to run that evening. "Has Geordie got any leads?"

"Helena, I know very little about the case and I've got a lot on. If you'll excuse me . . ."

"Evasive, as ever . . ."

"I don't mean to be."

"Yes you do. I don't mind. I'm busy too, you know. In fact, I'm on the way to the matinée at the Arts."

"The pantomime? Are you reviewing it?"

"I'm in it."

Sidney felt sick. "Oh God, oh Montreal."

"It's not that bad . . ."

"No. It's something else." Sidney had completely forgotten that he was due to attend a performance that very night. It had been Hildegard's idea of a Christmas treat.

"Although it is a bit embarrassing, I must confess," Helena continued. "I'm playing the Fairy."

"I don't suppose anyone would think that was type-casting."

"You're too kind, Canon Chambers. At least it's only three scenes."

"Perhaps it will bring out your feminine side?"

"For the first and last time, I can tell you. It's only because the director happens to be my boyfriend. He thinks it's going to soften me up, playing the Fairy, but believe me; it's going to do the exact opposite. I'm going to come out of this even tougher."

"Has the man any idea of what lies in store for him?"

Helena smiled. "He hasn't a clue."

"Then he has my pity."

"I tell you one thing: he deserves everything that's coming."

"You always did have a strong sense of justice."

"It's about the only thing you and I have in common, Canon Chambers. I do hope you will feel you can inform me as to how your enquiries progress."

"How do you know I am investigating anything at all?"

"Because I know you, Sidney Chambers," Helena added almost flirtatiously. "I can read you like a book."

"Then I hope it's a good one."

"Oh yes," she said. "It's a *classic*."

Sidney wondered if he had deliberately forgotten about the planned visit to *Dick Whittington and his Cat* because he hated pantomimes. He remembered that he had promised his wife the trip to take her mind off what she had started to call "God's little joke": the uncomfortable, sleepless ninth month of pregnancy. Hildegard had said that if she laughed enough at all the antics then perhaps it might bring on the baby.

267

"I don't think it'll be that funny," Sidney warned. "But I'm sure we'll be taking the little one soon enough."

"You will have to explain what happens in the story," his wife said. "You know how I can't concentrate on anything at the moment. My brain is like strudel."

"It's quite simple, although these Christmas shows never make much sense anyway. It's more about the interruptions than the plot," Sidney began. "They're essentially fairy stories: morality tales for the people . . ."

"Like *Hansel and Gretel*."

"Exactly. They're often about money too, in which the poor are ultimately recompensed for their virtue."

"Unlike real life."

"Reward for virtue, Hildegard, is at the heart of the Christian message. We cannot scorn popular entertainment. People love these shows. They are feasts of foolery."

Sidney knew that he should just get on with it and tell his wife about Abigail's baby before she read about it in the local paper, or anyone else mentioned it to her, rather than wittering on about a bloody pantomime that he didn't even want to go to but Hildegard was in a relatively good mood and he didn't want to spoil it.

"What is the story of this play?" she asked again.

Sidney was relieved to continue; although he knew that he was not off the hook by any means and merely prolonging the ultimate disclosure. "In this case, Dick Whittington, who is played by an actress . . ."

"Dick is a man's name. Why does a girl play a boy?"

"Because the Dame is always a man."

"So women are men, and men are women?"

"That is, allegedly, what makes it so very amusing. The roles are reversed. It's like Shakespeare."

"The confused English relationship to sex . . ."

"You have to know all the time that it is a man being a woman otherwise it isn't funny . . ."

"Already this is complicated."

"They say it's all in the eyes and the knees." Sidney stood up from the kitchen table in a desperate attempt at humour. He opened his eyes wide and put his legs apart, demonstrating the role of the clown. "The eyes look everywhere and the knees knock together. Like this."

He began a frantic clown impersonation. He could hardly postpone his news any longer but he wanted his wife to be cheerful. Besides, he liked her laugh.

Hildegard clapped her hands. "You are doing your best, my darling, but it doesn't sound so amusing."

"It's very English," Sidney explained. "Although they have it in Scotland too. I suppose it's something of an acquired taste."

"Like cricket."

"Or bread and butter pudding. A boy, played by a girl, falls in love with a real girl and is either helped, distracted or obstructed by a man playing a woman, the Dame. Then there are the talking animals. Traditionally it's a horse with one man at the front and another at the back, but in *Jack and the Beanstalk* it's a cow, and in *Dick Whittington* it's a cat."

"And it is for children?"

"Yes. But there are adult jokes and a singalong."

"The audience have to join in?"

"They do, Hildegard. That's the bit I don't like."

"You are used to being in charge. You want to be the star of the show, not its victim."

"I'll let that pass. But I suppose it's all part of my duty to support such a venture. Many of our parishioners are in it and a lot of the schoolchildren are the rats."

"I look forward to it."

"Really?"

"I do, Sidney. It is you who are being anxious."

"I'm not," her husband replied grumpily. He really would have to get on with it and tell her about Abigail and her baby.

"It's Christmas, *meine Liebe*. We should be happy. What is wrong with you?"

"I don't know."

"You do. Tell me."

Sidney looked at his wife. "Well, Hildegard, there is something . . ."

And so, at last, he broke the news of the stolen child.

The Arts was packed with an expectant crowd who cheered as the lights came down, the music began and Dick Whittington introduced his cat Tommy and explained how he was going to London to seek his fortune. The stage cloth lifted to reveal a busy scene that was soon entered by an enormous pantomime dame weighed down with carrier bags.

"I've just been Christmas shopping in Market Square. It's terrible out there. It was so crowded. Men were rubbing up against me and touching me in all the places they shouldn't. I'm going back again tomorrow. *Anyway*, boys and girls, mums and dads, ARE YOU HAVING A NICE TIME? We'll have a bit of a sing in a minute. I've asked the orchestra to check their parts. They're a lovely lot of men down there. I like the one with the horn. *Anyway*, I'm here to see Dick — it's been a long time — and I do love playing with his Tommy. Are you looking forward to Christmas? We're having an extra large turkey this year so everyone gets a good bit of leg and a nice bit of breast. I just need to make sure I get plenty of stuffing."

The audience laughed and the Dame feigned shocked surprise. "What? Oh stop it. You are *awful*. At least I've done my shopping. The only thing is that I don't think I need all these sweets. I'm sweet enough already. Would you like some, boys and girls?"

The children in the audience screamed out that they did.

Blimey, Sidney thought, once our own child is born there's going to be years of this.

As the Dame opened her shopping bags and started to throw sweets to the audience, Hildegard asked if Sidney was enjoying himself.

"You have not been laughing," she observed.

"No, I have been too worried."

"About what?"

"The thing that is going to happen next. Right now, in fact. Saints preserve us!"

271

Sidney was in an aisle seat near the front of the stalls and the Dame was already advancing towards him. He was going to be singled out for audience participation; he could tell.

The actor waggled his bottom, plumped up his false breasts and sat on the edge of Sidney's seat. The follow-spot was already on them.

"Hello, sweetheart, what do you do for a living?"

"I'm a vicar."

"You're not wearing any knickers? That's not a very nice thing to say. A man in your position? What's your name?"

"Sidney."

"If you were called 'Kidney', I could put you in one of my puddings. I've got a very hot oven."

There was no escape. Even Sidney's friend Fergus Maclean, the usually morose undertaker, was laughing.

"Will you marry me, Sidney?" the Dame continued. "I've already had three husbands. The first one died of mushroom poisoning, the second one died of mushroom poisoning; the third one jumped in the River Cam. He wouldn't eat the mushrooms! Anyway . . ."

She moved on to taunt a man with no hair. It was always the men she picked on, and one of them complained that he hadn't come to be insulted.

"Where do you usually go then, darling?"

As the show rolled on to a rousing chorus of "Oh! What a Wopper", Hildegard enjoyed Sidney's discomfort. "At least she didn't make any jokes about the holy roast or shepherds washing their socks by night."

272

"Well it'll soon be over for another year. Then I can get on with the next thing."

"There's always a next thing, Sidney. Perhaps we should enjoy the present without concerning ourselves over the future." Hildegard touched her stomach. "We have more important things to worry about."

After Dick had been blamed for stealing all the Alderman's money and was leaving London for good, Fairy Bowbells, in the guise of Helena Randall, called him back.

"I didn't know she was in it," said Hildegard. "Is that why we've come?"

"Of course not."

"She sings very nicely. A thin voice but at least it is in tune."

By the interval, Sidney had become quite agitated about the time he was spending in the theatre, away from news of the case of the stolen baby. Hildegard put his restlessness down to hurt pride after his humiliation at the hands of the Dame and told him that she needed to get out fast so that she could join the queue for the Ladies' while Sidney bought the ice creams. As he did so, he was interrupted by Inspector Keating.

"I didn't know you were at the show," he said.

"I'm not. I've come to see you, Sidney."

"Then you've timed it well."

Geordie was in no mood for small talk. "A witness has reported someone behaving suspiciously."

"Who?"

"A woman in a headscarf wearing a long camel coat and high heels. Have you been to see Miss Redmond?"

"Not yet."

"Well, get on with it, man. She's not keen on talking to the police and you can get things out of her that I can't."

"I'm not sure that's true."

"You have your ways, Sidney. I want to know how long she thinks she was asleep for at the time her baby was taken; and if she has friends who want children and can't have them or who have had miscarriages recently. This inquiry needs your gentle touch. I'm relying on you."

"I'll do my best."

Hildegard emerged from the Ladies' and was surprised to bump into the detective. "Surely you're not off duty?" she teased.

"No, Hildegard; even here, I am vigilant. I was just passing and saw Sidney in the foyer. There's nothing to worry about. Good evening to you both."

The couple returned to the auditorium. The actors were on board the *Saucy Sally* on its way to Morocco. The Dame was mopping the decks before the drill routine and complained that she was used to rubbing down with something bigger. "Is she impersonating Mrs Maguire?" Hildegard asked.

"The Dame is her brother-in-law."

"She has a sister? You mean there are two of them?"

"I am afraid so."

At last Dick Whittington reached the shores of Morocco to be met with a chorus of dancing gorillas. Dick went into the palace of the Sultan where the Dame had already joined the ladies of the harem.

"Sidney?" Hildegard asked.

"What is it?"

"You seem distracted. What did Inspector Keating want?"

"Nothing much."

"He wasn't 'just passing', was he?"

"No."

"So how involved are you in the case of the stolen baby?"

Sidney pretended to be concentrating on the pantomime. "I'm just helping out. It won't take up much of my time."

"I don't believe you."

"It will be well. All manner of thing shall be well, my darling."

"I am not so sure. You are up to something."

"Not at all. I am doing my duty . . ."

"Which takes you away from me."

The show neared its conclusion as Alice the heroine walked on stage hoping for the return of her beloved. "Christmas Eve, and still no sign of Dick."

Hildegard nudged Sidney in the ribs. "Now I understand the humour! I know how she feels."

Her husband was appalled.

The Redmond farm was a twenty-minute bicycle ride from Grantchester and Sidney had already made sure that Hildegard had the telephone number of every place he intended visiting should there be any sudden developments during the late stages of her pregnancy. Dr Michael Robinson was just leaving as he arrived.

"I've given Abigail something to settle her down," he said. "Try not to ask too many of your direct questions. I know what you are like."

"It is a pastoral visit."

"Then it's just as well you are in the countryside."

Sidney smiled wearily. Dr Robinson was always partial to puns.

On entering the kitchen, he discovered that Agatha Redmond was in no mood to shilly-shally. "I don't know whether you've come to collect your new puppy or ask some questions about my missing grandchild?"

"I have a sense of priority in these matters," Sidney replied, "and I was hoping I might have a word with Abigail."

"She's sleeping. The doctor has just given her something to help her do so. No doubt he told you. It's been like Piccadilly Circus round here. However, I know she wants to see you so you'd better get up there before she's out like a light."

Sidney was shown upstairs and knocked quietly on the door. Before he said who it was he was told to "go away" but then, on revealing his identity, he was allowed in. He sat on the edge of the bed. Abigail Redmond lay on her side with her face pale and blotchy. She was already drowsy. "I know I look ugly," she said. "But I don't care. I just want my baby back."

"The police are doing all they can."

"But are you, Canon Chambers? You're the one I trust. You know things."

"But I don't understand enough about this case yet, Abigail. I need to ask you a few questions. I won't be long."

"I don't know if I can tell you anything. I was so tired. I didn't know what was going on. It's all my fault. I should have stayed awake."

"You've done nothing wrong."

"I have. I lost my baby."

"He'll come back."

"Do you think so? How will he do that? He can't walk. He's so little. I love him so much and I need him to be here."

"I understand and we will find him for you. Try to remember. When exactly do you think it happened?"

"I'd had something to eat, so it was after six thirty and I was just off to sleep. Like now. Mum was leaving. She said goodbye, but there was so much coming and going and I was so tired it was hard to know what was happening."

"Could it have been around eight o'clock at night?"

"Yes, I suppose so. Why do you ask?"

"That's when the nurses change shift. So if no one knows quite who's in charge around then . . ."

"I'm sure they have a system. I remember there was always at least one nurse there all the time," Abigail said.

"Of course we must remember there are the porters to consider."

"I don't think it can be a man . . ." Abigail had thought through all the possibilities. "Although it might be a couple working together."

"We need to pin down exactly who was there at the time of John's disappearance; when your mother left and who was on duty. I'll have to have a word with the ward sister. I am sure we will find him soon." Sidney was determined to remain positive.

"There were three of them looking after me in all. There were Sisters Bland and Foster. I didn't like either of them very much. They were a bit creepy, to tell you the truth. Sister Bland took over from another one called Sister Carrington. I remember getting confused and not being sure which one was which." Abigail slid down in the bed and turned away.

"I'll need to speak to all of them."

"Sister Bland's got a moustache. The other one's got fat legs. Sister Carrington was all right. She was kind."

"I am sure they are good at what they do."

"Will I get my baby back safe?" Abigail asked.

Sidney tried to reassure her. "I am sure you will."

"Do you think if I close my eyes and sleep now then it will all go away? Then when I wake the cot will be back by my side with John sleeping in it?"

"We will find him," said Sidney quietly.

He gave her hand a little squeeze and, as he left, he remembered holding her baby's. "'There was a man sent from God whose name was John,'" he said to himself. "'The same came for a witness, to bear witness of the Light, that all men through him might believe.'"

Sidney hoped and prayed for a witness, as well as a little more light.

★ ★ ★

He headed for Trumpington Street, worried about returning to the hospital and treading on the toes of a chaplain who regarded Addenbrooke's as his personal fiefdom. The Reverend "Call me Stephen" Drabble always made it clear that he was far more practised in the diurnal rounds of birth, sickness, recovery and death than any fly-by-night clergyman who popped in and out of the hospital as he pleased. It was yet another area which required tact, and Sidney was determined to give his visit, as well as his investigation, as low a profile as possible. He also knew that people were not going to take kindly to yet more questioning when their main priority was the care of patients. He would have to wait for the tea breaks and hope for the best.

Sister Samantha Bland was a large Leicestershire woman with strong forearms that made her look as if she could have been as successful a blacksmith as a nurse. As she sat down opposite him in the staff canteen, Sidney remembered what Abigail had told him and realised that he had made his first mistake before opening his mouth.

He had promised himself that he would not look too closely at Sister Bland's upper lip but found that as soon as he had clapped eyes on her moustache he could not avert his gaze. It was amazing that she had done nothing about it. She had dark hair, too. It reminded him of the one Leonard Graham was attempting to grow the first time he had met him. They were such ridiculous things, Sidney thought to himself; but at least it would be something to tell Hildegard when he

279

got home. He remembered the myth of the great female Saint Uncumber who had sprouted both beard and moustache in order to get out of, or "unencumber" herself from, a betrothal she hated.

The nurse spoke with an unexpectedly high voice (Sidney had been anticipating something deeper) that drew power away from the firmness of her opinion. She told her inquisitor that the reason he hadn't seen her in church was that she was, in fact, a Roman Catholic and she wasn't about to have a change of heart now. She had taken over from Sister Carrington at eight o'clock on the night of the abduction and was praying for the return of the baby in her every waking moment.

"And it was you who discovered the child was missing?" Sidney asked.

"Around half past eight. I've told the police this."

"I think you said that you saw a figure disappearing."

"Yes, I did. Have they briefed you then?"

"I have read your witness statement."

"Then why are you here?"

Sidney evaded the question. "Could you describe the person you saw?"

"I can't be sure. She had her back to me and was hurrying to the end of the corridor but I thought she was carrying something. She was wearing high heels, I can say that, and she didn't have a handbag which was strange. She wore a smart coat. It was camel-coloured. You don't often see members of the public moving that quickly in the hospital. She must have been keen to get away."

"So she looked like she knew where she was going?"

"I suppose so. Although there are signposts to all the exits."

"That's true but I have noticed that people are often confused when they come to Addenbrooke's. They can never quite find what they're looking for."

"They can always ask."

"I think that they worry that everyone is too busy."

"That's because we are."

Sidney pressed. "But do you think the confidence and speed of her movements suggested a familiarity with the hospital layout?"

"I couldn't say. So many people come and go. I just noticed the haste and the high heels."

"But you didn't see an actual baby?"

"No."

"It would be dangerous to move at speed and in high heels while carrying a baby down a hospital corridor."

"Yes, I suppose it would."

"And you're quite sure you saw this woman?" Sidney persisted.

"Of course. Are you accusing me of lying, Canon Chambers?"

"Not at all, Sister Bland. Only some people might imagine that the sight of a mysterious woman disappearing down a corridor could be a case of wishful thinking."

"I saw what I saw. I don't need to feel bad about that. I only feel guilty about the child disappearing on my watch. Obviously I feel responsible and upset. In fact you are distressing me."

"I'm sorry. I don't mean to. I only have a few more questions."

"I don't see why I should answer them."

"You have been very kind, Sister. Could I just ask at what time you arrived for work on the night in question?"

"Around seven forty-five. I always try to get to work early. I don't like to rush."

"Unlike the woman in the camel coat. Did your husband bring you?"

"I'm not married, Canon Chambers."

"And is Sister Carrington?"

"She was." Sister Bland finished her tea. She clearly preferred being on duty to talking to Sidney. "Why are you asking? That's a very personal question."

"I was curious."

"I don't see how it's relevant. Sister Carrington is separated from her husband but not divorced. I am a spinster and perfectly happy to be so. I don't need the distraction and vanity of men."

Sidney checked himself. "I'm sure that is a wise choice. But I wondered if I could also ask if you saw anything untoward before eight thirty?"

"No."

"By which time Sister Carrington had gone home?"

"Yes. It was the end of her shift. Grace left on her own. I can tell you that. She's not the type to go round stealing other people's children, if that's what you're implying. Baby John was in his cot when she went."

"I'm not sure there is a type. Although you've told Inspector Keating about those unfortunate people . . ."

"Who have lost a child? Yes, I have. I don't think they need any more misery, do you? The police have been poking their nose in with them already, asking personal questions. Now you are doing it as well. I should get back."

"These are very sad times, Sister Bland, and we all have to remember that a living child is still missing."

She stood up to go. "You are assuming that the person responsible is someone who has suffered a misfortune?"

"What do you think?" Sidney asked.

Sister Bland was clearly irritated that she was expected to give an opinion. "It's not that simple, Canon Chambers. The culprit could equally well be someone who has had one child and can't have any more; a woman with daughters who has always longed for a son; someone suffering from post-natal depression . . ."

"How easy would it be to pretend to be a nurse?" Sidney asked quickly. He knew that he was running out of time. "Could you buy a uniform or steal one from the staffroom?"

"We all know each other here. But it would be easy enough to steal one from the laundry. It could even be someone who works there."

"You mean it could be anyone?"

"Any woman. Yes, I do. Although I'm certain it's not one of us."

"What makes you so sure?"

"Faith, Canon Chambers. You have to trust people."

If only it was that simple, Sidney thought.

★ ★ ★

There was no time for backgammon but he met Keating for a quick debrief in the Eagle before he went home. Sidney had no leads other than that he thought that the culprit was a woman who knew her way round the hospital and she wore high heels. Geordie told his friend that he knew this already. They discussed the possibility that the thief was either a nurse or had disguised herself as one, taking advantage of the change in shifts, and made a quick exit at the back entrance where she had either effected her own getaway or was driven off by an accomplice. But who was this woman, and was she still in the vicinity? Sidney suggested that a watch was kept at the Cambridge chemists and at the shops that sold baby clothes. They should be particularly vigilant at looking for women who bought supplies but did not bring their child with them, and they should circulate photographs of any suspects. The police should also find an excuse to search their homes.

Keating was in a curiously defeatist mood. "It's not as easy as that. I think we should concentrate on the nurses. I bet they're not telling us everything. Have you been to see the others?"

"I was hoping to visit Sister Carrington tomorrow."

"I wish you'd get on with it, man."

"It's difficult for me at the moment, Geordie."

"I don't mean to be hard but I've come to rely on you. I acknowledge that it can't be easy and I'm sorry this is taking you away from Hildegard. It's bad timing."

"It's never good," Sidney replied. "But I think she's all right about it. I always tell her where I am."

"You mean she knows you are in the pub with me now?"

Sidney hesitated. "Well, to be honest, I am not sure that's strictly true."

"That means it isn't the case at all."

"She knows the number of the police station."

"That's not the same thing."

"Finding me could be a matter of moments . . ."

"It's about as easy as locating a missing child. Half of the time no one knows where you are, Sidney."

"Nonsense. The church services are posted on our noticeboard. Tuesday nights are bell-ringing."

"You don't ring the bells yourself."

"Wednesday is the PCC. On Thursday nights I am with you. It is a life of considerable routine and I have a very tolerant wife."

"Take that tolerance for granted and you might end up regretting it. She's going to need a lot of looking after."

"Her mother is arriving tomorrow and she wants to get the house in order. I am told that I tend to be in the way. So I thought I'd steer clear for a little while so she can do what she needs to do and then mother and daughter can have a good chat about all things baby."

"You mean you are trying to pass off your negligence as benevolence?"

"It has worked in the past, Geordie."

"That's no guarantee of the future."

"Never mind all that. Let us see. Have you any news of the case yourself?"

"There's no sign of the child. And it's no good asking for help from the useless boyfriend, Colin Sampson. He couldn't organise a stag party for a herd of deer. So now I'm thinking that if it's not a mother that's been bereaved, and we've been to see the ones we know, then, as we have discussed, it has to be an inside job at the hospital."

"I agree," Sidney replied.

Keating was adamant. "But it's important we don't make the perpetrator panic. We don't want to find the baby dumped in a dustbin."

"I am aware of the sensitivity of the situation. Everyone we speak to must be given the impression that they will be helped."

"Even to the extent of getting away with it."

"It's not the apprehension of the culprit but the protection of the child that matters most. Do you think we're running out of time?"

"I hope it's one of the nurses. They are more likely to take care of him."

"Do you know if any of them have lost a child recently?" Sidney asked.

"It's not a question we can easily ask. But what about that doctor friend of yours, Michael Robinson? Doesn't he owe you a favour? I remember we turned a blind eye after he bumped off his mother-in-law a few years back."

"He didn't 'bump her off'."

"We both know he did. Isn't he your missus's doctor?"

"I hardly think either of them will appreciate my interrupting one of his visits."

Keating finished his pint. "I'd have thought you'd be used to that. No one 'appreciates' what you are doing except me. A prophet is without honour in his own land, don't you remember? Just ask the doctor a few decent questions, if you don't mind."

It was fortunate that Sidney had seen plenty of Michael Robinson recently and that the doctor had been vigilant during the later stages of Hildegard's pregnancy, popping into the vicarage to see that all was well before returning to his home in nearby Eltisley Avenue. However, Sidney still knew that he was going to have to be at his tactful best to elicit any breach in patient confidentiality.

"This situation has been a very distressing business," the doctor said on his next visit. "But you must not worry unduly, Mrs Chambers. These things never happen twice."

"That is what they say about the lightning," Hildegard answered. "And sometimes people say it about love too, but I have only loved properly once and it is now."

Sidney smiled uncertainly. He was uneasy with public pronouncements of private affection.

His wife continued. "I try not to worry about bad things happening, Doctor, but of course, I still think about them all the time."

"I am sure that your husband will look after you."

"When he is here, yes, he does. But he is often away."

Dr Robinson hastened to reassure her. "A baby changes everything. I'm not sure that Canon Chambers is aware of that yet."

"I live in trepidation and hope," said Sidney in rather too pat a fashion.

The doctor picked him up on his tone. "I hear you are involving yourself in the investigation into the disappearance, as usual."

"It's not that usual."

"It must be difficult for you to continue your enquiries, I imagine. Especially now that everyone knows what you are up to. Perhaps people are less willing to tell you things. The line has become blurred between privacy and the public good. The secrets of the confessional and the problem of indiscretion is something that we have in common, I think?"

"Indeed it is," Sidney concurred. "Although I think it's fair to admit that one cannot keep any questioning of the people involved a secret. Particularly in this case."

"Some of those being the nurses who were on duty that night?"

"It's a delicate situation, as you can imagine. Those who give their lives to the care of others do not take kindly to any kind of inquisition. They feel they are doing enough as it is."

"And yet you must continue. You cannot give anyone preferential treatment."

"We have to think it through, Dr Robinson. It's not enough to contemplate what happened on the night in question. We have to find out what went on before that night, anything that might have led to the taking of the baby, perhaps as a replacement after a tragedy . . ."

"Indeed."

"And so patient history becomes an issue."

"I am sure you can't expect me to provide you with any clues, Canon Chambers?"

"I wouldn't dream of asking you. That would be unprofessional."

"And, as far as the hospital is concerned, I cannot give you any hard information. I am merely a GP. The nurses there are very reliable and I have no doubts about the women who were on duty that night. Sisters Bland and Foster, together with Miss Carrington, are admirable in every way."

"Are you their doctor?" Sidney asked quickly.

"I don't think I can answer that question, Canon Chambers. But this is a small community. I am sure that you can jump to a conclusion or two."

"I have already been warned about that."

"Ah yes, perhaps one can make too many leaps of faith. It's so easy to be mistaken. But it is important to live on the side of the angels. I assume you have no further questions?"

"I do not. Thank you."

"I am sorry not to have been of any more help. Look after your wife, Canon Chambers. We don't want another mishap. Any fall from grace."

After the doctor had left Sidney cleared away the teacups and began to wash up. He was doing his best to help Hildegard around the house but was not known for his ability to concentrate on domestic chores. There was always so much more to think about.

"By the way," he asked his wife before picking up a tea towel. "Don't you think it strange that Dr Robinson hoped that we didn't suffer any 'mishap'."

"No. I didn't notice anything unusual. I thought he was just being careful and kind."

"'Mishap.' It's an odd word to choose. A man doesn't normally go round hoping that people don't suffer 'mishaps'."

"Perhaps that's just his way."

"But he stressed the word 'Miss'. As in 'Miss Carrington'. Not 'Sister Carrington', which is her proper professional title. Miss Carrington. As in 'miscarry'; and 'Grace' as in 'fall from'."

"Sidney, really." Hildegard looked at her husband but knew that any attempt to stop this flight of fancy would be futile.

"There's no harm in going to see her, is there?" Sidney asked.

Grace Carrington lived in a terraced house a mere five minute's walk from Addenbrooke's Hospital. The Christmas tree in the window looked welcoming enough, but Sidney knew that he was going to have to be at his tactful best if he was to gain entry to a home that might well be harbouring the missing child. He said that he was just passing, he made it his duty to

290

wish all of his parishioners a happy Christmas and he just wanted to ask a few questions about how he could best support his wife through the final stages of her pregnancy.

The nurse was reluctant to let him in. "Couldn't we discuss this at the hospital? It is the most appropriate place."

She was a tall woman with the slightest of stoops, and she wore a tartan skirt with a dark green cardigan and a cream blouse with a silver thistle brooch, although she did not sound Scottish.

"I was not sure when I might find you," Sidney began.

"There is always Sister Bland."

"You never know who is going to be on duty."

"I'm on nights at the moment, so I admit it isn't very convenient. And I've been off work this week."

"Have you not been well?"

"I was owed holiday. I'm going to see my mother tomorrow."

"I see. Does she live nearby?"

"Just a few miles down the road."

Sidney had wondered how a nurse who worked nights could keep a child at home. This could, perhaps, explain things, especially if her mother was aiding, even unwittingly, the concealment. "I am preaching a sermon on what it means to have a baby, on Christmas Day, you understand, and I was hoping that I could benefit from your wisdom."

"I don't know why you are asking me. I don't have a child myself."

291

"But you have known plenty of mothers and seen so many children brought into the world."

"That is true. Do I take it you want to come in and talk about it? It's not a very convenient time."

Sidney had already decided not to care whether he appeared rude or not. "It won't take long."

She stepped back and showed Sidney into a small lounge where two tabby cats made their hostility known by refusing to move from sofa and chair. A side plate with half a mince pie was on the table next to a copy of *Modern Knitting* magazine and an unfinished cup of tea. The wireless was playing dance music. "I haven't finished tidying, I am afraid."

Three or four twigs of holly had been spread across the mantelpiece, twisting round a few Christmas cards and a ticket to the pantomime. Sidney decided not to tell her that the show was dreadful.

"It doesn't matter. I've seen all sorts of houses and this is very congenial."

Grace Carrington took up Sidney's original theme. "Some of the mothers don't have a clue, of course. They expect us to do it all for them." She moved one of the cats. "Sit down, won't you?"

"I suppose they don't appreciate how lucky they are."

"That's just the thing, Canon Chambers. Some of them don't know they're born."

"Do you ever think, then, that some mothers don't understand what it means to have children?"

Grace Carrington was surprised by Sidney's boldness. "That's a very unchristian statement, coming from you."

"I was just wondering. They perhaps don't ever realise how fortunate they are."

"I try not to think about it. Sometimes it's best just to get on with your work. If you ask too many questions you end up worrying."

"I was thinking of someone like Abigail Redmond," he continued.

"She's not very fortunate, is she?"

"I gather you were on duty on the night her child was taken."

"I'd just come off. I made sure Sister Bland saw that everything was in hand. Then Sister Foster arrived."

"And you went home?"

"Of course. I had finished my shift."

"You didn't need to go back for anything?"

"Are you the police, asking questions in this way?"

"No, I'm not, I'm sorry."

"I know you help them from time to time."

"An occupational hazard."

"I have already told them everything I know."

"This is a very nice room," Sidney blundered. He was looking for family photographs. "Is it just you here?"

"It is now. My husband left, but I'm happy enough without him, to tell the truth. These things happen. I don't really like talking about it. You just have to get on with your life."

"And you don't have children?"

"No. I've already told you that."

"I'm sorry."

"We couldn't, if you must know."

"Do you have nephews and nieces?"

"My sister has a little boy."

"It must be comforting to have a nephew at least."

"It's not the same as having one of your own."

"No, I imagine it isn't. Did you ever think of adopting?"

"I wanted to but Ben wasn't having any of it. We'd had such a time . . ."

"You lost . . ."

"Three miscarriages. I just couldn't hold on to my babies. I gave them names. I think of them every day." Grace Carrington stood up. "I would offer you tea but I've got things to do. Will that be all?"

"Yes, I think so. I was just wondering if you had any tips about looking after a child. Something I should bear in mind. My wife is about to give birth, as you know."

Grace ushered Sidney to the door. "You have to love them unconditionally, that's all. And you have to put their needs first. You can't be the child in the house any more because a real one has just arrived."

"And how does a home change when it has a child in it?"

"Well, it should be warmer at this time of year . . ."

"Your house is nice and cosy."

"I prefer it that way. Although it is expensive."

"And children are costly too, I imagine."

"I imagine they are. Now will that be all, Canon Chambers?"

"Yes, of course. I am sorry to have kept you. I apologise. I'm rather nervous. Such a pity about the

Redmond boy. It makes for a very uneasy atmosphere at the hospital. All the mothers are worried the same thing might happen to them."

"Let's hope it doesn't."

"Or, on a more positive note, let us pray that the child is returned."

"Yes, of course," Grace replied. "We all want that."

"It would be a shame if things turned out unpleasantly," Sidney continued.

"What do you mean?"

"If the child was harmed in any way . . ."

"I don't think that's likely . . ."

"Or if the perpetrator was found and apprehended."

"What do you think would happen to him?"

"You think it's a man?" Sidney asked.

"I wouldn't know," Grace said, her face expressionless as she opened the door, letting the December wind sweep into the hallway.

"I imagine that if the culprit is caught then a prison sentence is likely. But if the baby is returned, perhaps even anonymously, then the intensity of the search might be called off. If the baby is safe after all then perhaps the person who took it might even get away with it . . ."

"That's not something, I imagine, that you would countenance."

"Allowances might be made. People might have sympathy for the person who took the child." Sidney was careful not to say the word "thief". "They might feel if, for example, they were acting out of desperation or distress, or he or she couldn't understand what they were doing at the time, that they had suffered enough. The best thing for everyone concerned would be the safe return of the baby, whatever the circumstances. But I am sure you know all this, Sister Carrington. You don't need me to tell you either about morality or the sorrows of the world. Might I see you in church at Christmas?"

"I find it a bit difficult at this time of year. All those carols about a little tiny child."

"In the new year, perhaps. But I do hope you can find peace this Christmas, Miss Carrington. It can be a difficult season for so many people. I'd like you to know that I am always available should you ever need me. You can pop in unannounced at any time, just as I have dropped in on you."

"I am sorry I wasn't more hospitable. And now I really must close the door. I don't want the house to become too chilly."

"Indeed we must all keep ourselves warm on these bitter nights," Sidney agreed. "You have been very kind; and I am only sorry that you have clearly suffered so much in your marriage. There can be an end to those sorrows, I promise."

"Do you think so?"

"A new life does not always begin with a birth, Sister Carrington. There are other ways of starting again." Sidney took her hand. "God bless you."

The following morning Hildegard's mother arrived. Sibilla Leber had once had the same short blonde hair as her daughter but it had turned grey as it curled down to the level of her dark green eyes. Her nose was slightly more upturned, her face thinner and gaunter, and her mouth had gathered lines around it; the result of smoking. She had produced both her children when she was very young, been widowed at the age of twenty-seven, and had just celebrated her sixty-seventh birthday. She was not a woman of doubt, combining folk tradition, communist extremism and Protestant Christianity in a unique stream of opinion. Her English was as erratic as Sidney's German. Her son-in-law met her at the station and said that Hildegard was doing well.

"I see her myself. Men do not know things. She eat?"

"Like a horse."

"My daughter is not horse."

"It is a form of expression."

"I do not understand. You cannot say my daughter is like animal. Perhaps better we speak German?"

"*Ich tue mein Bestes.*"

Sidney made sure Frau Leber's two weighty suitcases were stowed in the back and that his guest took the front seat of the taxi. She was wearing so many layers of clothing that she appeared to have doubled in size since he had last seen her.

By the time they arrived back at the vicarage Sidney was ready for the return to his study and a bit of peace while mother and daughter unpacked, caught up on their news and prepared the lunch. It was Frau Leber's opinion that her duty was to make sure that her son-in-law was well fed and kept out of the way. His only function was to eat and then, as soon as he had finished, keep a low profile.

He was doing just that, and settling down to concentrate on his sermon after their first lunch together, when Hildegard popped her head round the door. "I forgot to tell you that Mrs Redmond stopped by."

"Any news?"

"Our new puppy is ready. She hoped you could pick it up today."

"Gosh. A puppy and your mother at the same time."

Hildegard touched her stomach and grimaced. "I know. I hope they like each other."

"What's wrong?"

"A little kick, that's all. It won't be long now."

"Are you all right, my darling?"

"Don't worry about me. I have my mother."

"I know. But I still don't like leaving you on your own. She's not familiar with Cambridge."

"But I am. Go and fetch the dog."

"Are you sure you want me to?"

"I agree that the timing is not ideal. But Mrs Redmond was insistent, Amanda has arranged it all, and you know I think it's good for children to be brought up with pets."

Sidney wondered what on earth they were doing. Surely they were bonkers to think about a replacement for Dickens at Christmas when there was so much else going on? Amanda promised that she had organised the whole thing but that had not included delivery; and so Sidney found himself bicycling out to the Redmond farm on a day of drizzle and depression that marked the depth of winter.

Although her grandchild was still missing, Agatha Redmond was practical. "I'm sorry not to have been able to bring your dog in person, Canon Chambers, but I don't like to leave our Abi."

"I understand."

"I could have let you have him earlier, but I wanted him checked over, wormed and vaccinated. Normally my brother-in-law would have done the necessary but, as you are aware, he is indisposed." This was a euphemism for prison if ever there was one. "Fortunately, the new vet has given all the puppies the thumbs-up. I know that in the past you haven't been, what shall we say, *diligent*, about a Labrador's daily requirements, and with a new baby on the way I wanted to set everything up for you in case you forgot anything. You will remember what to do, won't you? It's a long time since Dickens was your puppy."

"Believe me, Mrs Redmond, I remember it all too well. I am looking forward to the stage when the little chap can fend for himself and has developed a bit of character."

"Oh, little Byron has got quite a lot of that already. Even Miss Kendall noticed. That's how she picked him out."

"It is very kind of her."

"He's been properly socialised and she's paid all the bills so you don't need to worry. All you have to do, Canon Chambers, is concentrate on looking after him. Do you think you can manage?"

299

"I do have quite a bit of help. My mother-in-law is staying with us."

"And does she know about dogs?"

"I haven't asked her yet."

"Haven't you even mentioned it? Most people are beside themselves with excitement when they bring a puppy home."

"Perhaps I'm too old for that."

"Nonsense, Canon Chambers. A new Labrador and a longed-for baby: what could be more thrilling? I'll just get him for you."

"I should have a word with Abigail . . ."

"She's resting now, but I doubt she's asleep. She still blames herself, Canon Chambers, that's the trouble. She thinks that if she had kept an eye and hadn't fallen asleep then baby John would still be with us. Why don't you go upstairs and see her and provide a little reassurance? I won't be a jiffy."

As Agatha Redmond made her way to a little room off the kitchen, the telephone rang. Sidney heard her complain, "Well if it's not one thing it's another. I suppose I'd best answer."

He wondered if it could be Hildegard but dismissed the thought. She was perfectly fine when he had left and he was hardly far away. He started to climb the stairs when there was the sound of the doorbell. Agatha Redmond called out from the back. "Do you mind letting in whoever's at the door, Canon Chambers? Unless it's the carol singers . . ."

Sidney went through the carpeted hallway and was surprised to see no shadow behind the frosted glass. He opened the door. There was no one there, but on the step, in his Moses basket, lay the tiny figure of baby John.

He picked him up and held him against his chest.

"There," Sidney said.

A note fluttered to the ground. It contained one word. "Sorry."

Sidney lifted up the basket and placed it in the hall. He closed the front door, and made his way up the stairs to Abigail Redmond's bedroom. When he was halfway up, Agatha Redmond walked into the hall with Byron under one arm.

"Good heavens, what's that?" she exclaimed.

Sidney looked down at the child and replied as simply as he could. "It's baby John."

Agatha Redmond took in the moment and then managed to burst into tears and fluster at the same time. "Oh, Abi, Abi. Here, Canon Chambers. Give me the baby. You hold the dog. On second thoughts, don't. Just let him scamper. He'll be perfectly all right. Oh, Canon Chambers. This is my grandson back at last. My beloved little boy."

She took the baby from his arms. "Hello, little John! Hello, little baby!" Then she hared up the stairs. "Abigail, Abigail, baby John is back at last!"

Sidney followed and watched as mother and baby were reunited. The two women inspected baby John again and again to see that he was all right. They marvelled at his toes and fingernails and noticed that his hair had grown and the mark under his left eye had faded. Then they asked questions that the poor baby could not possibly answer: had he been fed and was he warm enough and did he want to put on the new clothes waiting for him? Was he excited to see his mummy again? Did he know it was her? And did he understand that from now on she would never let him out of her sight, not ever?

Abigail rocked him in her arms and sang him a little hush-a-bye song while Sidney said a quiet prayer of thankfulness. Some things really did turn out for the best, he thought, as he sat calmly with mother and daughter, enjoying the peace and the respite of the reunion.

What a day it had been.

After about twenty minutes, and just as Sidney was thinking that it was probably time to go, Abigail asked her mother in a dreamy fashion, "By the way, who was that on the telephone? Was it Colin? We should tell him."

Mrs Redmond's face paled instantaneously. "Oh my! I'm so sorry. I clean forgot in all the excitement. It was the hospital, Canon Chambers. Your wife's there with her mother. You'd better get a move on. She's in labour. You don't want to be late for the birth of your own son."

Sidney looked at the sleeping child in Abigail's arms and realised that he was going to have to move very fast indeed.

The roads into Cambridge were busy with last-minute shoppers. Christmas trees protruded from car boots that would not close, couples with tired children waited at bus stops and an ambulance sped past. For a moment Sidney panicked that it was Hildegard inside but then reassured himself that he had been told that she was already at the hospital. As he parked his bicycle outside he was grateful that he was familiar with the location of the maternity ward and he hurried past reception, fully aware that his life was soon to be changed irreversibly. You cannot ever stop being a parent once you have begun, he told himself.

It did not take him long to climb the stairs but, as he did so, his stomach cramped with anxiety. What if all was not well? What if he had to choose between saving the life of his wife and that of his child? What were the chances of disaster as well as joy?

Sister Bland emerged from the maternity ward and let the door swing behind her. "You can't go in. She's not there. You'll have to sit in the waiting-room."

"Where is she?" he asked. "Is anything the matter?"

"It's been trickier than we thought, Canon Chambers, and that's quite a large baby you've got there, but I am sure that mother and baby will both pull through."

"I need to know everything," he pressed, leaning close to Sister Bland and catching yet another sight of the dreaded moustache. "What on earth is going on?"

"The doctor thought a Caesarean section would be safest."

Sidney felt his insides turn over. "I thought they were dangerous. Hildegard wanted to give birth herself."

303

"She will still give birth and she has agreed to the procedure. This way, we can control what happens and keep the baby safe."

"Are they in any danger? What's wrong?"

"The baby is in breech. So we can't wait any longer."

"Is Hildegard's mother in there with her?"

"We can't have anyone watching, Canon Chambers. Frau Leber is in the waiting-room. I'll show you where to go."

Sidney thought he should ring his father. As a doctor, he could tell him the right questions to ask. It was, however, too late for that now. He should have seen him earlier. He could have sought out his advice and prepared for all eventualities instead of roaming round Cambridge in search of missing children. "Oh, damn my stupidity," he muttered. "Damn, damn, damn."

Sister Bland, in an unexpectedly kindly fashion, put her arm around him and tried to reassure him while still retaining her brisk manner. "We are quite used to this kind of thing happening. The operation takes time and patience but it is best for everyone concerned. I'll ask someone to fetch you a cup of tea."

Sidney had never felt so useless. He could not discern whether he was being told the truth, even though he had no reason to believe the nurse would mislead him. That would be unlikely, he thought, before wondering if perhaps Sister Bland had known anything at all about the theft of baby John, or suspected that anything was amiss with her colleague, Grace

Carrington. Perhaps she had covered up for her, or turned a blind eye?

He stopped himself. *Concentrate on this moment, Sidney. This is your wife and child. Nothing else matters.*

He tried to control his fears but still they ran on. What if this all went horribly wrong? What if it was punishment for life going well, for all their happiness, an ultimate test of faith? Hadn't Hildegard gone through enough suffering? What about the loss of her father, the war, the murder of her first husband? Surely that was enough pain for one life?

He walked into the waiting-room to see Frau Leber knitting a red blanket. "If I do this, I do not think," she said.

She was sitting next to an elderly woman who told them that her husband was recovering from a heart attack. "I'm wearing my lucky coat," she said. "I can't take it off or something will go wrong."

A young mother was trying to keep her three-year-old daughter from playing with the fake Christmas tree. Its lights had already broken. "My sister's in the same ward as your wife," she said. "I just hope no one steals any more babies."

Sidney had forgotten that the news of baby John's return had not broken and that he had failed to inform Inspector Keating of this essential fact. He was not sure that the Redmond family would think to do it for him but he could hardly pop out and make a telephone call now. He tried to concentrate only on what lay ahead of him. "I think I might pray," he said to Hildegard's mother.

"Then I will pray with you."

Sidney remembered an old American song in which a man offered to die in place of his wife and child, and then was immediately furious for thinking only of himself and for the idea that he might make any kind of bargain with his creator.

"Peace be to this house, and to all that dwell in it," he began. "O Lord, look down from heaven, behold, visit and relieve this Thy servant. Look upon her with the eyes of Thy mercy, give her comfort and sure confidence in Thee, defend her from the dangers of the enemy, and keep her in perpetual peace and safety, through Jesus Christ our Lord."

They waited several hours. Between them they drank six cups of tea, started on a second packet of digestive biscuits and paced over a mile of hospital flooring. After Sidney had, at last, managed to telephone Keating and tell him that baby John was safe, they were joined by a father who chain-smoked in the waiting-room as he held on to find out if his son who had come off his motorbike would live or die; a woman whose husband had poked himself in the eye while doing the Christmas decorations; and a restaurant owner whose chef had burned himself with goose fat.

At last, just after three in the morning, Sidney and his mother-in-law were allowed into the ward. There were four beds and the lights were bright. An exhausted Hildegard lay with a drip in her arm and a child beside her.

"Meet Anna," she said.

Sidney's eyes filled with tears as he could not decide which he loved the most: his brave, beautiful, indomitable wife or the frail miracle of creation that was his baby daughter.

On Christmas morning, Sidney preached a sermon on the advantages of recognising fragility in ourselves and all those we love and care for. He had not had time to prepare properly and so he spoke off the cuff in front of his parishioners, his family and his friends. Hildegard and her mother were in attendance with his parents Alec and Iris Chambers and their new grandchild. He could look out from the pulpit to see his sister Jennifer and her fiancé Johnny Johnson, members of the Redmond family, nurses from the hospital, Geordie and Cathy Keating and their three children sitting in front of Helena Randall who was with a beleaguered-looking man whom Sidney took to be the director of the pantomime. Amanda Kendall was late, of course, but she had promised to bring plenty of champagne to wet the newborn baby's head.

He began by talking about the Christ child as the representative of all children and what it was to be childlike. He was arguing in favour of the need for times of weakness and vulnerability in our lives. An always invincible, strong, resistant humanity would have no room for growth or learning. It would have nothing to do. There would be no test because there could be no failure. Humanity needed its failings in order to understand itself. This was more than a matter of learning from mistakes. It was about acknowledging weakness, denying pride, and beginning any task from a position of openness, aware of the possibility that we often fall short. We must learn from the appearance of the Christ child in the world, as ready for companionship as tribulation, a blank canvas on whose surface life was painted and where depths contained mysteries yet to be understood.

"The fragility of a baby is a reminder of our own responsibility," Sidney continued. "He, or she, is at our mercy, as we are at God's. A child can either be crushed to death or fed, nurtured, cradled and allowed to grow. We see ourselves in each new birth and remember our own childhood. A society is judged by how it treats its children and its old people. Do we offer a favourable climate for a flower to grow, or do we provide impossible soil, harsh rains, and constant darkness? Christ tells us that it is we who must provide the light to see and warm the child in the cold black nights of the soul. The candles of Christmas represent the hope of our own flickering humanity against death and despair, and no matter how frail the flame, we must trust in its ability to illuminate our fragile state. For the light entered the darkness, and the darkness comprehended it not.

"This is the message of Christmas," Sidney concluded. "Light against darkness, vulnerability against brutality, life against death. We pray that under the inspiration of the child of Bethlehem, we may shine in a way that will lead others to the true source of peace and joy. May God bless you this Christmas time — you and all those whom you love."

"Not bad," said Amanda after the service. "You got through it even if everyone could tell you were pole-axed."

"A good night's sleep would be a help."

"I've brought the promised champagne to revive you."

"It's more likely to send me to sleep."

Sidney greeted the last of his parishioners as they left. Among them was Dr Michael Robinson, the punning doctor. "Happy Christmas on this 'miss-ty' morning," Sidney smiled at him knowingly. "I am so grateful to you for your advice."

"I don't recall providing any assistance?"

"You helped to solve a miss-tery."

Dr Robinson shook his hand before moving away sharply. "I'm only glad the miss-ing child was found."

Amanda had made sure that there were enough drinks for everyone and she invited the Keating family to come to the vicarage. "We haven't been asked," the Inspector worried.

"But I'm inviting you now."

"Just as long as you don't let in that journalist," Cathy Keating muttered to Amanda.

"Don't worry," Amanda replied. "I think her boyfriend is punishment enough."

Her chilled champagne was a sparkling challenge to the hot punch made by Hildegard's mother but the extra guests meant that there were sufficient numbers

309

to prevent any embarrassment about choice. There were a few raised eyebrows when Frau Leber offered pickled herring on cocktail sticks, the English contingent preferring the current craze for the similarly skewered cubes of ham and pineapple, but after the drinks guests had departed there were plenty of takers when it came to the roast turkey, potatoes, red cabbage and Brussels sprouts with Frau Leber's Germanic addition of bacon and chestnuts. This was followed by a choice of Christmas pudding or stollen and then coffee with a selection of chocolates Amanda had brought from Fortnum and Mason. She had quietly replaced Inspector Keating's gift of After Eight mints.

After the meal and, as they washed up and waited for the Queen's speech, the Chambers family listened to the news. The Soviet Union was conducting rocket tests in the Pacific, British troops were leaving for Cyprus, and the Scots Vigilante Association had threatened a revolt if Dr Beeching's proposals for the reorganisation of the railways were allowed to proceed. One of its spokespeople complained that the country was now being run by "Cockney leatherbottoms". Sibilla Leber asked what a "leatherbottom" was and Sidney explained, unconvincingly, that although it was not widely known, several members of the British Cabinet had taken to wearing lederhosen. His wife did not think that this was funny.

The National Anthem played and everyone, including Hildegard's mother, stood up. The Queen talked of her campaign to free the world from hunger, and said that the only ambition that mattered was to be good and honourable. The message of Christmas, peace on earth and goodwill to all men could not be achieved without determination and concerted effort.

Sidney remembered that his sovereign was pregnant with her fourth child and wondered if she felt the same anxieties as he did about the future of the world. Those born into this nuclear age would form the first generation to live with the possibility of its own annihilation. What was the human capacity for good, for evil?

The end of the speech became the cue for present giving, as bottles of wine, boxes of chocolates, fiendishly complicated jigsaws and games of Scrabble were distributed amongst the family. Sidney's father gave him the traditional copy of Wisden, his sister furnished him with a pair of cufflinks, and his mother had knitted him an Aran jumper which had, she told him, "taken simply ages". The puppy scampered amidst the detritus of unwrapped parcel and loose ribbon as Hildegard excused herself to give Anna a feed.

"You know that Byron is your present," Amanda told Sidney, "but I thought that I should give you something to open on the day."

"It's too much," said Sidney.

"Nothing is too much," Amanda replied, handing over a set of spoons. "I'd like to be able to say that Anna was born with a silver spoon in her mouth. There are advantages to that, you know."

"That's too kind."

"I trust I will be her godmother?"

"You didn't have to ask."

"And I assume Leonard will be a godfather?"

"And Geordie, I hope. With Hildegard's sister that will make up the four."

"I always think having a family member as a godparent is such a waste. You might as well ask that journalist girl."

"Now, that would be controversial . . ." Sidney smiled.

There was no evensong on Christmas Day but after all the presents had been opened Amanda said that she should be getting back. Although she had seen her parents the previous evening there was a little soirée in Mayfair that she had promised to visit, if only for the chance of meeting a few rich bachelors who had abandoned their dutiful attendance at family Christmas.

Hildegard returned from the kitchen and turned off the radio to bid Amanda a proper goodbye. A critic had been discussing the way the Beatles had translated African blues and American western idioms into "tough, sensitive Merseyside" in "Baby It's You" while using a Magyar 8/8 metre.

"I don't care what he says," Amanda said airily. "They can borrow as much as they like but they'll never be any match for Mozart. So lovely seeing you all. Don't let me break up the party."

"It was so good of you to come," said Sidney.

"Anna's such a wonderful baby. You must be so proud."

"Yes," said Hildegard. "We are."

"I never thought I would see the day."

"She is the greatest gift," said Sidney.

"You'd better keep a close eye on her then. I'm tempted to steal her away with me."

Sidney remembered that he had not told his friend anything about the theft of baby John and was momentarily pleased with his own tact. It was one less thing about which he had to defend himself. He kissed Amanda on the cheek and let the other guests know that this was, indeed, a cue for their departure as well. It had been a long day and he was looking forward to a peaceful night.

However, just after nine o'clock that evening, when all the inhabitants of Grantchester were surely sated by Christmas and watching either *Mr Pickwick* or *Christmas Night with the Stars*, and when Hildegard was giving Anna her last feed and Byron had been settled in his pen, the vicarage doorbell rang. Sidney was told by Hildegard very firmly not to answer it, but after a second ring he thought that, in all conscience, he had no choice in the matter. He was, as he still told anyone who would listen to him, never off duty.

He opened the door to find Grace Carrington standing before him in a dark navy coat with a matching beret. She held a soft package wrapped in white paper with holly and red berries. "I brought some things for your new daughter. To welcome her into the world . . ."

"That's very kind."

"And to say thank you for everything."

"I haven't done very much."

"We both know you have."

"We had a conversation. That was all."

"You saved me from myself."

"That may be true. Or, of course, it may not. We don't need to tell anyone else."

"I hope not. Thank you for what you did."

"I can't recall doing anything" Sidney replied. "But I'm glad you stayed for an answer."

Grace Carrington shook his hand. "Happy Christmas, Canon Chambers."

Sidney picked up the package and thought quietly, yet unavoidably, about desperation, guilt and redemption. It was a brave and risky thing for Grace Carrington to do, appearing at his door and quietly acknowledging her wrong. He would discourage Inspector Keating from pursuing a conviction. He would also try to be a better priest by going to see her and letting her know that he would always be willing to listen. That was something he had to learn so much more about: listening rather than speaking.

He left the package on the table in the hall and went into the kitchen to make some cocoa. He would bring a mug up to Hildegard and reassure her that the call at the door had been nothing serious. There would be no further adventures that night.

"Thank you, O Lord," he prayed as he stirred the milk over a low heat, "for your gifts; not least, the gift of life itself."

Outside the wind began to pick up. There was rain at the window. Byron stirred in his basket, and Sidney knew that he would have to walk him on a loose leash on Boxing Day. It was yet another thing to do, and it